Destiny in Wild Africa

Jean Mary Bonsor

authorHOUSE®

AuthorHouse™
1663 Liberty Drive
Bloomington, IN 47403
www.authorhouse.com
Phone: 1-800-839-8640

Published by AuthorHouse   01/17/2012

ISBN: 978-1-4685-4466-4 (sc)
ISBN: 978-1-4685-4465-7 (ebk)

Library of Congress Control Number: 2012901087

TO GET OVER a break up with her boyfriend, Suzanna Scott reluctantly agrees to accompany her cousin Sally on a week's holiday to a remote bush camp in the Zambezi Valley.

She is unprepared for the beauty of the camp and, despite her initial resistance, discovers deep in her heart an awakening love and compassion for the rugged bushveld and the animals that live within it's fascinating confines.

One person keeps upsetting her, though. The brusque and intolerant manager of the camp seems intent on clashing swords with Suzanna. Why can't she just walk away and ignore his unsettling influence? How can she possibly know that their destinies are linked together? A die cast without their knowledge.

This is a charming story that takes the reader deep into the wilds of northern Zimbabwe—an area that many people can only dream of visiting—and leaves them with a warm and memorable glow of satisfaction.

Chapter 1

THE CAVE STANK of the detritus of hundreds of years of rotting material. He peered ahead into the dim light, looking at a deep layer of stinking bat dung, black and revolting, heaped in piles against outcrops of jutting rocks that littered the cave floor. A constant twittering vibrated through the air indicating that thousands of the furry animals were hanging in clumps from the roof, wings folded, heads swivelling this way and that, beady eyes staring, waiting for darkness to release black clouds of bodies into the night to forage for food.

Somewhere in the dank depths, where the light didn't penetrate, he heard a steady dripping of water. Green slime hung from a crag, like forgotten mermaid's tresses, droplets dripping steadily off the trailing ends.

He had climbed for hours to get here, struggled to the summit of the precipitous cliffs to discover this place. For the last part of the climb the fog had swirled round him, blanketing the whole area in a clinging dense mist that seeped through his clothing and glistened wetly on the surface of the sharp rocks. Carefully he released each hand in turn and wiped the wetness of his palms against his shirt, knowing how vital it was not to lose his hold even for an instant. A trickle of sweat ran down into his eye, despite the high chill, and his heart lurched as he disturbed a loose stone with his shoulder when he tried to wipe away the stinging salt. The stone bounced against rocks below, pinging and skittering into oblivion.

His research had taken years. He had investigated thousands of leads, discarded most of them, and slowly sifted out all but a few that had finally led him here, to this foul smelling, dank opening under rock that had been split open millions of years ago.

Wide eyed in horror she watched as he crawled forward on all fours. One slip, one rash or impulsive move, one hand-hold that wasn't secure, and he would plummet hundreds of feet downwards. He would slide over the loose and slippery scree and fall. He caught a whiff of sea spray and threw a fearful glance over his shoulder taking in a brief glimpse of the fate that awaited him should he go down. His body would be torn into shreds, scraped raw as over a giant cheese grater, and there would be little more than a bloodied mass to feed any sharks or other roaming shoals of fish patrolling the thunderous surf pounding ceaselessly at the rocky jaws lining the base of the sheer cliffs.

He had put all this time, all this effort, all this research and almost his entire savings into trying to capture a series of photographs on the legendary Yeti-like creature that supposedly lived in this remote and desolate area—perhaps in this very cave. Vague sightings had described the Being as half man half beast. It was reported as having huge hands and long rank hair that covered a large head and over-long arms. All the hours of research had placed him here in this very spot.

Now he cautiously approached the mouth of the cave. His progress was slow and painstakingly careful. His camera was primed and ready, hanging on a short strap round his neck to prevent it from banging against a rock and getting damaged. He hadn't come all this way only to find he could not obtain the evidence he needed.

He stopped, fumbled at his belt with one hand and checked that his knife was still tucked into the protective sheath—his only weapon of defence. The blade was a full eight inches long, curving and vicious, and the steel was honed to a razor sharp edge.

He was cautiously gaining ground, creeping steadily forward. One knee of his thick climbing trousers caught and tore, and immediately the skin was sliced open. Blood spurted out in a thick glutinous glob, staining the ground and leaving a bright red trail behind him. But he ignored the pain and kept going.

The sound from the disgusting depths of darkness began as a low hissing noise. It gathered in intensity, ominous and threatening. The hiss deepened, the tones thickening into a growl, and then the growl developed into a furious roar. The vibrations echoed off the walls before him, resonated from the dark, obscene mouth of the cave, reaching out to wrap his senses in a confusing cacophony of noise.

And then it stopped.

And so did he.

The heavy silence was almost more frightening than the noise had been. Rigid with fear he peered into the gloom ahead. Could he see a light? Was there the echo of heavy footfalls approaching?

Now, for the first time, it occurred to him that his life could be in imminent danger, not from losing his grip and falling over the cliff, but from the approaching creature. He had no idea of what to expect—what size the beast would be, or whether it would instantly attack him. Although he had visualized finding the Yeti, he had never actually been able to mentally picture the setting or how close he would be able to get to his quarry. All he had hoped for was a good shot, a clear series of photos that he could carry triumphantly down the cliff and present to the news media of the world. Instant fame would be his, the pictures worth a fortune. The rest of the world would clamour for copies, he would sell his story to travel magazines, wild life film makers would make him rich overnight.

But in all his planning he had not seriously considered that he might be risking his life and that he may never return to boast of his success. Now the thought banged into his brain, and the sweat gleamed across his forehead and prickled in the small of his back.

He managed to wedge his feet against a rock and leaned backwards. His body was awkwardly placed but secure. He reached round and drew the knife out of it's sheath, lifted the camera and held it in front of his face

The growling resumed, soft and ominous, growing once again in volume. It swelled until it vibrated in his chest and his head. It echoed all round the cave, humming and resounding into a hollow crescendo. A sinister form was taking shape in the darkness, increasing in size, threatening and powerful. She clenched her hands together, not able to look away or even blink. Her eyes were glued to the photographer's back, drawn to the flash of the long blade in his hand. His face was streaked with dirt, his fingernails broken. The sweat soaked his shirt, sticking dark to his shoulders. All attention was directed towards the mouth of the cave from where the ghastly creature must once and for all surely emerge.

Slowly the figure took shape. It grew in size as the whole body began to take on more substance. Eyes that gleamed like vast living coals, set in a gaunt face that was almost covered in shaggy, filthy, unkempt hair, slowly materialized out of the murky darkness. The thudding steps slowly approached, matching the heavy thudding of the man's heart. The photographer held his breath, trying to keep the shaking camera steady.

And then there was blackness. Total and all enveloping darkness.

Overcome with fright, she flung out her arms and screamed out loud.

Dave jumped and yelled, "Jeez, Suzanna! You almost gave me a heart attack!"

"Oh my God! What's happened? Why is it dark? What's happened to the TV?" She was trembling and angry, perching on the edge of her seat. The occupant of the cave had been on the verge of emerging into the daylight, to face it's destiny and expose it's terrifying form to the world of avid viewers—and right at the wrong moment there had been a power cut.

All the lights had gone out, plunging the living room as well as the entire house into darkness.

This soap opera had been going on for months. Week by week, program by program they had been heading to this point of revelation—and the now power had gone off. Miles worse than someone forgetting the punch-line in a complicated joke.

Suzanna opened her eyes wide, trying to see beyond the sudden darkness. She stood up to check the light switch, risking falling over the coffee table. She flicked it up and down. Nothing!

"Damn! This is unbelievable. Where are your candles, Dave? Do you have any matches?"

"Sit down before you fall over something. I know where they are, I'll get them."

The street lights outside were still working and Dave fumbled his way in the dimness to the pantry cupboard, found the candles and matches and soon the warm yellow flame was flickering in it's holder on the table.

Usually she loved the enforced candlelight when the power went off, and she and Dave often deliberately switched off all the lights to enjoy a soft romantic evening. But tonight of all nights Suzanna needed the electricity. She thumped her fist on the arm of the sofa.

"We've watched this program for weeks and now we'll miss the main part of the whole story. It's really too bad." She knew she sounded strident, but she was mad enough not to care. "I've been hanging on this episode for ages. It's enough to make you spit. And we can't even make a cup of coffee until the power comes back on again."

"Well, sit down. I need to talk to you anyway." Dave's jaw stuck out and his eyes glowed in the candlelight. "Sit down, Suzanna."

Suddenly aware of the serious note in his voice, she turned to look into his face. A frown puckered between his brows and his mouth was set in a straight line. A tiny frisson of alarm slipped down her spine.

"What's the matter? Has something happened?"

He hesitated, carefully choosing his words. "Well, I've been trying to wait until the right time to tell you this, but there really is no right time."

"Right time for what? What are you trying to say?"

He squirmed, ran his hand through his hair and moved a little further down the sofa. The street light threw a pale yellow pool onto the carpet, picking out the mottled patterns and throwing long shadows across the room. The candle flame flickered at his movement.

"I need some space, Suze. I want to go out and explore a few other horizons—meet new people. I don't want to be harsh, but I hope you can understand . . ." He trailed into silence.

Suzanna's expression was incredulous and her hands clenched as the penny dropped. Her mouth was suddenly dry and she ran her tongue over her lips before she could speak. Her eyes were huge in her face, more black than dark brown in the candlelight.

"What are you saying? Are you telling me it's over between us? Are you breaking up with me?" His face was closed and he picked at a loose thread, refusing to meet her eyes.

"Why would you want to do that? How long have you felt like this?"

"I don't know how I feel—mostly confused, I guess." He clasped his hands together. Like a priest about to give a sermon, she thought. The gesture irritated her.

"I think, in fact I'm sure, that I still love you, but lately I've been wanting to break out and go crazy. Do some radical things that I've never done before." He gave a wry smile. "Live wildly before I'm middle aged."

"You're only twenty two. You've got years before you're middle aged."

This could not be happening. They'd been going out since high school. They were an item. She had never contemplated life without Dave.

"Are you saying I'm too boring for you now? Have you met someone else? I can't believe you're doing this to me."

Her voice was rising. "Did you feel like this on Friday when we spent the night together? Was that wonderful night just a sham—like all the others? Were you pretending you loved me just to get some sex? That's despicable!" She was beginning to get worked up, letting her temper take hold. She grabbed at a cushion and pummelled the stuffing into a round ball.

"Suze. Please don't take it like this. All the times we've been together have been wonderful, you know that. You're a beautiful girl—stunning in fact. It's something that has been growing inside me and I can't explain it. I just need some space for a while. Perhaps, later, we can get together again."

"Is there someone else? Have you been lusting over another girl all this time?"

"There's no-one else, Suze. It's only ever been you. Somehow that's part of the problem."

He sounded so pathetic. She peered at him, trying to see his eyes. He kept his glance down, and the muscle at the side of his jaw jumped. Was this her strong handsome boyfriend talking? His face was shadowed, his profile appearing subtly altered and for a second she felt she didn't recognise him. They had been going out for almost four years, and now, in this half light, he seemed totally different. Like a stranger.

She tossed her hair back and abruptly stood up. "Right! Well. Could you take me home now?"

He looked up, startled. "Please don't be like this. I never meant to hurt you. Let's talk it over. There's so much to be said."

"I think you've said it all, Dave. What else is there to talk about? You've made up your mind, that's quite obvious, so just take me home."

She flung the words at him as she paced furiously around the lounge, almost gutting the wavering candle, avoiding the dark furniture, picking up a few of her possessions. She grabbed her handbag and opened the lounge door. Damn this power cut! The passage was dark, but she knew the way—how could she not after so long?

They sat silently in the car, each stewing over thoughts that remained unsaid. As he drew up outside her flat, he stretched out a hand in a last attempt to get her to stay and talk things over. He wondered, in fact he knew, that he would regret all this tomorrow. He hadn't thought beyond the words that had churned in his mind for several weeks now and couldn't visualize what would happen after his announcement. Had he secretly expected her to plead with him, make him feel wanted and necessary once more? His emotions had been in a muddle for ages, but, typically, Suzanna had not noticed anything different. Or if she had, it hadn't been mentioned.

If their relationship had become this cosy now, what would it be like if they took the next step and got married? He had made a stand but already he was regretting voicing his thoughts. He switched off the car and turned to her.

"Suzanna, can't we just talk about this? Don't let's part this way."

Without saying another word she almost tumbled out of the car and slammed the door with a satisfying bang that rocked the vehicle on it's wheels. She fumbled her key in the front door lock, afraid that he would get out and follow her, afraid that he wouldn't get out and follow her. She didn't know what to expect from him, but she certainly was not going to turn back and be the one to give in and hold out her arms. He made no move to open his door—just sat completely still watching her. Damn him! He had started all this and she had no idea why. The tears swelled behind her eyes, began to drip down her cheeks, but she kept her face turned away as she let herself in.

Even after she had opened the door and disappeared inside, he sat on, reluctant to drive away and make his decision final.

The flat was dark and quiet. Automatically she reached out and flicked the switch, and thankfully the power came on, bright and reassuring. Sally was still out. She had gone to dinner with one of her friends, and Suzanna was glad she hadn't got home yet. She wiped at her wet face, needing to be alone. She dropped down into her chair, hearing Dave's words in her head. What had he done? Why had he broken up with her? She sniffed, leaning forward over her knees, knowing that the strange numbness inside would soon give way to grief that would make her howl and cry.

Her mind drifted back to last Friday. He had been tucked into the corner of the sofa, and Suzanna had been snuggled up with her back against his chest. His arm held her close. Slowly, tantalisingly, his fingers had stroked a lock of her hair, progressed to trace small circles on her neck and then descended down inside her shirt to touch the swell of her breast. Finally they had found a nipple, teasing and deliberately lighting a fire that sparked and burned between them, carrying them into a hot furnace of desire and fulfilment.

The reality hit her. They were really through. Over! Their relationship was done for. How could he have thrown it all away? Had she meant so little? A flame of anger burned in the pit of her stomach and licked hotly at her innards. It was a temptation to give in to it, hurl all her shoes at the wall or smash something.

She had been proud of herself for not breaking down and crying in front of him. At the very least she felt she had managed to keep her dignity and not give him the satisfaction of a tearful scene, but now she wished she had had the satisfaction of throwing something at him while she could. The shock of his announcement had struck deep, too deep for tears.

But now they started in earnest, rolling down her face in a steady stream.

How could he chuck it up so easily? What new horizons had he meant, and why couldn't they have explored them together—whatever they were? Was he so callous and shallow? They had been so right together, but perhaps she hadn't noticed what he was really like. Had she taken him for granted? Presumed he would always be there? The questions drummed through her mind, and a savage headache took hold, boring a red-hot hole in the back of her head. The tears gathered force until the sobs shook her shoulders. Gulps of air convulsed her chest. What would she do without Dave? She felt utterly miserable and alone.

The box of tissues was on the side table and she dragged out a handful to mop at her streaming face. Her hand dislodged the bottle of sleeping tablets and it fell to the floor, scattering small white pills in every direction. Ever since she could remember she had been prone to periodic bouts of nightmares that tore her nights apart, destroying any chance of sleep. Lately it had been better, but when things got bad a couple of the little tablets relaxed her and helped her descend into sweet oblivion.

Now they lay scattered at her feet. A few had rolled into a line, lying like beads from a broken necklace. She sniffed loudly, wiped her eyes, and peered fuzzily down at them. As she watched them with a mounting morbid fascination they seemed to glow, sparkling like little jewels, inviting her to swallow them, each one calling, 'Eat me first. Me first. Me first.'

It would serve Dave right if she ate the whole lot. She wouldn't feel a thing—just drift off into a deep and dreamless sleep, never to wake again. Her soul would lift up and fly away, leaving her body to be discovered and mourned over. Everyone would ask Dave what had happened, and he would have to front up—tell everyone how he had broken her heart, and caused her death. It would be on his conscience forever.

Suzanna didn't consider how Sally would feel, or what Toby's reaction might be. All she could think about was hurting Dave. Getting back at him for throwing her over like something worn out and useless. How could he have done it? Had she meant so little to him after all this time? Well, she'd show him. He wasn't going to get away unscathed.

Slowly she leaned down. Her hair hung forward over one shoulder as she reached out and picked the nearest tablet off the floor. It lay in her palm, white and pure. Like a tiny drop of snow. Merging and blurring through her tears.

The flat was quiet. No sounds came in off the street. She would make sure she got to her bed, not just fall onto the bathroom floor in an untidy heap. She sniffed and pushed her hair back, wiping at her face with the palm of her hand. She would tuck herself up for her final sleep and arrange her limbs so that she would look presentable to anyone who found her—probably Sally. Poor Sally! But she would just have to understand. She wondered if she should leave a note, then decided that would be too dramatic and let Dave off the hook.

Let him field all the questions and take the blame. He deserved it.

As if in a trance, she opened her palm again, picked up the tablet, put it into her mouth—and swallowed, grimacing at the bitter taste. Then she leaned down and stretched out her hand to reach for the next one lying in the broken chain at her feet.

Chapter 2

THE ENVELOPE HAD slipped onto the floor, lying unnoticed between the table leg and a small pile of magazines. Sally sat on the carpet, cross-legged, frowning over a pile of monthly accounts. She chewed her lip, her pen poised in midair.

"Did you put something on our account at Goldfields?" She looked over her shoulder and raised an eyebrow at her cousin.

"How much was it? I can't remember." Suzanna's reply was listless and disinterested.

She was curled up on the pile of cushions in the window seat, her long legs tucked underneath her. The sun streamed in, warming and cheerful, but her mood remained bleak. The book she had been trying to read lay open on her lap, the pages unturned. Her gaze was fixed on the twisted tree outside the window, and the last thing on her mind was what she had bought, or when. The weekend stretched before her, empty and endless. Sally had tried to persuade her to join a group of their friends heading to the pub later, but she had cried off, hating the thought that she might bump into Dave—or worse, see him laughing and flirting with someone else.

"Suze, concentrate! Did you get the gift for Mum from Goldfields?"

"Um, yes. That must have been it."

The depression had taken root in her soul, gripping her in a relentless hold like being tied up in wire, and it was too much of an effort to do anything that wasn't immediately essential. She twisted a strand of hair round her fingers and battled against tears of self-pity.

Sally went back to her work. The clock on the mantle-piece ticked steadily away, the only sound. There weren't many envelopes to open, but they all had to be attended to. Suzanna was more than happy to leave the unpleasant chore to Sally to finish.

Eventually Sally sighed and straightened out her legs. "Well that's it for another month. Let's have a cup of tea."

"You've missed one."

"What?"

"You've missed one." Suzanna's voice was dull. "It's down there on the floor."

"Drat it!" Sally's skirt pulled up her slim thighs as she scooted over to pick it up. She tore the envelope open, impatiently pulled out the letter and glanced at it. She read it once, gasped and read it again.

Then she leapt to her feet with a loud yell, whooping and dancing round the living room. Her face was lit up in a wide smile, and she waved a form in the air, inches from her cousin's face.

"I've won. Oh my God, I can't believe it. Look at this."

"Steady on. Don't take my eyes out. What have you won, anyway?"

"Don't you remember that raffle ticket I took? The prize was a trip for a week to a bush camp down on the Zambezi River? It was ages ago. I had forgotten all about it, and I certainly never thought I would win it—but look, here's the proof—I did win." She pranced around, kicking up her legs and swinging her arms over her head.

"Oh—that!" Suzann's weak grin faded and her face fell. What was a trip to some remote bush camp when her life was still in tatters. Once again the tears burned the back of her throat, threatening to overflow. How could Sally talk about a holiday when one good night's sleep would have been enough for her.

"Come on Suze, cheer up. You can't go on moping around and feeling sorry for yourself forever. At least try to show some enthusiasm. I've always wanted to go down to one of those camps but never been able to afford it. Now I can go for a whole week, all expenses paid. I'm thrilled to bits."

Suzanna tried to look a bit brighter. "It's great. I know you'll love it. That sort of rough living in tents and so on is just up your ally. Unlike me. Give me a comfy hotel any day."

She leaned backwards as Sally dropped to her knees in front of her, her face alive with excitement.

"Suze—what about coming with me? Think of the fun we'd have."

"Are you kidding? You know I'd hate it. How can you even suggest it? Anyway the ticket was for one, not two."

Sally sat back on her heels, studying the letter closely. "Yes, unfortunately it is for one. But how about considering it? The break will be good for you—get your mind off things. I know it'll be a bit expensive, but your savings are looking healthy at the moment. You haven't spent anything on yourself for ages, so why don't you come with me?"

She pulled herself to her feet and plumped down on the window seat, making the cushion wheeze in protest. The book fell onto the floor, pages in a mess. She gently gripped Suzanna's chin and made her turn to look at her.

"Listen, Suze, you have to get yourself back together again. I know you loved Dave and thought he was the one and only for you, but now that he's gone you have to get over him and just move on with your life. It still gives me goose bumps to think what you would have done if I hadn't got home when I did last Sunday night. Would you really have swallowed all those sleeping tablets?"

"You've asked me that a hundred times, Sally. I wasn't thinking clearly. I don't know how many I would have taken. Knowing what a ninny I am, probably not a lot."

In fact, when she thought back to that night, it scared her. Would she have carried on to eat all the pills? A shiver ran down her spine. Was Dave worth sacrificing her life for? What could she have been thinking? Sally had returned home, in the nick of time so to speak, bounced into the flat and discovered her cousin crouched over with the pills in her hand.

"What's this? What the hell are you doing? Are you crazy?" Fright made her voice loud and she slapped at Suzanna's hand, scattering the pills once again.

Once she had prised the whole sorry story out of her cousin, she had dragged the vacuum cleaner out of the cupboard and, in a frenzy of activity, swept the carpet twice over, making sure no pills were left.

"How many did you take? Get up. You will damn well walk up and down this room for the next hour until I'm satisfied that you're OK. I can't believe you."

Now she stared into Suzanna's face, noting the fine lines of strain that had recently appeared at the corners of her eyes. The full mouth was turned down and her hair, usually so vibrant with colour, hung in neglected tangles. Despite all this Suzanna's natural beauty was hard to disguise.

"Suze, you are a gorgeous girl. You have been blessed with the kind of looks that most people only dream about. It's time you pulled yourself together. Mr Right will be out there somewhere. You can't sit here feeling miserable for days on end. You'll wind up with wrinkles and grey hair!"

Suzanna swallowed the lump in her throat in an effort to please.

"I'm still so angry with him but I miss him so much Sal. I don't know how to do anything without him. I can't believe he hasn't even rung me to apologise—not once."

"You two have been going out since High School, Suze. I've told you over and over, you didn't do anything wrong and neither did he. You had no excitement left between you. He needed to get away for a bit, spread his wings. If you were meant to be a couple he'll eventually come back, but I think you'd be crazy to sit around and wait for him. Take this time to get out and explore a few horizons of your own. There are heaps of yummy fish in the sea, and you need to be sure Dave is the right man for you. Your relationship had become as exciting as . . . ." she waved her hand in the air, "I don't know, about as exciting as plum pudding."

"Oh Sal, you are the end!" Suzanna leaned over to give her a hug. "Never-the-less, I still don't want to come to your camp. I'm terrified of all those animals, not to mention the creepy crawlies like scorpions and spiders. It would just be my luck to get bitten by something and come up in a great rash. You go. You'll have a good time, and I'll be fine here without you." Her tone was teasing. "I should be able manage for a week by myself."

Sally scraped a hand through her hair, making it stand up in golden ringlets that framed her face. They had both inherited their mother's features and colouring. Sally's blue eyes and blonde hair contrasted with Suzanna's thick auburn locks and dark eyebrows. Sally was the shorter of the two and although she was a few months younger, she had always been the more forceful.

Once again she looked at the letter in her hand and sighed in frustration.

"You could do with some adventure in your life, Suzanna Scott. You have lived way too long in a nice little cocoon and it's about time you did something radical. Plus you should take the leave due to you before you lose it."

When Sally used her whole name it was a sure indication to Suzanna that she was in for a lecture. The feisty little blonde head would tilt at a stubborn angle, the blue glint of determination framed by her long lashes evidence that she would try to get her own way at any cost. But today Suzanna didn't feel like letting her get away with it.

"Sal, I'm truly pleased for you, but I'm not in the mood to be told what's good for me. I've told you already—you go. You won the ticket and you'll love the experience."

She swung her legs down and left Sally re-reading her precious letter while she went through to the kitchen. For a second she stared blankly at the wall, and then like an automaton she sploshed water into the kettle and thumped it into the base to boil.

Amazing how a cup of tea was the solution to so many problems. When she'd fallen off her bike on the rough gravel, Auntie Ann had scooped her up, straightened the handlebars, loaded her plus her bike into the back seat of the car and given her a hot cup of sweet tea to sip while she cleaned up the scraped and bloody knee. A hot cup of tea had been the answer to a whack on the shin from a hockey stick, a celebration after her first—narrowly survived—driving lesson, and a triumphant toast when the cousins' exam results had come out.

"Sit down dear, and let me make you a nice hot cup of tea." Auntie Ann's voice would echo through Suzanna's life.

As she waited for the kettle to boil she watched her cousin stride up and down in their tiny living room. Her lovely features were glowing with an animated smile, and a row of even white teeth chewed at her bottom lip. The blonde highlights in her unruly curls caught a few sunbeams, and as she paced she turned the pages of a coffee-table book on the Zambezi Valley. Her precious letter had slipped to the floor and lay with one edge slightly turned up, issuing a silent challenge across the room—are you brave enough to come with us?

Suzanna wished for the millionth time that she had Sally's energy and drive. Somehow she seemed to breeze through life with a smile and a toss of the head, disregarding anything that might cause a problem in her road. And, more often that not, the problems seemed to melt away and resolve themselves with minimum input from her.

Sally fell into and out of love with a carefree attitude that left her boyfriends reeling. But the male species was drawn to her happy, vibrant nature, and didn't seem to mind standing in line for her attentions. She always had several blokes hanging on a string, and was never short of an escort.

Unlike her, Suzanna had been a one-man woman and her perfect man had been Dave. He was tall and slim and wore his clothes well, and his easy manner had always made her feel attractive and confident. He hung on her words and said she looked good, no matter what she wore. So what if they had been going out since High School? She reasoned that lots of couples date in High School, and go on to get married and live long and happy lives together. Dave had been the head student, plus the captain of the rugby team and plenty of girls would have changed places with her in an instant. He had been popular with everyone.

Similarly, the admiring glances that his friends sent Suzanna's way hadn't escaped her notice. She told herself that if she'd wanted to take any of them seriously she could have crooked her finger and beckoned to any one of them—not that she ever did. Even when he went away to College, Dave's beat up old Citroen would valiantly tackle the miles to bring him home to see her at least twice a month. They had lived for each other's emails and spent hours running up their phone bills.

And then, out of the blue, a few words had destroyed everything that had existed between them.

The loud hissing of the kettle brought her back to the present. She glanced through to the lounge. Sally was on the phone, animatedly waving her hands as she broke the news of her win to Toby, her brother. Her smile was wide and she was fairly bouncing off the walls.

Sally, Toby and Suzanna had grown up together. Toby was almost two years their junior and looked to the more knowledgeable and worldly-wise girls for advice and guidance. Although they were first cousins, Sally and Suzanna had been as close as sisters since both of them could remember. Their fathers were brothers so they even shared the same surname.

As little kids, before the accident, they'd had a happy childhood, secure in the knowledge that the carefree times would last forever.

Uncle Bill helped the three of them to build a tree-house in the fork of a bent and twisted willow tree. It was the children's' most favourite place. To get to it they rode on their hobby-horses, rhythmically clicking tongues stained red or green from fruit ices, in a clip-clopping sound as they held the sticks between their legs and compared the way the horses' heads bobbed as they walked along. They'd each made their own horse—days devoted to stuffing a sock with cotton wool to make the head, securing the head onto a smooth stick, attaching pieces of knitting wool to form the mane and forelock, designing the way the bridle curled round the mouth and getting the string for the rein exactly the right length. Sally and Suzanna had refused to sew Toby's eyes on for him, telling him it was good for a boy to learn to use a needle. So his horse always wore a lopsided look with one eye button higher than the other. Not only that, but it had a permanent wink as the button on the left was smaller.

They almost always took a back-pack filled with drinks and snacks to the tree-house. The girls reasoned that since Toby was the only boy around, it was up to him to carry the load. On occasion, when the pack was extra heavy, they'd had to threaten to whack his horse in the rump to make him catch up with the girls' longer legs and not linger so far behind.

Toby had to pull the pack up onto the platform and they all carefully unpacked and spread the feast out on a flat piece of board. Then they'd set about eating and drinking the whole lot. Afterwards they would lie back, staring up into the leafy canopy above and discussing important subjects such as what they would do when they grew up, or how they could possibly increase the size of their tree-house. When it was time to return home, the girls argued about which one would carry the empty bag, assuring Toby that they were doing their share.

Toby often got the short end of the stick. When the mangoes in the neighbour's garden were ripe Sally hatched a plan and stuffed an empty plastic bag into his pocket, then held up the fence so that he could crawl through.

"Quick, Toby," she instructed him. "We'll keep a look out for Mr. Mitchell. Make sure you fill the bag with golden ripe ones now."

Trustingly he did as he was told, while Sally and Suzanna urged him on from a safe distance.

Even before the accident that had re-shaped her life, Suzanna had spent most of her time over at their house—a huge rambling building with a garden full of secret and exciting hiding places. A child's paradise.

The memories drifted. Mechanically she dropped teabags straight into two cups.

She had been unofficially adopted into their family at the age of eight, after her mother was killed in a car crash that had shattered all their lives, and most especially Suzanna's.

"Suzanna? Come and sit down, sweetheart, I'm afraid I have something really bad to tell you." Uncle Bill had taken it on himself to break the devastating news. A terrible band of fear had squeezed the little girl's heart and closed her throat and exploded pieces of her soul into darkness.

"It was a lorry—going too fast. He couldn't take the corner properly—swung out too wide. Your Mum was forced to swerve. She went down a steep bank . . . ."

Her father's shocked and pale face swam in and out of her vision. He was unable to speak or to move—a shell of a person who's living, breathing core lay smashed and broken in the tangle of a red sedan.

Auntie Ann's saucer rattled uncontrollably and tea slopped over the edge of the cup. She stood with a frozen expression of wide-eyed disbelief and shock on her face. Her jaw hung slightly down and her shoulders were stooped. She looked old and bewildered, and couldn't get anyone to accept the proffered solution to all dilemmas and crises.

Slowly, Suzanna's father withdrew into a place that only he could access, and he moved like a robot that had lost it's connections, scattered like the pieces of a picture puzzle dropped onto the floor. His grief was so deep that he was unable to comfort his distraught daughter, or provide an answer when she asked why such a terrible thing had happened to her sweet, beautiful mother.

Her nights were haunted by nightmares and the tears were never far away—she even cried when the gardener sucked up a tiny frog that instantly clogged the swimming pool vacuum system. The family were there to console Suzanna but it was Sally she'd clung to—two little girls, one with a black hole at her feet, and the other determined to try and fix the problem—suddenly realizing that life was big and terrifying, and the awful things that happened were beyond their parents' control.

The weeks that followed the unspeakable tragedy remained a blur in Suzanna's mind. At the funeral she clung to Auntie Ann's hand and refused point blank to look into her mother's open coffin, terrified of what she'd see.

"She looks so peaceful, Suzanna. She's beautiful."

"How can she be beautiful when the car smashed her to bits?" The child's distress upset everyone around her. It was hard to maintain a balance and encourage her to face what had happened.

"Leave the child to make up her own mind. Give her time to heal."

Over time, Uncle Bill and Auntie Ann slowly and gently filled the aching emptiness, and Sally and Toby were her lifeline back to some sort of sanity. Scars on the body and in the heart eventually become fainter. But sometimes they only fade and become hidden, never totally disappearing.

Her father never did manage to fit himself back together again. He eventually decided to sell the house and took off—alone on a sea of unhappiness. He drifted from place to place, unable to settle down or forget the love of his life, and his infrequent visits back to his pale and wraith-like daughter left them both feeling restless and unhappy.

Despite everything, they had had to go on. Sally and Suzanna had sat next to each other in class, shared all their secrets, all their problems and all their friends. Sally became her cousin's rock and anchor.

After school both girls had attended the same Secretarial College and proudly graduated at the same grand ceremony. Afterwards Uncle Bill and Auntie Ann had taken them to a local hotel for the predictable cup of tea. They didn't find it necessary to tell the proud adults that they'd had a wild time the night before, drinking wine with their friends. And of course Dave had been there, celebrating and laughing and congratulating Suzanna.

Sally landed a good job as receptionist to a lawyer in a family firm, and Suzanna loved her niche in a small advertising agency. The girls found a tiny flat to share, and although they were a little cramped, it's central position was most suitable.

The main bone of contention between them was Sally's unquenchable adventurous spirit. She was always planning to go somewhere exotic or do something extreme, and often dragged her reluctant cousin to places she would never have dreamed of going to by herself. Once they arrived they generally had a good time, but the price was a few prior sleepless nights of worry on Suzanna's behalf.

Like the time Sally dragged her to the mountains in Inyanga for a three day cross-country walk. Suzanna was dreading it and stressed like mad beforehand on what she should take, what shoes she would wear and whether she would be able to keep up. She packed and unpacked her case several times, but still didn't manage to take all the right gear. Sally suffered no such qualms and was on fire with enthusiasm for days before they were set to go. She flung a suitcase of stuff together at the last minute and, of course, everything she packed was exactly right for the occasion.

They were collected by bus, and, to Suzanna's distress, checked in to a very mediocre hotel in what seemed the middle of nowhere. The party was scheduled to walk through rough and precipitous mountain trails to find the next hotel on the route, spend a night there, then make their way in a rough circle until they finally staggered back to the original hotel.

The party of walkers clustered together and set off in a straggly line to follow the guide, everyone hitching at clothing and packs and adjusting straps, energetic and full of anticipation. They had walked for no more than an hour along the first trail when Suzanna missed her footing, stumbled on the rocky path and fell awkwardly in an embarrassing tangle of backpack, spilled supplies, legs and arms. An excruciating pain shot through her ankle and she felt the tears spurt into her eyes as she struggled to control herself. There was immediate consternation, and one of the men had used the opportunity to paw Suzanna's arm and slyly brushed her breast with his hand as he attempted to help her up.

She had to be taken back to the mediocre hotel and wait it out there for the rest of the party to continue their hike and eventually return to base. Three days lying around with her foot heavily bandaged, reading and being bored out of her mind. Then, when Sally returned with the rest of the exhausted party, she had had to suffer all Sally's reports of the fun they'd had, the gorgeous guys she'd met and the wonderful things they had done en route. Suzanna could only think of getting back to the comforts of home and putting the whole unfortunate incident out of her mind.

If ever there was a creepy-crawlie in the flat or the garden it was Sally who calmly rescued or dispatched the creature as necessary, while Suzanna was backed up, shuddering with revulsion and fear.

She would never forget the occasion when she closed her bedroom door, only to behold an enormous black and revoltingly hairy spider crouched mid way up on the inside. A great black body hung between bent spiky legs that would almost have covered a saucer. She totally freaked out, and her hysterical scream had Sally racing to her rescue. She found Suzanna flattened against the far wall, her hands clamped to her mouth, shaking in fright.

"Oh for goodness sake, Suzanna, it's just a spider! What are you making such a fuss about?"

"Kill it, kill it!" She screeched. "How in heck could it have got in here? My God, it might have crawled into my slipper or inside a pair of jeans. Look at the size of it. It could have jumped off when I opened the door and bitten me. Kill it, Sally, quickly!"

"We can't kill it, it can't help being a spider. Besides, it'll make a huge mess. Go to the kitchen and get me a large jam jar. Quick—while I watch it."

"What are you going to do? What on earth do you want a jar for? Watch out, it'll leap off there and run under the bed or something."

"Suze, just get me the jar. One with a wide neck. Move it."

Suzanna edged her way past Sally, her back to the wall, and was only too happy to be out of the room and away from the ghastly hairy monster. Her skin was icy and she felt quite sick. Hastily she rummaged in the pantry cupboard and found a glass container half full of sugar. It was the best she could do and she emptied it straight into the bin in her haste to get the jar back to Sally. Sally hadn't moved and almost seemed to be admiring the gruesome creature. Without taking her eyes off the monster, her hand reached out and she took the container out of Suzanna's shaking hand and unscrewed the lid.

Calmly she stretched out and in one swift move she neatly placed the jar over the revolting thing. Suzanna screamed again as it folded it's legs and obligingly leapt backwards to crouch in the bottom of the glass. Sally deftly closed the lid above it.

Then, of course, she couldn't resist holding her prize aloft.

"See, it's only a spider. I'll take it out to the garden and let it go."

"No! Don't you dare. It'll come back in. Take it to the end of the street and let it crawl into someone else's house. Please don't put it down in our garden."

"Are those it's eyes?" She peered into the bottle, loving torturing her long suffering cousin. "I think it must be a female. In general they're bigger than the males."

"Just take it away. Get rid of it. Take it miles away." Suzanna clamped her hands over her eyes and refused to look or listen to Sally's attempted biology lesson on the attributes of a spiky, hairy black spider with it's knees round it's ears.

No—there was no way Suzanna would let Sally talk her into going on this crazy bush trip. She was determined to resist all the persuasive looks and arguments that she knew she would be subjected to. With a deep sigh, she took the mugs of tea through to the lounge, pushing the letter under the table with her foot as she passed.

"I've decided that I definitely won't come on this trip with you," she announced.

Sally glanced up and Suzanna's spirits immediately sank. She knew that look so well. It screamed of manipulation and devious cunning.

"Oh no you don't!" She looked at the blonde head, now turned and innocently gazing out of the window. "Don't even try. I've been saving for a holiday in a lovely plush hotel I have yet to choose. I am not going to spend my savings staying in a rough camp by the side of the Zambezi River where, incidentally, there also resides a vicious range of crocodiles, hippos and other dangerous wild animals."

Sally glanced over her shoulder and her eyes opened in mock innocence.

"That's fine. You must do what you're happy doing. I will support your decision—possibly!"

"Huh! Don't think I am going to be fooled by your wide-eyed innocent looks. You know I'm hopeless when I'm out of my comfort zone. Just leave me here and go on your own."

"You love being depressed, don't you?" Sally shot back. "Very well. I won't say any more. You stay here and be miserable. I hope you have a good time wallowing in your self-pity. You can think of me having a ball and meeting a whole range of gorgeous men. I know you'll be sorry."

Suzanna sipped at her tea, regarding her cousin over the rim of the cup. She decided not to reply. On occasion she had scored in a battle of wills between them by maintaining a silence that got under her cousin's skin. Sally could out-argue the best of them, but she found it more difficult to battle against a wall of silence and non existent responses.

Good! Sally could go and leave her in peace for a whole week. She was entitled to mope around and be miserable if she wanted to. Without Sally forever drumming at her to pull herself together she could be left to get over the break-up with her boyfriend of more than four years in a quietly healing and restorative manner. She had no intention of going to the camp. She would make sure to stick to her guns and resist all her cousin's scheming plans and continuous arguments.

It wouldn't be easy but she was determined not to change her mind. In Suzanna's book the words 'holiday' and 'a touch of luxury' definitely went together.

Chapter 3

THE ROAR OF the engine drilled through her head and vibrated her internal organs. She felt as though her bones were being so rattled about there was a very real danger of permanent damage. The noise confused her senses and she wondered if the occupants of the vehicle would live to tell the tale of this washing machine experience, or wind up like a tangled heap of old abandoned clothing, flung carelessly on the side of the road to rot in the dust.

Long ago she had taken part in a school concert. The young group of performers had been attired in black body suits painted on the front with a white skeleton. They'd done a dislocated sort of dance to jangly music, and now she felt as though she was repeating the dance moves, but to the tune of a roaring vehicle, billowing clouds of dust and violent motion.

Suzanna wondered if the truck they were travelling in had fallen off the Ark when Noah landed on shore. It rattled and shook in every joint. The corrugations of the road had loosened every part until surely it would fly apart at any given moment. It was certainly manned by a maniac with very little sense of passenger comfort or vehicle longevity. The road was not only knee deep in clinging sand and gravel, it was also littered with more than it's fair share of stones and rocks. The driver constantly changed his grip on the steering wheel as the tyres of the truck bounced and jolted as though trying to fling them all into the dense bush that flashed past on either side of the narrow road.

Sally and Suzanna had done the first part of the journey in the comfort of their own car on the smoothness of the tarmac highway. They had reached the pick-up point and been met by the cheerful driver and, trying to ignore the dusty interior, they were loaded, along with their luggage, into the camouflage coloured Land Rover. Hardly allowing them to settle, the driver had raced off and they were now hurtling at break-neck speed along the rough road leading towards the vast area that formed the Zambezi Valley.

Suzanna's knuckles strained white as she held onto the rail of the seat in front. Her tongue was dry and her teeth closed on a thick layer of grit that crunched unpleasantly between them. The dust billowed in clouds behind them, and permeated through the entire vehicle, coating the occupants from head to toe. Her hair felt lank and lifeless, and her skin was gritty and dirty. She glanced over at Sally and felt wild with anger to see her smiling joyfully while she hung on to the seat in front of her, letting her body roll to the jolts and bumps of the bucking vehicle.

The driver threw a look over his shoulder and grinned happily at Sally's enthusiasm. His white teeth flashed in direct contrast to his black face, and his khaki uniform seemed smart and crisp despite the heat and the overwhelming dust.

"How much longer do we have to put up with this?" Suzanna's voice came out in a staccato as they hit the millionth bump. It was impossible to open a window—she had tried already. Even the smallest gap encouraged more stifling dust to swirl in and make her cough and choke.

"Not long till we get to the gate," he yelled, "then we can slow down a bit. They close the gate at 5.30 each evening and since we have left late we have to hurry to get though. If we don't make it in time we will have to turn round and come back tomorrow."

Suzanna leaned forward to hear his words over the roar of the engine, and another bump took her by surprise. Her chin came down hard on the handrail, and she struggled not to yell out in fury as the tears popped into her eyes. She wiped them away and left a grey smear down the side of her face. The thought of turning round to go back over this awful stretch of road, and then set out to do it again tomorrow was unthinkable, and she almost wanted to spur him on to a greater speed just to get the journey done with.

She knew she shouldn't have agreed to come on this crazy trip. She had been so determined, used every excuse she could think of, and tried to devise every sort of plan she could, just to avoid enduring exactly what she was enduring at this precise moment. Sally had gone on and on, wearing her down and countering every move she made, each excuse she could think of. She hadn't let up for a moment, and once she sensed that Suzanna was beginning to weaken she increased the pressure.

"OK, I'll tell you what," she'd said. "If we can get our leave dates synchronised you'll come with me. If our dates clash I'll leave you alone, and you can stay here while I go to the camp."

Miraculously of course, once Suzanna had sorted out a vague date to take her leave, Sally announced that that was the exact time she could take leave as well. She made sure

Suzanna approached her boss to take the week off, and she did the same.

"Look, if you're unhappy and really hate it, which I'm sure you won't, I'll try to make sure there's a vehicle handy to bring you home early," Sally had promised. "It's only a few hours drive and they're sure to do several trips a week to bring in stocks and supplies for the camp."

In sheer desperation Suzanna had given in.

"OK, OK! Enough already. I'll come with you."

Sally had danced about in delight, hugging her cousin and spinning her round.

"It'll be great, Zannie. We'll have a marvellous time. I feel certain it will be an adventure neither of us will forget."

But Suzanna knew it would be a disaster. She knew she would hate every moment. The so-called few hour's drive had dragged on and on and they had been in perpetual motion for almost six hours, with more to follow. She closed her eyes, hung on tightly and willed the next half an hour to fly past.

At last the vehicle slowed and drew up to a metal boom that stretched across the road, closing off any further access. The truck hissed with an audible sigh of relief as the driver killed the engine, and a hot, stuffy silence descended on the occupants.

A tiny round hut with a tin roof was set on the side of the road. This was the official office and as they waited, now mopping at damp foreheads, a khaki clad officer sauntered out. His round black face shone with sweat, a testimony to the roasting heat trapped in the tiny office. He scratched at something that irritated his neck, his expression unwelcoming. The top button of his uniform was undone, and the rest strained to keep the front of his jacket closed over the round paunch. He held a clipboard with all his important papers firmly clamped in place and a pen dangled from a piece of string that swayed from side to side as he strolled towards the vehicle, laces undone on his scuffed and dirty boots.

Making an obvious statement he raised his arm, pulled back the cuff of his sleeve and took a long and deliberate look at his watch, deciding whether he could be bothered to raise the boom this late in the evening or send the truck back and demand they return tomorrow.

"Surely he'll let us through? We can't possibly do that trip again." Suzanna was filled with panic. She stared out of the window, considering whether to get out and speak to the officer. If she knew it would help she wouldn't hesitate, but he looked imposing and rather frightening.

"Keep your voice down, Suze. Hopefully he's just showing us how important he is." Sally's tone warned Suzanna to stay where she was.

The driver had had this treatment before. He knew what was expected of him when he arrived at the gate just before closing time. He leaned his elbow out of the window and called out a cheery greeting. The rotund figure sauntered closer, his full lips pursed and his eyelids half closed against the low sun that shone directly into his eyes. Undaunted the driver repeated his greeting and drew the officer into a rapid conversation in their own dialect, hands waving and fingers pointing. Neither Sally nor Suzanna could follow the discussion and they watched the changing expressions flit across the face outside the window with concern.

Then an envelope magically appeared in the driver's hand. He held it up like he'd pulled a white rabbit out of a hat and extended it out of the window. The sight of it cracked a huge grin across the official's perspiring black face. He grabbed the bribe, quickly tucked it into his side pocket and held out the clipboard. The driver scribbled a signature across the bottom of the blue form, and to the girls' relief the boom was raised to let them through. They set off once again, taking another dusty track that wound westwards.

The surface of this narrow road wasn't as bad as the one they had just travelled, but the bush on either side was thicker and in places seemed almost impenetrable. They passed an occasional baobab tree that sat fatly on the dry ground with it's grossly thick trunk and misshapen branches looking thousands of years old. The driver had slowed down somewhat, and now that they weren't in dire danger of an accident, Suzanna took more of an interest in the passing scenery, trying to catch a glimpse of any animals that could have been browsing on the edge of the road.

Even so, she was taken by surprise when the vehicle suddenly stopped in a flurry of dust opposite a clearing off to the left. Quietly the driver pointed to a small herd of zebra that lifted their heads and stared back in silent intrigue at the faces of the people staring at them. The perfection of their painted black and white stripes contrasted with, and yet seemed totally a part of, the dusty, dappled setting.

"Our first lot of game," Sally breathed. "Aren't they lovely? I wish I had my camera. I'll have to get it out of the suitcase as soon as I can. Listen to the insects trilling as well."

The zebra were accompanied by some delicately beautiful brown antelope, heads adorned with elegant twisted horns, glistening black noses with flared nostrils and soft ears that twitched backwards and forwards, alert to every sound. They bunched together, regarding the humans with large brown liquid eyes, skittery and anxious on tiny pointed hooves—poised for instant flight. A shaft of late afternoon light shone through the trees like the golden beam of a celestial torch, and lit up the pale hides marked with a white stripe down their flanks. Suzanna was caught by the beauty of the scene.

"They're beautiful," she breathed. "What are they?"

"Oh, those are impala with the zebra," the driver replied. "They are so plentiful in this part of the Zambezi Valley that some people refer to them as the goats of the area. They form a vitally important part of the predator food chain, but their beauty is often overlooked. See now, how they leap into the air when they run. Not all antelope can jump so high—it helps them to escape."

Suzanna's heart went out to the delicate graceful creatures.

"It must be awful to be so nervous all the time." Her voice was soft and low. "Any one of them could be here one moment and dinner for a lion or leopard the next."

It occurred to her that for the first time in her life she had felt a sense of empathy and concern for any animal living in the wilds of Africa, and she hugged the feeling tight inside. Another thought sprang into her mind. She had lived her whole life in this Country and yet this was the first time she had seen any wildlife close up and in their natural element. She tried to burn the scene into her mind, so that she could remember it forever—take it out and hold it close like a precious photograph.

Now that they weren't speeding and bucketing over the rough terrain she felt more relaxed, but even so she wasn't looking forward to spending the next week in this remote area. They were miles and miles from anywhere. Suzanna glanced over at Sally. Her cousin smiled encouragingly at Suzanna's worried look and squeezed her hand.

"Don't look so concerned. We must be almost there now. Weren't those zebra and impala gorgeous? We should have some wonderful game viewing over the next few days."

Suzanna had a sudden vision that it could have been Dave next to her on this brown backseat and her heart gave an involuntary lurch of longing for him. He would have loved seeing those two small herds. Unlike her he had been into the bush with his family and had tried to get Suzanna to go with him, doing his best to persuade her. But she had steadfastly refused. Perhaps that had been one of the marks against her?

Against her will the memory of their first fumbling attempt at making love together popped into her mind. It had been at her eighteenth birthday party. She'd had way too much to drink, had danced with every man in the room, and loved every moment of her special evening. Dave had kept his eyes on her, envying the flirtatious looks she had bestowed on all his friends. She was his girl and should only have had eyes for him, he'd reckoned. It was a long wait until everyone had left and they were finally alone. He took her into his arms, insistently kissing her and encouraging her to relax and let herself be undressed and loved. Carried away on the emotion of the evening, and a fair quantity of wine, she had felt the fire build in her belly. But the experience hadn't been entirely what Suzanna had been lead to expect from any of the romance novels she'd read. They had got better at it—or at least he had. Suzanna was never really certain what role to play, or how forward she should be. Dave hadn't appeared to be concerned and always took control. He constantly stroked and admired Suzanna's slim naked body and couldn't wait to get her alone.

Now her hand circled her throat as she wondered who he was with at this very moment. Into her mind came a picture of a girl with long blonde hair and adoring eyes, hanging on to his every word as well as his muscled forearm.

Part of her hated the thought, but suddenly the other part threw the idea aside. 'He doesn't want you, my girl. What do you care who he's seeing—let him get on with it. Why should you care if he sleeps with half the girls in his office? Best of luck to them. Perhaps they'll find out that he's not prepared to commit himself, and he's only out to have a good time. Good riddance.'

The driver swung the vehicle round a corner and stopped, interrupting her string of thoughts. Several other similar vehicles were parked under a spreading canopy of trees. It seemed they had arrived.

Stiffly the girls stepped out of the truck, brushed at the dust on their clothing and walked a few paces for their first look at the mighty Zambezi River. It was instantly impressive. It flowed past, half a kilometer wide, smooth and slick. Here and there the water broke and swirled round hidden submerged rocks, displaying the potential surging power of the current. Further on gentle wavelets lapped at the edges of a series of shallow islands of sand, carefully built up and left behind by the never ending flow. The trees on the far side grew green and dense, dark shadows nestling under the clustered trunks.

"That's Zambia across there," Sally observed. "Funny how the bush is so different to our side. The trees this side seem to be more sparse, but perhaps it's just this particular area."

Suzanna glanced around. There was no sign of any form of building or tents—or anything.

"Where's the camp, Sally? We won't have to walk there, will we? We can't possibly carry our luggage anywhere in this heat."

Sally ignored the question and turned to go back to the vehicle. A low red boat bobbed at anchor next to a square wooden jetty on the edge of the river. It was already well laden with boxes and crates, but the driver set about heaving their cases out of the truck and piling them on top, making the little craft tilt alarmingly to one side.

"Sally, what's all this? What's going on? You didn't tell me we were going anywhere by boat!" Suzanna glared at her cousin as she staggered under the weight of a large suitcase.

"Just give me a hand with this case, Suze. What on earth have you got in here anyway? No wonder you took so long to pack, you must have brought your entire wardrobe."

"You didn't answer my question, you devious minx. What other surprises have you got up your sleeve? You know I don't like being out on the water. What if we get turned over by a hippo or something? How much further do we have to go? It's almost dark, too, so doesn't that make it all the more dangerous?"

Sally just grinned and continued to wrestle the last of the packages and boxes across to the boat.

"You could help a little here, Suze. If we all lend a hand we'll be able to get going quicker."

She stepped down into the boat and settled herself cheerfully on top of Suzanna's case.

"You'd better hop in Cuz. Once we leave, this landing will be deserted and you won't want to be here by yourself. Get in or get left behind."

Suzanna placed her hands on her hips and stood on the bank glaring down at Sally.

"You can't seriously expect me to get into that boat," she retorted. "It's over-laden as it is. Ask them to find another one. You never told me I had to go in a boat, so the least you can do is find a bigger one."

"This is the only boat going to the camp, Miss." The African driver flashed Suzanna a grin, thoroughly enjoying her discomfort. He stooped down and made to untie the rope holding the front of the boat.

"It is perfectly safe," he continued, "and the one we use all the time. But we need to get going right now—they will be worried about us at the camp. We are very late and have already radioed them several times."

"My life is forever on your conscience," Suzanna growled at Sally. She was met with an unrelenting cheeky smile.

"Come on Suze. It'll be fine. You heard the man, they only use this boat and we're late. So move it along now and get in."

Nervously Suzanna held on to the driver's proffered hand and stepped down into the bobbing craft. It swayed and rocked with her weight, making her heart jump.

"You will owe me forever for this, and you'd better save me if we capsize."

She squeezed herself uncomfortably between a box of supplies and a crate of drinks, convinced that the heavily laden little boat would never make it safely up river. The driver stepped in, rocking the boat once again. He started the engine and they roared in a curve of spreading wake away from the jetty, heading upstream.

Suzanna's hair whipped round her face in the wind created by the flying little craft and she clutched at her wildly flapping clothing. She tried to crunch down and make herself as small as she could, but there was no shelter on the open deck. Sally, of course, loved every moment and had a smile as wide as a house on her face. She caught Suzanna's eye and gave an infectious laugh that was instantly blown away in the wind. Slowly Suzanna relaxed to the motion but she wasn't going to give Sally the satisfaction of admitting that it was actually fairly exhilarating, with the foaming wake spreading out behind and the tossing wavelets in front that caught the dancing beams of the setting sun. The banks unfurled to either side of the wide river, sometimes hundreds of meters away.

The driver followed the deeper channels, keeping a sharp watch out for the shallows of the sandy islands that dotted their path like giant footprints dropped into the fast flowing water. Suzanna was concerned to see a pod of hippo lazing on one of the islands ahead of them and frantically flapped her hand in their direction.

The driver nodded. He'd seen them long before she had.

"Won't they come into the water in front of our boat?" she yelled.

"As long as we keep our distance we'll be safe enough." The wind whipped his words away but he drove confidently past the pod of fat bodies without disturbing them. Neither of the girls had seen a hippo in the wilds before, but they had read plenty about them and knew of their unpredictability.

Wonderful pink and golden light reached out across the sky and turned the fluffy clouds above into huge puff-balls of candyfloss. The passing banks and trees welcomed the approach of the cooler evening air. The travellers glimpsed three elephant standing knee deep in an inlet, trunks curled under and heads tipped back as they enjoyed a cool drink, but sadly there was no time to stop and watch them.

As the boat drew into the landing at the camp, several smiling attendants dressed in crisp whites were waiting to welcome the party. The girls were offered steady hands that helped them step onto the landing and immediately the workers started to unload the boat. Suzanna looked beyond them and was amazed by the sight of sweeping green lawns and immaculate stone clad buildings, all neatly laid out and maintained. The luggage was efficiently carried away while the girls were escorted along a gravelled pathway up to the little office to check in.

An enormous jaw bone, picked clean of every tiny scrap of flesh and bleached white from years of abandonment in the hot sun, was placed outside the office door. It was a bleak reminder of the harsh reality of life and death and predation in the animal kingdom. Inside an overhead fan slowly stirred the air and a wide wooden counter dominated the room. The floor shone with red polish and in a corner another series of dried out whitened bones were neatly arranged. A crocodile's skull lay amongst them, huge white teeth protruding along the jaw line, an indication of the dangers hidden in the waters of the huge river. A broken elephant tusk was propped in the corner, and the stark black horns and hollow-eyed skull of an antelope stared forever sightless from the wall. The faint smell of formaldehyde hung in the air.

A tall, broad shouldered man stood with his back to the girls, studying a map on the wall. He was dressed in the khaki uniform of a National Parks official, shirt neatly tucked into close fitting shorts that reached knee length. His arms were crossed and he made no effort to turn and greet them. Sally threw Suzanna a glance, lifted an eyebrow, tossed her already dishevelled hair and loudly cleared her throat. He glanced over his shoulder and slowly turned to face the newcomers. His face was stern and his whole demeanor was definitely unfriendly.

Suzanna's gaze was instantly riveted to his face. He was the most handsome, most gorgeous man she had ever seen. Suddenly off balance, she reached up and hastily dragged a hand through her wild hair, hitched her handbag up onto her shoulder and smoothed her shirt into some sort of order.

Sally flung her another sideways glance, giving her a silent "Wow" behind her hand.

The bush green uniform set off his wide shoulders, his eyes were perfectly placed in his tanned, square jawed face, and his mouth, with a bottom lip that was full and promising, had been sculpted by a master craftsman. He emanated raw masculinity from every pore.

However there was no welcoming smile to greet the women. His jaw stuck forward and his lips were set in a hard straight line. He unfolded his arms and reached for a pen lying on the large register in the center of the counter. It seemed he was battling to hold on to his temper and an angry glint sparked in his hazel eyes. Before he spoke a single word, both Sally and Suzanna shrank back like school children who were about to be reprimanded for some misdeed.

"Good evening ladies. I hope you had a good trip, but may I inquire why you are so late?" His deep voice was icy. "I must point out that you have put my drivers, not to mention my vehicle and boat, into danger, by delaying them so much. Perhaps you are unaware of the hazards of being out on the roads and the river after dark? If anything had happened to your party it would have been almost impossible to send a rescue team out until the next day. Another few minutes and the boat would have had to leave without you."

His clipped words dropped like hard pebbles into a still pool, sending cold ripples through the room. Suzanna's eyes widened and the breath caught in her throat in disbelief. Blankly she tried to process why he was so angry with them. What sort of welcome was this? Who did this bloke think he was anyway? She couldn't recall ever having been spoken to in such a manner while checking in to a holiday resort of any nature. Guests should be made to feel welcome, late or not. Obviously this arrogant man didn't hold to the same theory and he wasn't afraid to tell the guests where to get off.

Sally wondered if she should explain. She looked uncertainly at Suzanna, knowing that her fiery cousin would probably make things worse by taking him on in a verbal battle.

Before she could speak, however, the handsome officer stared directly at Suzanna. He swallowed, cleared his throat and said, "I think you will find that several suitcases of clothing, plus the high heels and the hair dryer will be unnecessary here. This is a five star camp, but we work to a well laid out routine, and although we accommodate our guests to the best of our ability, we do appreciate a little punctuality in return."

Suzanna's admiration for the handsome features and extraordinary physique vaporized instantly in the face of this further rude and unnecessary attack. A flush rose in her cheeks and she flicked her hair back behind her shoulders. Sally cringed, waiting for the words she knew would spill out, but she was unable to think of anything to say to stop them. Suzanna straightened her spine, and her brown eyes glinted. She clenched her hands and stared directly back at him.

"Well! I have to say that that was the warmest welcome I have ever received! Do you greet all your guests in such an unwelcoming way?"

Her voice had icicles hanging off every syllable and her expression would have done justice to a stone sphinx.

"For your information," she continued, "I have just spent the last few hours being half battered to death in a rattle trap posing as a vehicle, covered in a layer of choking dust, and blown to bits in an open boat. I never wanted to come to your wretched camp in the first place, and I couldn't give a damn how many stars you have. I can assure you that if there was alternative accommodation close by we would be off to stay there, and leave you to stick your five star camp where you want to. The least you can do now, however, is to cut the lecture and show us to our rooms so that my cousin and I can take a long hot shower."

His expression softened a little but he held her gaze. Sally wondered if there was more to come, or whether he would apologise, but he glanced over Suzanna's shoulder to address one of the smartly clad men who had silently entered the office, and who was standing behind them.

"Solomon, could you show Miss Scott and Miss . . ." he glanced down at the register, "Scott, to their tent." He looked up at them both again and added, "Dinner is in 45 minutes. Pre-dinner drinks will be served to those guests who are present on the top lawn in front of the dining hall in thirty minutes."

They got it in one—either be on time, or miss out on the pre-dinner drink and possibly dinner itself. Suzanna spun on her heels to stalk out of the office, but she couldn't resist having the last word. She stopped and turned in the doorway, tossed her hair behind her shoulder once again and looked back at him.

"And just in case you haven't noticed, there is still at least an hour of daylight left. And for your further information, I don't use a hairdryer!"

Sally was right on her heels. This last comment appealed to her sense of humour and she gave a barely suppressed snort of amusement. With an apologetic glance directed towards the handsome profile, she followed her cousin out of the office.

"That was quite a performance, Suze," she muttered. "You sure told him his fortune. Not that he didn't deserve it, though. Mind you, he's certainly drop dead gorgeous, isn't he?"

"What do you mean?" Suzanna demanded. "He is rude and boorish. How dare he tick us off like two naughty kids. It's incredible that anyone bothers to come to this camp if that's how he greets his guests. It wasn't entirely my fault that we were so late. If I'd known how far we had to travel to get to this God forsaken place—well, I would never have agreed to come. And as for his looks—I don't think I noticed."

"Come on, Suzanna, you noticed alright. Your knees were practically knocking! And he was right about us being late. If you had got your cases ready when I told you to, we would've been on time. You know you always take ages to decide on what to pack for a trip." Sally grinned and tried to smooth Suzanna's feathers. "Anyway, don't lets argue. This must be our tent—wow, some tent!"

Solomon stopped outside their room. The girls looked at a wall made from vertically placed black painted poles. Each one had been cut into half length-ways with the rounded side neatly laid on the outside, leaving no spaces between each long length. The roof was a high, elegant A-frame of thatch that swept right down to ground level, overlapping the low stone side walls. The farm style front door had the top half open to let air into the room, while the bottom half was closed. Solomon stepped forward to open the wooden door for them.

"Welcome to Inkuni Camp, Miss Scott and Miss Scott. We hope you will be comfortable."

"Thank you Solomon," Sally grinned.

Suzanna bit off any more comments as they were shown into a spacious bedroom. The only similarity to a tent was the high pitch of the thatched roof. The combed grass had been immaculately tied over huge black beams and that ran down the length of the room. The low stone walls were wide enough to double as seats and were strewn with brightly coloured cushions and cotton throws. There were also deep fat cushions placed on heavy comfortable looking wooden armchairs sitting solidly on either side of the room. A huge circular rug covered the stone floor, roughly woven in some kind of thick grass or sisal, and a round table was placed in the center of the mat, gleaming with dark varnish.

The far end of the thatch roof was open and the room was completed by a wooden verandah enclosed with a rail. Suzanna walked out onto the deck and stood admiring the glimpse of the river through the trees—a calm and beautiful sight in the last deep purple rays that touched the edges of the high cloud. She took a deep breath, calming herself as she absorbed the lovely view. Green lawns ended a few yards from the front of the little house and were outlined in deepening shadows that looked both tantalizing and scary at the same time. She could imagine unseen eyes watching from the growing darkness, and Suzanna shivered in the suddenly cool air.

Whilst the front of the long room formed the lounge area, at the rear there were two large beds immaculately made up and covered by patterned bedspreads. A variety of bright pillows complimented the colour scheme and the beds were both draped with 'Out of Africa' style mosquito nets. A beautiful solid wooden dressing table, two wooden stools and a large wardrobe completed the array of furniture. The whole place had certainly been very well designed.

Sally wandered through to the immaculate bathroom attached at the back of the room.

"Hey, Suze, come and have a look at this. Talk about luxury—this is great."

Suzanna went through to join her. "Oh wow! What a lovely bathroom."

It was smartly decorated and clean. An oval mirror was placed above the hand basin and the shower cubicle was enclosed with a pretty curtain. The window, however, was open to the elements—no glass or screening of any kind.

"I hope nothing decides to crawl or slither over the window sill," she commented. "Just my luck to have another spider incident."

"You've never forgotten that spider, have you?" Sally grinned. "I still don't know why you made such a fuss about the poor little thing."

"Poor little thing, my hat! It was totally gross. I get the shivers just thinking about it."

"Well, we'd better get a move on, Suze. Do you want to unpack or shower first? On second thoughts, I'll unpack for you while you take a shower. That way we just might make it to dinner on time."

Suzanna left her cousin to the cases. With relief she stripped off her dusty clothing, and clad only in her underwear, she walked through to the bathroom and turned the water on in the shower. One of the luxuries of life, she thought silently, as she stepped under the pummeling needles and felt the water run over her bare shoulders, soaking her hair and easing her body. How did people manage without running water and access to a hot shower each day? What a joy to feel the water wash the dust and dirt of the day away. She soaped her skin and stretched her arms up, luxuriating in the hot water. Then she stepped out, wrapped in a deep soft towel, and briskly rubbed her hair into heavy waves that hung down her back.

As Sally went through to the shower, Suzanna dressed in a loose wrap-around skirt that fell to mid calf, with a soft pastel green blouse and open toed sandals. She applied the minimum of makeup to her eyes, a touch of pale lipstick that complimented her full mouth and then curled up on the cushions to wait for Sally to finish getting ready.

"Isn't it great to fell clean and refreshed?" Sally peered into the mirror and fluffed up her blonde hair. She wore white trousers with a loose top, slim and attractive.

Suzanna sighed, feeling at ease for the first time in what had been a very long day. "It certainly is," she replied. "Come on, I'm starving. Let's go and find this promised drink."

Chapter 4

NIGHT HAD FALLEN in the sudden way that it does in Africa and the camp was full of shadows. Thousands of unseen insects, ground frogs and tree frogs had awakened and were now vibrating the air with a huge range of chirping, clicking, squeaking and croaking noises. The air was warm and sultry, and the moon hung low on the horizon, looking like a pale slice of lemon.

Suzanna was unprepared for the beauty of the scene before them as the girls walked across to the dining area. Fairy lights were strung between several trees, and the path leading to the thatched dining hall was lined by candles set in brown paper bags held down with a base of sand.

In the middle of the trimmed green lawn lay an oval swimming pool. Underwater lights threw beams of sparkling blue diamonds through the clear depths. The pool was encircled by perfectly laid glitter-stone paving, and several long lounger chairs were placed next to tables beneath the boughs of spreading trees, inviting one to sit and relax while enjoying some cool refreshment.

The dining hall itself had only low stone walls round the perimeter and the same A-framed sweeping thatch rose steeply above. There were several guests standing around in small groups outside the dining hall and a few heads turned to watch them walk up. A smiling waiter approached and extended a tray laden with glasses of sparkling wine, and both girls gratefully took a glass.

Suzanna glanced around, admiring the romantic setting. She studied the people standing closest to them and was startled to notice that the hulk from the office was talking to a group of people a few metres away. The men were avidly listening to what he was saying and two of the women smiled up at him, heads tilted and eyes alive. Suzanna knew the look so well. It was obvious that they were hoping to get more than just a casual response from the good looking face.

She studied him beneath lowered lashes. He had changed into casual clothing and looked even more handsome than before, if that was possible. He wore his clothes like a rugged male model. His shirt hung easily off the wide shoulders. The sleeves were half rolled up above strong forearms, and the collar was open at the neck, showing a triangle of tanned throat. Her glance took in the well fitting dark jeans, the slimness of his waist and the line of his thighs below a tight butt. He stood with one foot slightly forward, his head bent, listening politely to what was being said and contributing to the conversation. His tawny hair curled down over his collar, and fell onto one side of his forehead. As Suzanna watched he put up a hand and scraped it back off his face—a gesture that was unconsciously sexy. Against her will, and slightly to her irritation, the muscles in her pelvis tightened.

Suzanna was still smarting at his rudeness towards them earlier, however, and despite the fact that he was very easy on the eye, she had no wish to talk to him. She watched one of the women in the circle laugh gaily at a remark, displaying a pretty dimple in her cheek and flirtatiously slanted eyes. Suzanna wondered what he had said, and secretly admired his broad smile, envying the woman who had caused it. As though he sensed he was being scrutinised, he suddenly glanced round and she quickly bent her head and dropped her eyes to study the drink in her hand.

Sally had turned to introduce herself to another couple and, feeling a little guilty and just a bit flustered, Suzanna turned away and joined them. She had the strangest feeling of being almost caught spying on someone. The back of her neck felt hot under her heavy hair. She wished she had pinned it up instead of leaving it in curls and ringlets down her back.

The two girls stood for a while, sipping wine and chatting to a circle of people. One of the men stepped towards Suzanna and held out his hand.

"Hi, I'm Steve Evans." He introduced himself with a smile, running his eyes appreciatively up and down her body and held onto her hand for longer than he needed to. Her discomfort increased, but he smoothly released her and disguised his gaze by turning to speak to Sally.

"I heard there were a couple of late arrivals this evening. Welcome to the camp. It's a lovely spot and I'm sure you'll have a good time. If there is anything I can show you or help you with, I would be delighted to do so."

"Thank you," Sally replied. "I'm Sally Scott and this is my cousin Suzanna. Yes, we were a little late, but we're glad to be here."

Steve grinned at them both, relaxed and self-assured. His dark hair was cut short and he had the rugged looks of a capable sportsman. He stood with his legs apart, balanced easily on the balls of his feet as he dominated the conversation. He held his drink to his chest while he spoke, and his keen wit soon had the circle of people laughing at a tale concerning a fishing expedition he had recently been on. Not to be outdone, Sally countered with an amusing story of their trip down to the camp, and happily made fun of Suzanna in front of the bunch of strangers.

"When she asked for a larger boat to be delivered I thought the poor driver would have a heart attack."

Suzanna tried unsuccessfully to distract her and get her onto a safer subject, but Sally loved being in the limelight and making the other guests laugh. Her cousin was relieved when one of the waiters pulled a small round tom-tom onto the steps of the dining room. He bent over the little drum and delighted the guests by beating out a hollow, driving and repetitive rhythm.

"That's a true touch of Africa, isn't it?" Steve was right behind Suzanna's shoulder, so close that she could feel the heat of his body and the puff of his breath on her neck. It flustered her to have him so close and she stepped sideways, trying not to appear rude.

He continued, "It's the signal that dinner is ready and we should go into the dining room."

"A really authentic touch," she agreed. "Far better than an ordinary dinner gong."

As she turned to walk away she glanced behind her to see where Sally was—swung back and bumped straight into the rock solid frame that she had been covertly studying earlier. She gasped as her glass tilted and wine slopped onto the front of his dark blue shirt. He involuntarily stepped backwards and for a second she thought she would trip over his foot and fall. His hand shot out and he grabbed her arm with an iron fist to steady her.

Time stopped still as they stood face to face, Suzanna's wrist burning in his grasp. His gaze was fixed on her face. She felt as though she had dropped into a whirling void and her cheeks flamed crimson as she stammered out an apology.

"I'm so sorry—I didn't see you. I turned too quickly—here let me help."

He looked down at his soaking shirt, opened his hand and let go of her arm. She fumbled in her bag for a tissue and dabbed ineffectually at the wet mark, only succeeding in making it worse. He stepped away from her.

"Don't bother, Miss Scott, I can manage without your help." His voice ground out between clenched teeth as he dragged a handkerchief the size of a small sail out of his pocket. "I was going to inquire if you had checked in alright and found the room to your satisfaction. I didn't count on being doused with wine."

Suzanna was painfully aware of the nearness of the wretched man. It flashed through her mind that he was over half a head taller than her, but the width of his shoulders made him appear bigger. Or perhaps he seemed larger than life due to his overpowering and aggressive manner.

"Our room is beautiful, thank you," she managed to stutter. "In fact the whole camp is extremely well laid out and very beautiful. You were right about the stars. I mean the stars for the camp, not the other stars."

What on earth was she gabbling on about? If she sounded like a fool in her own ears, she would not be coming across well. Her hands were shaking. The words were tumbling out and the longer she stood there, with his eyes boring into hers and that mouth only inches away from her face, the worse she felt. There was no softening in his dark hazel stare, however, and his expression remained severe. Suzanna made a concerted effort to pull herself together and clamped her jaw shut before any more inanities could spill out.

Sally's voice in her ear made her jump.

"Are you ready for dinner, Zannie?" She had been standing just two feet away and had witnessed the whole embarrassing encounter. She hadn't made any effort to come to her cousin's assistance and wasn't making any attempt to hide her wide grin. Suzanna instantly knew that her use of 'Zannie' instead of the usual 'Suze' meant that Sally had another smart comment up her sleeve. She let her hand drop and surreptitiously pinched her arm in warning. Suzanna did not need to give this arrogant man any more fuel to add to the fire.

Before either of them could say any more, a pretty woman walked up to join them. She tucked her arm possessively into the crook of the green clad masculine elbow with a possessive gesture. She was dressed in a long kaftan and her short dark hair was cut in a neat shining bob that framed her pretty face and accentuated large, kohl-lined eyes. More than a small amount of cleavage was on display in her deep plunging neckline. She tilted her head to one side, looking coyly up at the handsome profile.

"There you are, Gregg," she gushed. "I see you've met Sally. I'm Rachel, and you must be Suzanna, Sally's cousin?"

Suzanna stretched her mouth into a false grin, but her words were clipped.

"Hi there. Yes, I am Suzanna and no, we haven't been formerly introduced as yet. Such niceties haven't managed to enter the conversation so far."

Undaunted, Rachel's laugh tinkled out, making her nose wrinkle in a charming manner, and the tops of her pushed up breasts quiver happily. She held an empty wine glass in her other hand and the silver bracelets round her slim wrist tinkled as she waved it elegantly in the air.

"Oh, that's par for the course! Has Gregg been ticking you off already? Don't mind him, he means well. Nothing is more important than his beloved camp and equipment. He runs a very efficient outfit here, and his staff and most of his guests adore the ground he walks on." As she paused for a breath she noticed the wet wine mark down the front of his shirt. She clicked her tongue flirtatiously at him and Suzanna's cheeks went pink again as she trilled out,

"What on earth have you been doing? Your shirt is all wet."

Now it was Gregg's turn to look uncomfortable.

"Yes—I've noticed," he muttered. "Excuse me."

He disengaged her hand and hurried off towards the back of the dining room. Embarrassment washed over Suzanna, but it was all she could do not to follow his retreating back with a loud hurrumph of disbelief at this lovely girl's words. Adore the ground he walks on—indeed!

Rachel laughed lightly, "Oh dear! I think I just touched a nerve there. How did his shirt get so wet, anyway?"

"Oh that was my fault." Suzanna's hair draped over her cheek as she inclined her head. "I tripped over his foot and my wine slopped over a little. I didn't mean to do it, obviously, and I feel really bad about it."

"Yes, something like that wouldn't please Mine Host at all. He can get wound up by funny things quite easily."

She spoke in such an assured manner that it seemed evident that she and Gregg were more than just acquaintances. Suzanna bit her lip and swallowed the retort that sprang to her lips. If they were involved with each other she would have to be careful about voicing any opinions. She pasted her smile on a little more securely as she and Sally excused themselves from Rachel's attention and walked into the dining room.

A waiter immediately came towards them and courteously directed them to a table set for two. They thanked him, settled themselves and ordered another glass of wine to have with dinner. While they were waiting for the drinks and the meal to be served, they glanced around. Lines of softly glowing lights hung in trails from the heavy black poles that supported the high pitch of the thatch. The stone flagged floor was well polished and shiny, and doorways, as well as dining alcoves, had been artfully constructed into the interior design. The overlays on each table were crisp and white, and the candle centerpieces threw gleaming reflections onto sparkling glassware and shining, well laid cutlery.

"I have to say, this is a very well designed dining room," Suzanna commented. "A lot of thought has gone into the planning of it."

"The whole camp appears to have been well designed," Sally agreed. "I'm looking forward to exploring everything properly tomorrow."

The meal was delicious and the wine crisp and cool. Sally and Suzanna chatted easily and happily, recalling the day's events.

"I'm sorry I didn't tell you about the boat trip, Zannie. I was afraid you would refuse to come, and I'd had such a hard time persuading you. I thought you would change your mind. To be honest, I wasn't actually sure how long the boat trip would be, or how large a part of the journey it was."

"Oh well, we survived it, I guess. I wasn't very impressed with the reception we got from Mr. High-and-Mighty Gregg though. I wonder if he treats all his guests so curtly when they're two minutes late." She giggled. "And then I had to go and spill wine on him. Of all the things to happen!"

Sally grinned, "Yes, it was bad luck. But you have to admit we were slightly more than two minutes late. I think he was probably worried about us."

"More likely worried about his precious boat," Suzanna countered, sipping her wine. "Who are you looking at like that?"

"Ladies! I hope you are enjoying your meal?"

Startled, Suzanna jumped and almost tipped the glass over. He was standing right behind her chair. She turned and looked up at his handsome face and noted that he now wore a dark green shirt. Her cheeks burned once more to think of their embarrassing encounter earlier. She left the polite talk to Sally, who assured him that the girls had both wined and dined well.

"I'm taking numbers for tomorrow's early morning game drive," Gregg continued. "I only have a couple of others going out tomorrow, so if you can handle the early start you're welcome to come along."

Sally glanced at Suzanna and nodded her head. Without waiting for her to comment she said, "We'd love to come, wouldn't we Suze? What time do you leave?"

Suzanna wasn't at all sure she wanted to go anywhere with this self assured man, and she reached out to kick Sally's foot under the table. If he was going, she certainly didn't want to be there if she could possibly avoid it.

"The vehicle leaves the camp at first light, so you'll need to be outside the office just after 5.30am and we depart just before six. We have another drive going out at eleven, and then there's the boat trip later in the afternoon. So if 5.30 is too early for you, you can always join another of the options."

Jeepers, was there no end to his arrogance? Suzaana felt the last jibe was solely directed at her, and she instantly changed her mind. Who did he think he was? For all he knew she could have been up at 5.30 every morning and dashing about the place on an early morning run or something. Did she look the sort of person who would lie in at every opportunity, and only swing her legs over the edge of the bed at the crack of dawn when she had reason to do so? On sheer principal they would go on his beastly game drive now, even if she had to stay up all night so as not to be late.

She straightened her spine, flashed him a bright smile and smoothly said, "Oh, I don't think 5.30 is too early, is it Sally? We'd be delighted to join your early trip, thank you Mr . . . er . . ." She floundered to a stop, unsure of what to call him. She fiddled with a spoon and then reached for her glass to cover her confusion.

She looked up. Although his eyes were fixed on hers, his eyelids were slightly lowered and he gave the impression he could see into her mind and had just been reading all her thoughts. His broad hand tightened on the board he was holding, the knuckles standing out like ridges, and, for an instant, a muscle flexed in the side of his jaw. With a sharp gesture he suddenly turned and grasped a chair from the next table, dragged it across and sat himself down at the girls' table.

Suzanna's wine glass had been half way to her mouth, but she carefully set it back down, afraid that she would choke if she took a sip. As he swung the chair round and lowered himself onto it with his bent legs spread wide, her focus was drawn downwards. Despite her best efforts to look elsewhere, her eyes took in the firm spread of his thighs on the chair, and flicked across the zip in the middle of his pants that curved sexily outwards. His knee was inches away from her own, and she felt he was issuing a silent challenge, daring her to be the first to move backwards.

He emanated pure masculinity. A rush of heat spread through Suzanna's lower stomach, and she tried not to squirm on her chair, wondering if he knew what an effect he had just had on her. She crossed her legs, feeling as mesmerized as a rabbit in the headlights.

Gregg leaned forwards and propped a bent elbow on the table. A slow smile spread across his face making his eyes sparkle and totally transforming his handsome features. He stretched out and shook Sally's hand.

"I think I owe you both a small apology," he stated. "I over-reacted when you arrived because I was worried that perhaps there had been an accident of some sort. I'm Gregg Mayland."

As he swivelled towards Suzanna, her hand floated into the air of it's own accord and tucked itself into his wide palm. She was unable to look away.

"Please accept this formal introduction, Ladies, and may I wish you a belated welcome to Nkuni Camp. I feel certain you will enjoy being here."

He was making fun of her earlier remark, Suzanna knew it, but now he had her hand held firmly in his grasp and his gaze was fixed on her face, and she found she could not move a muscle. Her stare was totally encompassed within those hazel eyes. Her mind was a complete blank and, for the life of her, she couldn't think of a single reply.

Sally came to her rescue and filled the uncomfortable silence by introducing first herself and then her cousin.

"Please don't call either of us Miss Scott," she smiled, glancing from one face to the other. "It's far too formal, and confusing since we have the same surname. And we'd love to come out on the early drive tomorrow morning."

As if a thread had been suddenly cut, Gregg released Suzanna's hand and abruptly stood up. The wonderful smile had vanished, and a frown had taken it's place. Suzanna felt as though a cold wind had blown across her face. What had flipped through his mind to bring on such a radical change in his expression and manner? She pinched her lips together and smoothed her skirt over her knees, determined not to show how disappointed she was to lose the warm contact with his large hand.

He turned on his heel and rather curtly said, "Right then, I'll see you both bright and early tomorrow morning. It will probably be cool to start with so bring a jacket along."

Suzanna felt she could breathe again and she drew in some air as she watched him stride off across the room to speak to another couple. Her palm was on fire and she hunched forwards, hugging both hands under her armpits to hide the visible trembling. A strange weakness settled in the small of her back.

"What?" She demanded of her cousin. "Get that silly grin off your face—it would look good on a Cheshire cat. I still think he is overbearing and self-opinionated, and he sure runs hot and cold in a heart beat. I only agreed to go on the drive so that he didn't get the better of us. I certainly don't want to get up that early, but I'll be damned if I'll let him know that. Sally, will you wipe that silly grin off your face!"

"Oh Suzie, you are in trouble," Sally chortled. "You have been smitten by that gorgeous hunk. I have to say, I don't actually blame you. A little encouragement and I could be giving you a run for your money over him."

"What utter rubbish!" Suzanna felt flustered and hot. "You are talking through your hat. Anyone can see that he isn't on the market, and anyway, what about dear Rachel with her melting brown eyes? She is obviously his girl. Either that, or he's already married. Who would want to be involved with such a temperamental and grumpy guy, anyway? You'd have to be insane to fall for him. If you want him, you can have him, as far as I'm concerned."

"Cool down, Cuz. Let's go and have a night-cap at the bar before bed. If we have to be up before the crack of dawn we'd better turn in reasonably early. I wonder who else will be along tomorrow?"

Several sets of eyes followed them across to the bar. Suzanna told herself it was Sally's lovely tousled blonde look that drew the glances, but secretly she knew that they made quite a striking pair together. Her darker auburn colouring complimented Sally's blonde looks and they both had a long-legged way of walking that seemed to attract attention.

The barman welcomed them with a smile. He was standing behind a huge bar-top of solid dark wood. Suzanna marveled at the size of the tree that must have been sacrificed to construct this magnificent gleaming counter. It stretched a full twenty feet down the room, and was covered with a scattering of glasses and bottles belonging to people chatting and laughing in groups. Behind the barman more glasses of every shape were arrayed on wooden shelves and a colourful line up of half full bottles of brandy, whisky, gin and liqueurs waited to be measured and poured for thirsty customers. A happy and social atmosphere prevailed.

As the girls hesitated, deciding what they would drink, a ruggedly good-looking man came over to stand right next to Sally. He flashed them both a grin, sticking out his hand to shake theirs.

"Hi there! I'm Pete Walters. You must be the ladies who arrived late this evening. Can I buy you both a drink? Beautiful evening, isn't it?"

Sally laughed. "It seems the whole camp knows about our late arrival."

The girls introduced themselves, accepted the offer of a glass of wine, and spent the next half an hour chatting amiably to him. It was pretty obvious to Suzanna, though, that the focus of his attention was on her flirtatious cousin, so when her glass was empty she decided to excuse herself and slip away. The long day had caught up with her. Her limbs felt heavy and tired and she was more than ready to head for bed. She touched Sally's hand as she left the bar, not wanting to disrupt the party or make her departure noticeable.

She stepped outside, feeling the sultry air warm, and yet somehow cool, on her skin. After the lights inside, the path leading down to their room suddenly seemed filled with deep patches of shadow. Suzanna hesitated but she wasn't going to turn back and look like a ninny afraid of the dark. She walked lightly along, telling herself that nothing would come so close to human habitation, but her heart was beating rapidly and her ears strained for any unusual sounds.

She almost made it!

Just as she passed the soft lights of the pool area, an ominous rustling off in the darkness to her right made her stop dead in her tracks. She clasped her hands together and peered into the bushes trying to see what had made the sound.

The rustling continued, coming closer. All at once a huge grey shape emerged out of the shadows just ahead of her. An involuntary cry escaped her lips and she shrank back against a tiny tree that would give her no protection at all. Her heart was hammering, and she was struck by fear. She wondered if she should run back, but she couldn't get her wobbling legs to move. She recalled stories of people being chased and attacked the moment they fled from wild animals.

"Stay quite still!" A voice in her ear almost made her leap out of her skin and she gave another yelp of fright.

"Right, I've got you. Now move slowly back this way."

Gregg's strong arm was around her shoulders and her back was pressed to his solid chest. He held her against him and slowly moved with her, step by step, away from the great animal that was calmly munching at the green lawn. It was a very large hippo, and Suzanna could hear the grinding of it's awesome teeth in a huge wide mouth as it tore at the tender shoots. It lifted it's head and poised, motionless, staring in their direction. Suzanna was terrified it would charge. Her nails dug small crescents into the skin of Gregg's forearm and she squeaked in fright.

"Shh. We don't want to spook it. Just come this way."

Slowly, the couple retreated to the safety of the far side of the pool, Gregg's arm still holding Suzanna's slim shape close, and they stood for a moment watching the peaceful animal enjoying it's feed. For the briefest of moments she relaxed against his chest, holding onto his arm and enjoying the feel of the solid masculine frame, but now her knees felt weak for a different reason. She wasn't quite sure why she felt so off balance and why her heart was making funny irregular beats. A picture of Rachel's attractive, self-possessed smile popped into her mind. She stepped away from him and ran a shaky hand through her hair. She was suddenly on the defensive and a quick retort leapt to her lips.

"Were you following me? You almost gave me a heart attack! How come the animals can just wander at will through the camp, anyway? Don't you realize the danger to the guests?" The harsh words spilled out of her mouth. Where on earth had they come from? She hadn't planned to say anything so hurtful and ungrateful. Hadn't planned on saying anything at all really.

Even in the dim light she could see the flash of his eyes, and his whole being tensed up with anger.

"This is an unfenced bush camp, not some sort of zoo, Miss Scott," he ground out, "and I consider your remark about following you to be offensive. We are privileged to be able to share the natural surroundings and environment of the wildlife here. If guests are stupid enough to walk about on their own, without taking proper care and attention to things around them, especially at night when the animals move around more, they are asking for trouble."

He spun on his heel to leave. Suzanna regretted her quick, thoughtless words, but they were out now and nothing she could say would make the situation any better. His face was a pale mask above her.

"The hippo has moved away, so you'll be safe enough to go back to your room now. Good night."

She was rooted to the spot, feeling hot and cold at the same time. She watched his retreating form head back in the direction of the office and regret washed over her. Her sharp words hadn't been intentional. They had somehow fallen out of her mouth without prior thought from her brain. She wished she could take them back, make them disappear, never to have been uttered. It was not like her to be so confrontational and she was genuinely upset to have been so rude to Gregg.

She glanced carefully in all directions and then, with her shoes in her hand, she fled down the path to the safety of their room. She fell onto her bed, totally exhausted. Her head was splitting, and the events of the day crowded in on top of her.

She knew she shouldn't have come. She should never have let Sally talk her into it. She knew she wouldn't fit into this camp-style living, as beautiful and up-market as it was. She felt like a fish out of water here. She knew nothing about the bush or the animals that existed in this area. Both Sally and Suzanna had been born and brought up in this land that abounded with wildlife, but they had had no experience of anything wilder than the cattle on a commercial farm.

Suzanna lay on her side feeling thoroughly sorry for herself.

Then she remembered that she'd heard someone in the pub mention that a few of the guests were going home tomorrow. A short, balding man and his equally dumpy wife had declared that they'd had a marvellous time and were sad to be leaving. But Suzanna knew she would not have a marvellous time when everything was so against her. She turned it over in her mind, debating whether she should leave with them. Yes, definitely, that's what she'd do. The more she thought about it, the more determined she became. As soon as they returned from the morning game drive she would announce her plan, and pack her case. Sally could stay on here by herself. She'd be perfectly fine and there were enough other guests to entertain her.

This time Suzanna would make her own decision and not allow Sally to force her to change her mind. She should never have given in and agreed to come in the first place. Now she would stand firm and not give in. Still fully clothed, she drifted into a restless sleep.

Chapter 5

THE SHRILL TONES of the alarm sounded just as there was a discreet knock at the door. Suzanna rolled over to see a waiter enter, carrying a tray laden with steaming coffee and freshly baked muffins. It was still dark outside, although there were a few tentative rays of light easing across a cloudless sky, throwing patterns of light through the room.

She sat up, hair tousled and nightie twisted around her hips. She remembered waking during the wee hours and getting up to change out of her clothing. Muddled dreams had pursued her all night and she was tempted to tuck back down for another hour or so. It was an effort to get out of bed.

Sally felt the same way. "Oh boy, I don't think I can get up," she moaned, but she swung her feet onto the floor anyway and leaned forward with her head in her hands.

"Did you have too much wine last night?" Suzanna's voice sounded foggy and she cleared her throat. "What time did you get in? I didn't even hear you. Did you spend the evening with Pete? He seemed quite nice actually—very good looking."

"Yeah, we got on really well and seemed to have a lot to talk about. The evening just flew. But there were some other pleasant people in the pub as well, you should have stayed and had some fun."

Suzanna felt too tired to tell Sally about her experience with Gregg and the hippo. It could wait until later. She finished her coffee, went through to the bathroom and they both started to get ready for the day.

Without mentioning anything to Sally, Suzanna left a pile of folded clothes on her bed, determined to go through with her plan to leave the camp as soon as they got back from the game drive. She knew Sally would be horrified at her decision and she didn't want to mention it until she'd had a chance to put the plan into action. Suzanna knew her cousin would spend all morning trying to persuade her to stay, and she had made up her mind for definite this time. On the way to the office, to divert Sally's attention, she related the story of the hippo incident with Gregg, making light of the harsh words they had exchanged. As soon as she'd finished the story, she knew shouldn't have told her! She should never have mentioned it. Sally exploded into giggles, but didn't get a chance to reply.

There were a couple of other guests standing near the Land Rover in the dawn light. Pete was amongst them, and he walked over to greet Sally with a warm smile.

"Good day, ladies. You look happy for such an early hour."

Suzanna sent Sally a warning look and clutched her jacket across her chest in the chilly air. The sun was just about to creep over the far horizon and the rays stretched out across the sky to grasp the new day. The camp was just as lovely in the soft daylight and the pool had looked most inviting. The river was visible through the trees and the growing early morning light sparkled off the water, flowing strongly but silently on it's long journey to the sea.

Despite the gentle haze, the day promised to be hot. Silently Suzanna cursed herself for leaving her dark glasses in the room and wondered if she would have time to run back for them. Just at that moment Gregg walked up with his long stride and her opportunity was lost. After he'd pointed out so clearly last night that the girls were not to be late, she thought it would give him great satisfaction to leave her behind if she ran back for the glasses now.

"Morning everyone." He held his clipboard and briskly greeted the waiting guests.

Suzanna noticed that he avoided meeting her eyes, and when he directed everyone to climb into the vehicles she pulled Sally across to the one on the far side, feeling sure that he would drive the nearest one.

Both vehicles had two raised bench seats behind the driver's seat and were completely open to the sky and the weather—and to any wild animals they might encounter. Pete and one of the scouts headed towards the second vehicle, which pleased Sally. The men leaped nimbly up to the second row of seats, looking perfectly at home.

Sally followed Suzanna and they climbed up, choosing to sit in the first row. Suzanna made sure she sat in the middle with Sally to her left. She felt safer with a person on either side of her, which she realized was a selfish move, but she was nervous enough in the open vehicle without feeling as though she may fall out at any given moment.

"Make sure you hold on," she warned Sally. "You're a bit vulnerable on the edge there."

Steve Evans approached and climbed up to settle himself in the seat to Suzanna's right.

"Good morning ladies. Suzanna," he smiled, leaning right into her face. "I trust you slept well? We're in for a good day I reckon."

Suzanna greeted him back, stifling the feeling that he had grabbed that seat just to be near her. He had binoculars hanging round his neck and gave the impression that he was an old hand at this game-driving scene. He lost no time in telling her what they could expect to see.

"This is the best time of day to go game viewing," he assured her. "The game likes to have a last drink before hiding out for the day."

"Actually the evening is supposed to be better," Pete leaned forward and put his hand on Sally's shoulder. "That's when the nocturnal animals start to move around, and set out hunting."

Both men were displaying their knowledge to impress the women, and Sally giggled, enjoying the mini jousting competition. Suzanna glanced past Steve and her face fell as she watched Gregg stride over to their vehicle. She had been so sure he would drive the first one, but it was already pulling out of the parking area with a different scout at the wheel.

Gregg flicked a glance at his passengers, settled himself in the drivers seat, and with a curt, "Everyone OK?" he fired up the engine and they left camp in the inevitable cloud of dust.

Suzanna hung onto the handrail, determined not to brush against Steve, as they headed inland away from the river and drove towards the thicker bush.

Right away she knew she had chosen the wrong seat. She was sitting directly in line with the rear-view mirror. She could see Gregg's hazel eyes clearly framed and knew that all he had to do was to glance up and he would only see her in his mirror. She was trapped! He would think she had sat in the middle seat on purpose. Damn! Why hadn't she brought her sunglasses! She sneaked a peak but at the moment his frowning gaze was divided between the road ahead and the man chatting happily in the front seat beside him.

Suzanna tried to take an interest in Steve's running commentary but her glance kept returning to the mirror, watching the eyes framed there. She noted the way the brown hair at the back of his neck curled over his collar, lifting and blowing in the breeze. She almost had to sit on her hands to resist the temptation to reach out and smooth it down. Then she remembered their exchange of sharp words last night, and the regret washed over her again. Rachel was a lucky woman.

"Did you bring your sunglasses, Sal?" She kept her voice low and casual. "The wind is worrying my eyes a little and I've forgotten mine back at camp."

"No, I didn't think to bring them. Sorry about that. Isn't this bush beautiful? Look at the shadows where the sun is hitting the far hills through the gap there."

Suzanna followed Sally's pointing finger and tried to keep her eyes on the scenery. They wound through a narrow road, travelling more slowly, all eyes trying to pierce the bush and catch a glimpse of an animal or two. The sun was fully up, sending golden shafts of light through the trees, but the air was still cool and Suzanna was glad of her jacket.

Gregg slowed to a crawl and then stopped to point out a flock of guinea fowl sitting like huge ripe fruits in the branches of a tree. Their heads were tucked down against their breasts, and the multitude of white spots on their grey feathers merged with the colour of the bark. As the party watched, one of the fat birds fluffed out it's feathers and launched itself off it's perch. The rest followed and the whole flock flew away over the tree line, calling melodiously to each other.

"Oh, for a shotgun," Steve said. "Guinea fowl make very good eating."

"You have to be sure to get the pellets out of them first," Pete said.

Sally raised an eyebrow at Suzanna. They were still competing!

Gregg drove on, winding slowly through narrow roads. Ahead of the vehicle a large pool of water suddenly came into view. It was surrounded by sparse grass cover and trimmed at the edges with clumps of dark green reed beds. Thorny trees spread their branches spikily upwards, affording dappled shade. The Land Rover glided to a stop near to the edge of the pan, and the enchanted passengers sat transfixed, absorbing the peaceful scene laid out before them.

A selection of herons and other water birds dabbled in the shallows, and a cloud of yellow butterflies fluttered around a pile of fresh animal dung lying on the muddy beach. The water of the pan was dark and seemed murky, despite the increasing sunlight. The whole area appeared to be deserted apart from the birds doing their early morning fishing.

Gregg turned to warn everyone to sit quietly.

"This is a central pan," he explained. "Plenty of animal trails wind past here, and it is a favourite drinking spot for a variety of game."

They sat in silence, waiting, hoping that something would emerge from the bush. One of the herons darted forwards and triumphantly held aloft a small wriggling fish in it's long sharp beak. With an artful toss of it's head it flicked the little body about and swallowed it in one gulp. The progression of the lump that the fish made was clearly visible as it travelled on it's last journey down the long neck.

"Oh look!" Sally whispered. "Kudu!"

As if by magic, a superb kudu bull stepped cautiously out of the trees. The dark faun of it's hide blended perfectly with the dusty greys and greens of the bush. He was truly magnificent.

They all held their breath as another two younger males stepped out of the cover to follow him down to the water's edge. Everyone marvelled at the wonderful elegance of their proud heads adorned with three-foot spiralling horns. Large limpid brown eyes and ears trimmed with soft hair checked for signs of danger. The antelopes stood perfectly still, within reach of the safety of the bush, staring intently at the vehicle, every muscle bunched and tense. Then, one by one, the regal animals stepped gracefully out into the clearing, shoulder blades moving under the smooth skin, every cell of their beautiful bodies alert and on edge. Heads high, they studied the surrounding bush, but their attention kept returning in the direction of the people who had time to appreciate the sweep of their long proud necks, and the white line under their eyes that looked like it had been applied by a make-up artist.

Gracefully, with long steps, they slowly approached. It took all of twenty minutes but eventually they reached the pan, spread their front legs comfortably wide and lowered thirsty mouths to the refreshing water.

It was a sight Suzanna would remember forever. It was a profoundly intense moment for her, and she felt it had seared itself into her memory. She was totally wrapped up in the moment. How could anyone ever consider shooting one of these magical animals? They were a fabulous study in grace and beauty and elegance.

A movement from Gregg brought her gaze back and she realized with a flush that he had been watching her reaction to the perfect scene. Impulsively, a broad grin lit up her lovely face and for a while their eyes locked as they shared an uncomfortably intimate moment via the rear-view mirror.

Then they all jumped in fright as the huge bull snorted a loud warning. The three heads swung up, instantly alert and listening. Then, as one, little herd turned on long legs and, cantering in long strides, they were swallowed immediately by the cover of the bush.

"Oh, they've gone!" Suzanna felt a strange sense of loss. "What could have frightened them like that? It took them so long to get the confidence to come down to the water, and they've hardly had a proper drink."

"I heard branches breaking a little while ago and my guess is that a herd of elephant is approaching," Gregg replied. "This pan never dries up so it attracts a wide range of animals, especially in the early morning like this."

She felt he was talking only to her and she put a hand to her throat to still the pulse.

He pointed over the windscreen of the truck and spoke softly. "See over there, can you pick out the grey of their hides? They've been feeding in that thicket for a while."

"But they wouldn't pose any threat or danger to such large kudu, would they?" Sally asked.

"No, they wouldn't. Kudu have incredible hearing, and a strong sense of self-preservation, so perhaps they just decided to vacate the scene," he answered. "The elephant are moving closer. The matriarch will lead them to the water once she has checked it's safe for the herd."

Suzanna's vision turned towards his pointing finger, but her untrained eyes could only pick out a slightly denser patch within the dappled shadows. It was rather frightening to realize that they were sitting in an open vehicle with a herd of elephant about to come their way. The kudu had been wonderful to see, but elephant were quite another story.

"What about us? Aren't we too close? What if they walk over this way?" Her whisper was loud.

"They are quite used to this vehicle, so just sit still and they won't be alarmed." He reassured not only Suzanna but the others in the Land Rover as well.

Slowly, the bulk of five elephant materialized out of the bush ahead. One moment they were just forms blurred in the shadows, and the next they had taken shape and were clearly visible. The lead animal was the largest. She swung her head towards the vehicle, put her head back and lifted the end of her trunk high, trying to catch a scent and testing for danger. The strange v-shape of the double tip turned towards the humans, breathing the air in their direction. One large white tusk slightly curved over the other, gleaming in a shaft of sunlight. Suzanna shivered with a mixture of fear and excitement, and grabbed Sally's hand. Those tusks looked fearsome and dangerous and they were pointed in their direction.

Once again the observers held their breath as the big cow hesitated for long moments until she deemed it safe to lead her small family to the water's edge to drink. Her grey hide was criss-crossed with hundreds of wrinkles, and the huge ears fanned backwards and forwards, moving the air to cool the blood pumping through the rope like arteries visible behind them. It was fascinating to see how the edges hung more softly—reminding Suzanna of the draped edges of a mini tablecloth. The soles of the enormous circular feet were capped by huge toenails that seemed almost human in likeness, and she walked with a slightly bouncy stride that made her huge head swing slightly from side to side as she approached. Her lowered trunk dangled down loose with the tip curled off the ground.

Behind her was another smaller cow, a three quarter grown calf and two quite small babies. Once the two little ones caught the smell of the water, and had been given the silent go-ahead by the matriarch, they trotted with the dearest ambling gait, stubby trunks whirling uncontrollably in anticipation, down to the pan, waded a few paces into the cool brown water and started to tussle and play. They pushed at each other's bodies and splashed and blew spray at each other. They looked like roly-poly toys with their small flappy ears, short trunks and slightly hump-backed stance. The people smiled at their antics—they were a joy to watch. The adult animals concentrated on getting their fill to drink whilst keeping a benevolent eye on the youngsters.

The matriarch sucked up a bucket's worth of water into her trunk, tipped her head back and emptied it into her mouth. Streams of water ran out of the sides of her under-lip and cascaded back to the ground at her feet. She drank several times, and then the next trunk full was sprayed backwards over her head and back, turning her dusty hide into rivulets of mud.

She stood still, but the sensitive end of her trunk reached out in all directions to investigate odd tufts of grass and weeds at the water's edge. It had the agility of a hand as it wrapped round a clump, pulled strongly and then swished the greenery back and forth in the water to wash off any mud before lifting the morsel up to the pointed lower lip above. Again and again she cleaned off clumps of grass before depositing them into her mouth, chewing with a sideways motion of large unseen teeth.

The younger cow stood with one back knee relaxed and bent forwards, encased in the baggy folds of leathery skin. All of their backbones curved upwards to slope away over their hindquarters and end in a slim tail finished with thick long bristles. Her trunk also stretched out to seek edible grasses, which she cleaned in the water before lifting them up to eat.

Next to Suzanna, Steve had been watching the huge animals through his binoculars, despite the fact that they were so close. He silently handed the glasses to her to look through. She adjusted the focus slightly and was startled to find that the huge grey forms seemed to leap within touching distance. She studied the age-old brown eyes of the wonderful female, and noted that although the cow was drinking and feeding and appeared completely relaxed, her keen gaze never left the vehicle for an instant. Her trunk might have been picking up morsels to eat, but her attention was totally directed towards the humans. She was watching them watching her and her family. The concentration and focus of her intelligent brown eyes unnerved Suzanna slightly. It was as though she was conversing in a silent language with her family, discussing the observers.

A beam of sunlight shone across the front of the vehicle, lighting up trillions of dust particles hanging in the air. Suzanna's nose suddenly itched, and in a panic she raised her hand to rub her face.

Oh great goodness—she was about to sneeze!

She knew that she had a serious problem on her hands. All her life she had had a loud and explosive sneeze. One that was impossible to control, often overtaking her completely. She just could not help sucking in loud involuntary gulps before a blast of air burst out of her nose and mouth, often at least five or six times, and generally there was very little she could do to stop the noise.

"Has anyone got a hanky?" Her whisper was louder than intended. She was impressed at how quickly Gregg produced the small sail from his pocket. He waved it in front of her and she grabbed at it gratefully. The binoculars fell to her lap as she clamped the hanky to her face, just as the first huge explosion shook her shoulders. Despite her effort to muffle the sound and swallow the sneeze, the result sounded like a blow-up pillow that a small boy would put underneath Ancient Aunt Matilda just as she lowered her bulk to the armchair, embarrassing her with the rude noise.

Everyone jumped and Sally automatically pressed her hand on top of Suzanna's in an effort to help. One, then two sneezes rocked her.

It is impossible for anyone to keep their eyes open when they sneeze, so she was unaware of the instant drama she'd caused until a few seconds later when Gregg's urgent whisper reached them all.

"Sit absolutely still. No-one move!"

Alarmed by the sudden sound from the vehicle, the matriarch elephant had whirled round, spread her ears wide and taken a series of rapid steps in their direction. She was standing just a few paces from the front of the vehicle, ears out, trunk stretched towards them and legs spread wide. Suzanna's eyes flew open and she froze in horror. The rest of the sneezes instantly died in her throat.

They all sat like statues, realizing how tiny and insignificant they were compared to this awesome animal towering like a hostile grey mountain in front of them. Suzanna was terrified she would charge the vehicle and kill them all, and it would be her fault.

She was so huge. Standing head on, the width of her skull was immense, made even more menacing by her flared ears. Her tusks pointed forwards, lifted towards the vehicle, threatening and powerful. She was poised for instant action and one more sound would have her onto them in a flash. Suanna's heart raced in terror. Her hands were clamped so tightly into fists that her fingernails dug into the palms. No-one moved. They were at the mercy of the enormous cow, staring at the massive shape as she decided whether she would carry out her threat.

It seemed like an eternity before the animal finally lowered her trunk, gave her head and ears a huge dust-cloud shake, and swung away to lead her small group at a fast pace back into the bush. In less than half a minute they had disappeared.

None of the occupants of the Land Rover had drawn a breath for moments on end and they let out a huge collective sigh, sagging with relief against their seats.

"I'm so sorry, everyone," Suzanna stammered. "I just can't help sneezing loudly. I feel really bad to have spoilt the game viewing. I'm very sorry. It must have been the dust. I feel terrible."

Pete and Steve murmured their sympathy and forgiveness, but Gregg turned round and gave her the benefit of his icy stare.

"We may as well head back to camp now." His voice was as cold as steel. "All the game within miles will have been frightened away."

Suzanna cringed down in her seat, cursing herself for sneezing and wrecking this special moment for everyone. She stared at the back of Gregg's head, feeling like an admonished schoolgirl once again. It seemed she was destined to annoy this handsome man of the bush. Whatever she did seemed to irritate him.

'Let's face it though,' she thought, 'he's in his element here, you aren't. How were you expected to know a sneeze would scare the animals? It's really not fair of him to react like this and make you feel so awful. It's embarrassing enough without him adding his ten cents worth.'

She blew her nose into his hanky, feeling awkward and defensive.

Well, she had decided to leave camp after the game drive, and now, after this incident, she would stick to her plan. She had enjoyed the outing, and loved seeing the kudu so close up, but she had had enough of his rudeness, and was not going to take any more. She was definitely out of her comfort zone here, so she would chuck it in and go home.

On the drive back to camp she stared resolutely at the bush slipping by on either side of the track so that there was no chance of meeting Gregg's eyes in the mirror. Sally whispered a few comforting words to her, knowing how upset she was, but Suzanna barely said a word in return. As the vehicle passed a thick patch of bush the pungent smell of dead and rotting animal flesh wafted past, and she shuddered at the unpleasant smell. This was a harsh and unforgiving place with no room for anyone who couldn't take the pace, and she would be happy to leave as soon as possible.

As soon as the vehicle drew up outside the office she jumped out and walked quickly inside to approach the guide on duty before anyone could stop her. Trying to sound casual but determined, she asked if she could leave the camp on the boat going out later in the morning.

"I'm so sorry Miss Scott, that boat has already left," came the smiling reply.

"What? It can't have! I heard someone say it was going out in the middle of the morning. It can't have left yet. I would like to leave on that boat, please. I've made up my mind, I want to go home today."

"The boat had to leave a little earlier to allow time to pick up supplies. I'm sorry but it left about half an hour ago."

Suzanna felt flustered and angry and hot. She leaned forward on the counter, trying to get her point across as forcefully as she could.

"Well, when does the next boat leave? Is there one going out tomorrow, or perhaps this afternoon? Can't you organise one to take me downriver? I really would like to go home. I've made up my mind to leave today. Please can you arrange something?"

The deep voice behind her made her stomach sink to her shoes.

"The next boat leaves camp on Sunday, Miss Scott. Our fuel supplies are precious so we can't afford to send boats on long trips too often. We try to preserve our stocks so that we have ample fuel left for game drives for the guests, or for any emergency that might arise."

She turned to see Gregg had entered the office, still looking imposing and annoyed. Sally was right on his heels.

"Suze, what are you doing? Why do you want to leave?" she demanded. "I wondered where you had gone to so quickly. I've been looking for you. What are you doing?"

Oh God! Suzanna felt like shouting at the whole lot of them. She dropped her head down onto her hand, and made a huge effort to control herself. She didn't want to get into any sort of argument here, or have to explain herself in front of the interested staff, or this arrogant man. A million retorts flashed through her brain, but none of them made it as far as her mouth. It was obvious that they would not take her back downriver today, argue as much as she liked.

She straightened her spine, swung her hair back, and with a cool, "Never mind," she walked to the door and left with Sally right on her heels. She could feel several pairs of eyes glued to her back, but she kept going, striding down the path, ignoring Sally's questions.

Once they reached their room Suzanna flung the door open and turned to her.

"I'm just fed up with the way that darn man keeps speaking to me. I can't do anything to please him and he keeps making me feel like a fifteen year old. We haven't been here for twenty four hours yet but it seems like forever. I should never have come to this camp in the first place. I'm totally out of my depth here. I should never have let you talk me into it. I made up my mind this morning to leave once we returned from the game drive, and now the boat has already left and I can't go. It's just not fair."

"Suze! You're working yourself up into a state here! Settle down a little. You never mentioned that you had considered leaving. Why are you letting Gregg get under your skin like this? As you say, we've only just met him, so why go on like this?"

"Of course I didn't mention it to you. You would have spent the whole drive trying to change my mind. I'm not letting Gregg get under my skin. I'm just fed up to the back teeth with how he speaks to me. I don't think I've met anyone ruder than he is. I couldn't help sneezing out there today, and I apologized to everyone. I was as scared as heck that that cow would charge us, and I didn't need Gregg's input to make me feel even worse."

She realized she still had Gregg's handkerchief screwed up into a ball in her hand. With an angry gesture she threw it into the corner of the room and flung herself onto the bed.

"OK, enough already, Suze. Everyone realized you didn't sneeze on purpose. We'll go out again and see more game. It's truly not the end of the world. Perhaps Gregg was still bristling from your little encounter last night. It seems to me that he's not quite sure what to make of you."

She was referring to the hippo incident last night. She laughed again and teased in her most irritating voice,

"Tell me the bit where you were in Gregg's arms again—I think I missed a few details there."

"Jeepers creepers, Sally, I swear you're almost as maddening as he is," Suzanna muttered. "Thanks for the sympathy. Trust you to overlook the fact that I was scared out of my wits. And please don't talk about it in front of anyone else."

Now Sally made an attempt to mollify her. "Come on. We're both starving, so lets have a drink and some brunch next to the pool and cool off for a few hours. If you have to stay here till Sunday we may as well enjoy ourselves and make the most of the fabulous facilities. I've booked us for the late afternoon boat drive, so we can relax until then."

Suzanna knew it was useless to argue with her, or to say that the last thing she wanted was to go on the boat drive later. Sally would only poke more fun at her. Suzanna gave the smiling blonde head the benefit of her blackest scowl, but her cousin grinned cheerfully back, unfazed and aware that she had scored once again.

Chapter 6

THE GIRLS CHANGED into their swimming costumes—Sally's a bright bikini and Suzanna's a sheer electric blue one-piece that hugged every curve of her body. They both wrapped colourful sarongs over the top, grabbed the sun cream, hats and dark glasses plus other essential items and headed to the pool area.

A few of the other guests had had the same idea, and were already soaking up the sun, chatting, sipping long iced drinks and looking thoroughly relaxed. The sight of the cool sparkling water did wonders for Suzann's mood. The girls dumped all their gear next to two long loungers, ordered a drink and a few tasty nibbles from the ever-courteous waiter, and took a while to spread sun protection over every inch of exposed skin. Suzanna wound her hair up under her hat, stretched out with a sigh, closed her eyes and let the warm rays of the sun drench through her limbs.

Sally and Suzanna attended regular yoga sessions and now Suzanna brought a few of the relaxation moves into her mind. She concentrated on the present moment, and put the embarrassing incident of the sneeze out of her mind. She closed her eyes, took a few deep breaths and exhaled slowly, loving the feel of the sun seeping into her bones. She gloried in the full stretch of her long legs, and slowly her muscles responded and the tautness dissipated.

Were they never to be left alone!

Suzanna was on the edge of sliding into a half dozing state, delicious waves of relaxation smoothing her senses. Sally too, was stretched out with her eyes closed and hat tilted over her face. Neither of them wanted to hear the cheerful voice that asked if she could join them. Suzanna put her hand up to shade her eyes and saw the lovely Rachel standing over them.

Her slim figure was being shown off to it's best in a sheer costume that was brightly slashed with contrasting oranges and blues. The neckline plunged and two plump breasts were half squeezed out of the top, sexy and eye catching. Her limbs were tanned a light golden colour, long and shapely. She had a light sarong tied round her hips, a beach bag draped over one shoulder and a bright smile lit up her beautiful face. A fashionably floppy hat dipped over one eye. She was the picture of casual but alluring elegance.

Suzanna sat up with a smile and invited Rachel to pull up a lounger and join them. She thought of her tucking her arm into Gregg's the evening before, clearly indicating a prior claim to his attentions. Here was Suzanna's chance—she was busting to quiz her about their relationship.

Rachel spread her towel out, unwound her sarong and stretched out with a sigh, reaching for her drink.

"Did you go out on the game drive this morning?" She chatted happily. "I went on the drive yesterday so I decided to do the walk this morning. It was magic—quite hot by the time we got back though. I just love the bush in the early morning before the wind gets up and the dust starts. Everything seems to hold such promise for the day, and the light is so beautiful."

"That's brave of you—to walk through the bush, I mean," Suzanna replied. "Don't you find it a bit frightening being on foot with the possibility of getting too close to a large animal? I was nervous enough this morning in the relative safety of the Land Rover."

"The guide that takes you out always carries a gun, which makes you feel safer, but they have only had to fire into the air on a couple of occasions in the last year. They know their stuff and their first priority is the care of the guests. If you're not very experienced they won't take you through thick bush but will stick to open walks, and you'd be unlikely to be threatened by any big game. You should go out tomorrow, it's a wonderful opportunity that you shouldn't miss."

"Let's do it, Suze," Sally was almost popping with enthusiasm, "After all, it will be years before we'll be able to afford to get back here, so we might as well make the most of everything we can. I'll even take a spare hanky for you."

Rachel raised one elegant eyebrow at Sally's comment and Suzanna's darling cousin immediately launched into an amusing account of her sneezing episode on the game drive. As the tale unfolded she began to see the funny side of it, and the three women dissolved into hysterical giggles, each adding another silly comment and suggestion.

"Look on the bright side, you could have needed the loo and been left behind a tree with your drawers down round your ankles." Rachel exploded into laughter again, her head thrown back and teeth showing white against her tanned skin. She looked beyond Suzanna's shoulder and waved frantically at someone near the dining hall.

"Gregg, come over here. We're just talking about you."

Suzanna's grin became a little more fixed as he strode up, holding a clipboard with a sheath of fluttering invoices fixed to it. He had caught their laughter and there was a gorgeous smile on his face. It changed his whole appearance, and the breath caught in Suzanna's throat as she stared up at him. Rachel's voice faded into a background blur.

Oh Boy—aware of it or not, he radiated pure maleness from every pore.

A shiver ran through Suzanna's body and goose-bumps immediately rose up on her arms. Her breasts suddenly felt heavy and ripe and she felt her nipples harden and stand out against the sheer material of her swimming costume. She moved her legs and her first instinct was to drag her sarong around her shoulders and cover her bosom.

But her gaze was fixed to Gregg's face—and Gregg's gaze was fixed to her body!

A devil took hold of her soul.

Almost in slow motion, with her eyes glued to his face, she shook her hair out from under her hat, and instead of covering the evidence of a tremor of hot desire, she stretched her legs like a shameless feline and pushed her chest out in a decidedly flirtatious way. Her breasts strained against the silky material, every voluptuous curve brazenly on show. Her head tilted backwards, and the line of her throat drew his eyes to her mouth and the moist tip of her tongue that licked daintily at her top lip.

The sound of Rachel's carefree dialogue was drowned out by the silence of the battle of emotions going on between this tall imposing man and the beautiful brunette stretched out in his view. He was as unable to look away or to move as she was. They were both frozen into the moment that lengthened exquisitely in it's torment.

The evil thought flipped into her head and she sent him a silent message—'So there for being so mean to me. Feast your eyes and enjoy the sight!'

"Are you listening to me, Gregg?" Rachel dragged at his arm and her voice was loud. "I don't think you've heard a word I've said. Really you are impossible."

He almost seemed to shake himself as he tore his eyes away and turned to apologise to her.

"Sorry, Rachel. I was miles away. I have to get to the office to do a few urgent chores, so I'll see you all later. Ladies." He gave a mock salute as he spun on his heel to leave.

Typically Sally hadn't missed a thing.

"What was all that about, Suze? You had him pinned like a moth on a display tray."

She was very observant when it came to people and their emotions and actions, but Suzanna passed her off with a shrug. Rachel glanced uncertainly from one to the other of them, so wrapped up in her tale that she had missed the whole incident.

"I don't know what you are talking about, Sally. Please be quiet." Suzanna was afraid she would persist and ask more questions in front of Rachel. She hastily changed the subject.

"That's a lovely carry bag you have, Rachel, where did you find it?"

The question set her off into another story, and Suzanna lay back on the pretence of listening to every word. She suddenly felt drained and her limbs felt hollow and weak. Why did that impossible man have such an impact on her? One moment he had her almost in tears and the next she was ready to fly into space. She adjusted her dark glasses and fiddled with her hair to hide the smug look that curled her mouth at the corners. She struggled against a sudden desire to leap up into the air and shout with happiness.

Rachel interpreted Suzanna's wide smile as enjoyment of her tale and she waved her hands to emphasize her point. She had no idea of the thought that had just crashed into the other woman's brain.

'He looked at me! His eyes were fixed on me and he wasn't able to drag his gaze away. Rachel was right here with us, but it was ME that he looked at. Not her! Despite being angry with me on the game drive, his gaze and his attention had been riveted on me.'

"That's so amazing!" she said out loud.

Rachel stopped in mid sentence, her jaw slightly open, and both girls turned to look at Suzanna.

"What's amazing?" Rachel asked.

"Oh, um, sorry, I just thought of something else." Suzanna tried to backtrack, swallowed, and said as innocently as she could, "How long have you known Gregg, Rachel? You seem to know him quite well."

Rachel waved a hand in the air and said breezily, "I'm not really sure how long. Quite a few years, though. Actually I know his partner better than him. She's quite the social butterfly and knows how to party. Gregg can be good fun when he gets in the mood, but I've always found him to be a little unapproachable."

'Tell me about it!' Suzanna thought silently. And then, 'Oh God—I should have known he wasn't single.'

"His partner? He has a partner? Where is she? How long have they been together?" She strove to sound casual, but her heartbeat had definitely gone up a notch.

"She's lovely, well, beautiful really, and is good fun to be with. She does part time modelling and is always immaculately turned out—one of those girls who'd look good in a sack. Well, I suppose this is telling tales out of school a bit, but I believe they haven't been all that happy recently. She's a city girl and of course he's only at home in the bush. They don't see each other very often, and she loves to live it up in the bright lights. She's a stunning girl and the men flock round her like bees round a honey pot. I'm not saying she's been unfaithful to Gregg, but then again she wouldn't lack the opportunity."

Rachel could certainly gossip, but this time Suzanna wanted her to go on and on. She wanted to find out all she could about this man she had known for only a few hours but felt so inexplicably drawn to.

Drawn to? Exactly since when had she admitted that thought to herself? Her sneaky inner voice scoffed at her—'So far all you've done is fight with the man. Now you're telling me you're drawn to him. What's going on here?' 'Shut up and go away.' She squashed the voice firmly.

"And, er, what about Gregg? He must be inundated with women here in the camp throwing themselves at him?" God, she sounded like she was being strangled, even to herself.

Once again the hand waved elegantly, and Rachel laughed lightly.

"Well, I couldn't be sure of course. I for one wouldn't mind having his shoes under my bed some night. But no-one I know has ever been that lucky. I've been to this camp several times and never heard any rumours about him. He's either squeaky clean, or good at hiding any late night wanderings."

"He seems the sort who would have quite high principals." This was Sally's input. Her sharp gaze was making Suzanna's cheeks burn. She dabbed at a trickle of sweat that ran down her temple.

"I think I may just have a dip to cool off," she declared. "The sun is burning my shoulders. Are you coming in, either of you?"

Thankfully Rachel shook her head and declined Suzanna's invitation, but Sally swung her legs off her lounger.

"Actually, you do look hot. I'll join you. The water looks most inviting." Sally stood up and they walked together to the shallow end of the sparkling pool.

"Come on, Suze—give." She hissed furiously into Suzanna's ear. "You deliberately flirted with Gregg and practically did a one woman show for him. You were oozing more sex appeal than a stripper with nothing on. What are you up to?"

"Sshh!" Suzanna glanced around to check she hadn't been heard. They eased down into the refreshing water and she splashed water over her shoulders.

"I couldn't resist it, Sal. He's been nothing but awful to me since we got here. I suddenly wanted to show off in front of him, and make him sweat a little." She giggled, "I think I may have scored one against him. Serve him right for ticking me off."

"Jeez, you sure did that. You almost had him dancing on the spot." Sally suddenly laughed and a few heads turned to look at them. She lowered her voice again and swam towards Suzanna.

"But can't you see that he's smitten with you? He has been from the very first moment he saw you."

"Don't be silly, Cuz. I know smitten when I see it, and he is not smitten. And besides, you heard Rachel. He has a partner and is in love with her. I'll just try and keep on his good side, if I can, and keep out of his way as much as possible." Suzanna's throat constricted in a very strange manner as she added, "I'll try to be on my best behaviour and not wind him up. He definitely seems the sort who doesn't suffer fools gladly."

"Well, I suppose, when you're in charge of a big operation like this camp, you don't get much opportunity to let your hair down and just have fun," Sally observed. "It's probably not very easy for him. It's a huge responsibility for one person—having to be sure all the guests are kept happy, plus organise all the staff, and see that the office runs smoothly."

"Pity we can't arrange a yoga session, or a full body massage to relax him up a little." Suzanna's words were out before she realized, and both of them burst into laughter again as they visualized the unlikely picture of the broad, masculine frame stretched out in a beauty parlour with avocado goo spread over his face and body.

Chapter 7

THE DEEP ARMCHAIR was soft and comfy. Suzanna's legs were folded under her, and her finger curled through the handle of a cup of coffee that rested on the wooden arm. Sally had decided to read a book on her bed, but she had moved to the veranda when they retuned from the pool.

The lovely view from the front of their room stretched out before her. Two little finches with brilliant red throats hopped from an overhanging twig to the ground, back and forth, busily searching for tiny insects. A hippo snorted from the direction of the river, and another answered from higher up. A warm feather of wind caressed her skin and the peaceful scene wrapped itself around her, sending tendrils that anchored themselves into her soul. Just a few hours ago she had been desperate to go home, but now she was only too happy to be right where she was—absorbing every last sound and smell of the unique surroundings and the bush that extended in all directions.

Thoughts of Gregg slipped into her mind. She ran her hand down her forearm, remembering the strength and feel of his arm round her shoulders. She closed her eyes and let her thoughts wander further, imagining his hold tightening around her, his mouth descending to hers. His frown would smooth out under her touch, and his smile would melt her heart. She tried to analyse her feelings but she didn't know what to make of them. Why did her emotions soar up and down so dramatically when he was near? She had been thrilled to hear Rachel say she wasn't involved with him, and then devastated when she'd casually talked of his partner. She wondered how they managed their relationship long distance, and if his partner indeed had other affairs as Rachel had insinuated.

There was no doubt, Suzanna decided, that she had to keep clear of Gregg as much as she could. She told herself she was over-reacting, and that the heat had gotten the better of her. She decided that since her heart was still raw from her break up with Dave, she had better take care not to expose herself to being hurt all over again. She realized she had to reign herself in, and make every attempt to stay cool and do her best to keep out of Gregg's way.

But whichever line her thoughts took, a tiny voice deep inside Suzanna's mind kept repeating that it was she that Gregg had been interested in at the pool, not Rachel. He hadn't even acknowledged Rachel properly because his gaze had stuck like glue to her! She hugged the thought close. He had definitely given out the signal that he had been more than just a little attracted to her.

Her eyes closed and her head dropped back against the fat cushion. But a self-satisfied smile refused to leave the edges of her mouth.

It was a relief to find that another of the guides was on boat duty when the girls got down to the jetty that evening. Suzanna knew all her resolutions to keep clear of him would have failed if Gregg had been in charge. But her buoyant spirits took a knock when the guide greeted them by saying,

"Hi everyone. Welcome to our evening game drive. My name is Stanley Edwards. Gregg usually takes this drive out, but he has some office work to catch up on, so I'll be your host for the evening."

"More likely that he knew I was booked for the drive, so he decided not to come." Suzanna muttered to Sally. "Do you think that's a good sign or a bad sign?"

Sally lifted her shoulders resignedly, and gave a lopsided grin.

"Don't think about it," she whispered back. "He's probably busy."

There were three other guests on board. One of them was Steve. Once again he had booked to go out on the same excursion as the girls had. Suzanna hoped he wouldn't refer to her sneezing episode. She felt as though the whole camp must know about it by now.

"Hi Suzanna," he greeted her. "Did you enjoy your swim this afternoon?"

"You weren't at the pool, were you?" She looked up in surprise, knowing perfectly well she hadn't seen him. But then, she had been so preoccupied with Rachel and Gregg that she hadn't noticed anyone else.

"No. I went for a stroll with my binoculars and just happened to come back that way." He laughed lightly and leaned towards her, winking broadly. "I have to say you looked sensational in that costume."

"Oh! Thanks." She dug in her bag and fussed with her seat, trying to appear busy and turned her back on him to cover her embarrassment. Surely he hadn't seen her stretching in front of Gregg? Was nothing private around here?

The girls introduced themselves to the other couple on board and settled themselves into their seats. Steve chose a seat near to Suzanna, and sent her a private glance that only served to increase her discomfort. Was he just being friendly, or was he trying to make a play for her?

The boat was a large flat-bottomed affair set on two long pontoons with a roof providing shade. The seats were fixed to the floor of the deck, but could swivel freely around so that the occupant had an unimpeded view in all directions. The driver sat at a tiny dial-covered consul, which was also equipped with a wooden helmsman's wheel. The whole craft felt stable and safe.

They pushed off from the bank and Stanley drove steadily up river. The air was cooler out on the water and Suzanna gratefully let her hair blow about and the breeze lift the edge of her shirt. Both Sally and she had worn shorts and they felt light and free. They shared a grin of carefree happiness and looked about to take in the scenery along both sides of the mighty Zambezi River.

Sharply defined banks, cut through with secret animal paths, lined the river. In places the torrent had washed relentlessly at the high banks and eroded away huge amounts of soil to expose the long roots of towering trees, causing them to teeter precariously on the edge and lean out over the water. A few of the giants had succumbed and fallen heavily into the water, the remaining roots left exposed and twisted like exotic sculptures created by Mother Nature. Their branches, some still covered with green leaves, had crashed into the river and were being tugged and pulled by the eddying current.

They passed enticing inlets framed by green reed beds, bare stony beaches that stretched right back to the distant tree line, and dense clumps of bushes that held the promise of hidden watching eyes. Eventually Stanley drew up to a large flat pebbly island that was right in the middle of an immensely wide part of the river. He beached the boat and jumped out carrying the anchor, which he dug firmly into the sand to secure the boat.

"Right'oh," he declared. "Isn't this Heaven? Who'd like a drink?"

He opened a large cooler box stashed in the rear of the boat, and with a flourish he produced an array of frosty cold beers, soft drinks and wine, and offered each guest a glass or a bottle. Not only did he produce drinks, but out came an array of nibbles as well, and the six passengers relaxed back against the seats of the boat sipping and eating.

It was magic! Five star treatment on the banks of the totally impressive river.

Suzanna leaned back with her elbows on the back of her seat and her feet up on the rail. She could have spent hours sitting in the safety of the boat, absorbing the stillness of the far off bush and listening to the deep rushing gurgle of the swiftly flowing water as it streamed past the island, moving and swirling round submerged rocks.

They all took turns with the binoculars. Stanley pointed out a colony of brightly coloured Carmine bee-eaters darting in and out of hundreds of small holes that the birds had dug into a 20 foot cliff face slightly further on upriver. The beautiful carmine red of their wings flashed in the sun and their forked tails scissored open and closed as they wheeled and spun through the air. The twittering and cheeping that the bright flock made was ceaseless. They were catching bees and insects in mid-air, and everyone marvelled at the uncanny instinct of each bird as it returned to the right hole to feed it's hidden chicks.

A cry of 'kaa-aa, kwa, ka-ka' took their attention to a large bird that wheeled overhead and then swooped to land high on the bare branches of a drowned tree near the bank. It carefully folded in huge tawny brown wings, and then turned it's white head above a snowy chest to regard the people from it's lofty perch, as solemn as a judge with folded arms. They could clearly see the round bright eye and sharp yellow beak. It balanced on strong, feathered legs, regal and proud.

Stanley uttered a satisfied grunt, dug in a smaller cold box and pulled out a fair sized bream—dead, cold and bloated.

"Just who we're waiting for—the resident fish eagle," he announced.

Everyone watched, fascinated and intrigued, as he held the dead fish by the tail and then lobbed the carcass high and wide into the waters of the river. It landed with a splash, disappeared for a moment and then bobbed up again, floating gently downstream in the current with the white of it's belly uppermost and clearly visible.

"Fish eagles have incredible eyesight and can see bobbing prey from hundreds of feet up in the air," Stanley explained. "They love to be offered a free meal such as this one, but are fast enough to snatch live fish from just under the surface of the water as well. Watch him now."

The eagle had seen the splash and immediately launched itself from the branch and flew towards the dead and floating offering. It's wings spread wide with the tips curled upwards like fingers on a hand. With an impressive display of aerobatics it swooped down, turned on one wing, dropped low at the last second and deftly scooped up the fish with outstretched yellow talons as long as a man's fingers and as sharp as ice picks. Although the fish seemed too heavy to carry, the eagle managed to hold on to it's prize, and, with wings beating hard, carried it back to the fork of the tree. As it landed it threw back it's head and sent a triumphant cry echoing across the water and the landscape. Then it bent over and ravenously tore strips of flesh from the carcass with it's long beak.

The watchers cheered with enthusiasm. What a fabulous display.

Stanley was extremely knowledgeable about the different species of birds they saw. He told them about the destructive quelea moving in such tightly packed flocks they resembled giant black amoeba constantly changing shape in the air. They trained the binoculars on an elegant three-foot high Goliath heron, posed as still as a statue waiting for fingerlings in the shallows, and picked out a tiny iridescent blue-headed kingfisher, a jewel of nature, perched watchfully on a swaying reed.

He spotted vultures circling like tiny dots high above in the evening sky and explained that if one dropped from the heavens to investigate a kill, several dozen others would see the movement and follow it down. In no time the kill would be covered with birds jostling and fighting for a scrap of meat.

As the party started the return journey he described the types of trees and bushes they passed—those that contained nutritional bark, leaves or pods, those that could be used in some medicinal way and others that provided protection to large and small species. Sally and Suzanna were fascinated by his narrations, and suddenly Suzanna felt a definite connection with this ancient land of their birth. Stanley had lit an internal fuse that made her want to get out there and do something to protect the precious animals that remained in this huge tract of land, but were so vulnerable to the whims and greed of mankind.

Since they were now travelling in the same direction as the fast current Stanley held the motor to a crawling pace, just enough to control the direction of the boat. Their passage was quiet and peaceful. He lifted his arm and pointed to two enormous crocodiles lying motionless on the bank, mouths wide open to expose their yellow throats and rows of white, pointed teeth. The short legs seemed incongruously out of proportion to the bellies that spread sideways on the sand. Huge hard scales lined their backs and stuck up in ridges right to the tip of their powerful tails. It was easy to picture them existing since prehistoric times. In quiet voices the guests discussed how evil and incredibly strong they appeared, and shuddered to think of being stranded in the water with such beasts lurking nearby.

But the best was to come!

As they rounded a slight bend Stanley gave a sharp hand signal to remain quiet. He raised his finger to his lips and pointed to the base of a low bush on the Zambian side of the river. Quickly and quietly he cut the engine, threw out the anchor and the boat swung round in the current as the passengers twisted their heads to catch sight of a magnificent lioness lying flat out on her side on the top of the bank. She was out in the open about ten meters from the edge, but was perfectly camouflaged by the bush behind her. Stanley's keenly trained eye had picked her out.

Everyone shivered with excitement and couldn't wait to grab the binoculars to look at her close-up. She was alone, stretched out in the small patch of shade afforded by the scrubby bush. The white tip of her tail lifted lazily from time to time, but apart from that she didn't move. The silence was only broken by the clicking of one of the men's cameras, and the continuous gurgling of the restless river.

Suzanna wished Gregg had been there to share this special moment. 'Silly girl—why keep thinking of him? He didn't want to take the drive out, so why waste time on him?'

"I wonder where the rest of the pride is?" Steve commented quietly.

As he spoke, the wide tawny head lifted and she gazed straight at them with intense yellow eyes. She studied them for a few long moments, and then, with a slight grunt, she swung herself up onto her feet. They could see how distended the tawny skin on her stomach was, and how her back dipped low with the weight. The regal lioness continued to stare at them, round ears strained forwards, listening alertly. A shallow panting caused her whole body to rock gently back and forth, and the end of her long tail continued to twitch from side to side.

"Gregg and I have seen this lioness before," Stanley said. "See the scar on her shoulder? That's how we can identify her. She's pregnant and has possibly left the pride for a while to have her cubs. She'll look for a secret and secluded place and then leave the babies hidden for a couple of weeks or more. The cubs are very vulnerable to falling prey to hyena or even other male lions that pass through the area."

The tawny female was incredibly beautiful. She stood only a few meters away and seemed in no hurry to leave. Neither Sally nor Suzanna had seen a lioness in the wilds before, and to be this close, and yet be so safe, was an amazing experience. Steve leaned towards Suzanna. He stretched out his hand and touched her shoulder.

"Isn't she fabulous? Look at the size of her feet. She's certainly heavily pregnant."

"Maybe she'll have the cubs tonight," Stanley said. "She's very heavy."

The powerful muscles in the large cat's shoulders, neck and hind legs spoke of her innate strength. Her coat was smooth and golden in the evening light. A liquid ray of sun caught the tips of her neck ruff as she turned her head to listen to a sound behind her. For a long moment she stood motionless, as though she was assessing the level of danger the sound had held. Then she swung her head back in the direction of the boat, and to the humans' complete delight, she stretched her paws forwards, arched her back downwards, opened her huge mouth and gave a wide yawn that showed her impressive five inch canine teeth and a long pink tongue.

She seemed relaxed and unperturbed by their presence. Perhaps she was used to being observed by interested people floating in the middle of the river. After another few minutes, though, she decided to move away and padded with huge inward turned paws, stomach swaying, towards a dense thicket on the edge of the tree line.

They watched until she had disappeared, all of them sighing with satisfaction. It was a privilege to have shared a wonderful moment with the beautiful and regal queen of the bush.

Stanley dragged in the anchor and they continued on their way back to camp, feeling euphoric and fizzing high on adrenaline to have had such a special sighting. Six pairs of eyes scanned the banks on either side of the river for a sign of the rest of the pride, but they weren't to be seen. The last rays of red and gold sunlight stretched across the sky, peaceful and beautiful.

The boat skirted gingerly round a pod of hippo that clustered together in the middle of the river. Their backs were almost totally submerged, but their wide heads and broad snouts turned towards the craft. Bristly nostrils flared, bulbous eyes stared and round ears wiggled as they followed the progress of the people moving past them. With a sudden wash of water one, and then another, vanished from sight.

"Hippo have to be afforded the greatest of respect by boat users on the river." Once again they benefited from Stanley's knowledge. "They can move at great speed through the water, and will attack canoes and small boats, sometimes with fatal results to the occupants. Many a person has come across hippo grazing peacefully on the land, only to be surprised and even injured in the animal's headlong rush back to the safety of the water."

"Hippo apparently hold the record for the greatest numbers of 'death-by-wild-animal' in Africa," Steve chipped in, keen to show off his knowledge and compete with Stanley.

"Yes, I've heard that," Stanley replied. "I don't know that I entirely agree with the theory though. It could be that they are the best reported and perhaps the most dramatic incidents, whereas, death by crocodile for example is not so widely spoken about amongst the local people. They tend to be a bit more fatalistic where crocs are concerned."

Suzanna thought of her encounter with the hippo near the pool, and that of course made her think of Gregg again. She wondered if he had really not taken this trip out because of her. She thought how great it would have been to share the few unique moments watching the lioness with him. Once again she remembered the feel of his arms round her and recalled his fixed stare on her body at the pool. A little shudder ran through her limbs. Steve saw the motion and he raised an eyebrow in query.

"Are you cold?" He leaned forward and put his hand on her arm. "I have a spare jacket if you would like it round your shoulders?" He tried to hold her eyes with his.

"No, I'm fine. Thanks anyway." Suzanna smiled and moved her arm in the pretence of tucking back a strand of hair. "It was just someone stepping over my grave."

Chapter 8

SALLY AND SUZANNA showered and changed for dinner.

"I'm more than ready to eat," Sally declared.

"Well, we haven't had much all day, really." Suzanna leaned towards the mirror to finish her makeup.

"Shall we invite anyone to join our table this evening?" Sally glanced sideways at her cousin.

"Like who? I don't trust that look, Missie. Who did you have in mind?"

"Well, perhaps Pete? Or possibly Steve? He spent most of the trip this evening watching you, did you notice?"

"You're making that up," Suzanna protested.

"Funny how he's been on both the trips we've done. One could almost swear he has a hidden agenda. I don't suppose he's out to get your attention at all?"

Sally giggled. She knew just how to get under Suzanna's skin.

"Come on, Sally, ease up. We were all watching the game and so was he. I didn't take that much notice of what he was doing. To be honest I was relieved he didn't mention

my sneezing episode. The less said about that the better."
Secretly she knew Steve had been watching her, and that
he kept glancing in her direction, noting her reactions, but
there was no likelihood of her admitting it to her sharp eyed
cousin.

"Well, we'll see if they already have full tables. Perhaps
we'll just join them for a drink after dinner?"

As before, the guests were called in to dine by the
throbbing of the tom-tom. It was amazing how the hollow
sound carried so well, and Suzanna could understand how
messages could be sent for miles between African villages
in this way.

The dining room looked just as romantic as it had the
previous evening. The white overlays and napkins were
placed immaculately on dark green tablecloths, and sprigs
of greenery nestled amongst the flickering candles. Both
girls agreed that although this was only their second night
in camp, it seemed so much longer.

Somewhat to Suzanna's relief both Pete and Steve were
already seated at their tables. The girls headed to the same
one they had sat at before and ordered a glass of cold white
wine. Once again the meal was perfectly presented and each
mouthful was delicious.

"They must have a very good chef here," Suzanna
commented. "This meal is tops. We'll be putting on weight
if we keep eating like this."

"Mmm, it is good. Who cares about the extra pounds.
We'll have to do a stint at the gym when we get home. You
look lovely tonight, Cuz. The dark golds and ochres of your
dress compliment the auburns and lights in your hair. And
your shoulders are already turning quite brown. You look
the picture of health."

Suzanna flushed with pleasure. Sally's compliments weren't handed out lightly. Suzanna didn't spend much time looking in the mirror, but she knew when something suited her. She had chosen her dress to show off her new tan and it draped softly and slimly at the waist. The strappy gold sandals were a favourite and she had pinned her hair loosely back with a butterfly clip, leaving the ends to tumble down her back.

"Thanks Cuz," she beamed at Sally. "You don't look so bad yourself. This outdoor life must be good for us both. Didn't we cancel our gym membership, though?"

"Never mind. We'll lose the pounds soon enough." Sally leaned back and sighed with contentment. "What a great day."

Suzanna agreed with her. "I just loved that river trip this evening. It was so special to see that beautiful lioness. Did you hear Stanley say that even regular visitors to the camp don't get to see lion, so we were very lucky. Know something? Toby would love it here. We must get him to book a trip. He would have been so thrilled to see that lioness today."

"Toby has been a bit preoccupied of late with his new love, Amy. Remember you met her at Frances' party? She's lovely. But you're right, he would love it here." Sally gave one of her smug fat-cat smiles. "I knew you would fall in love with this place, Suze. Aren't you glad you came now? It's wonderful that we have another few days to enjoy. We haven't finalized what we're going to do tomorrow. We should decide and book something." She leaned forward and squeezed Suzanna's hand. "I'm so glad there wasn't a boat to take you home this morning. I would have hated it here without you. I hope you really do feel more settled? Aren't you glad you stayed now?"

"Well, put it this way—I think I can manage to stick it out until the end of the week . . . with a bit of an effort. Isn't it strange—this morning seems like another age. As though it happened in another lifetime almost." They laughed, happy and relaxed.

"That river trip was so wonderful I wouldn't mind going out again tomorrow morning," Suzanna continued. "I hope it's not too late to book. Perhaps we can ask at the office after dinner?"

"We can ask right now," Sally said, "Don't look behind you—Mine Host approacheth!"

His voice sent a thrill through her. Suzanna realized that subconsciously she'd been waiting for him to do the rounds of the tables, and her evening would have been ruined if he hadn't stopped at theirs.

"Evening ladies. I trust you enjoyed your dinner?"

Her fingers twirled the stem of her glass and she smiled up at him, trying to get him to smile in return. She wanted to ask him to forget their previous clashes, but the words remained unsaid. Instead she tried to convey her desire to forgive and forget with her smile. It seemed to be working. The corner of his mouth lifted and his eyelids dropped ever so slightly, softening his expression. Then she noticed his glance go to the ring on the middle finger of her left hand. In an unconscious reaction she twirled it with her thumb, swallowing the insane instinct to tell him that she didn't wear it for anyone in particular, that she had inherited it from her mother and that she wore it always.

Instead she found herself saying, "The meal was delicious, thank you. Did you hear we saw a lioness on our river trip? She was so beautiful. It's a shame you weren't there to see her." God, was she gabbling? She pressed her lips together and sucked in a steadying breath. Why did this man have the power to turn her into a jelly just by standing near her? It was ridiculous.

If he noticed her confusion, he made no sign of it. But the half smile had not left his mouth and Suzanna thought she detected a gleam of—was it satisfaction—in his eyes.

"Yes, I heard you had seen her. Sounds like she'll have those cubs tonight so we may not see her again for quite a while now. She'll probably only show herself once the cubs are a few days old and it's safe to leave them hidden while she hunts for food."

Suzanna couldn't take her eyes off his face as he was speaking. It was possibly the longest sentence she had heard him utter without throwing in a telling-off. She wanted to keep him standing here, talking only to them.

"Stanley gave us a very good trip. It was so relaxed and pleasant. He's very knowledgeable, isn't he?" She tried to speak casually as she added, "We haven't actually booked to do anything tomorrow morning. Would it be possible to go out on the boat again? We were thinking of doing the walk, but we've both changed our minds now. Is that OK?"

"No problem," Gregg replied. "Stanley is taking the boat out and I'm doing the walk. Sometimes we alternate, but that's what we've planned for tomorrow."

Blast! Blast! Blast! It was too late to change trips now, after her eloquent little speech.

He grinned, "You'll be able to have a few minutes longer in bed as the boat leaves a little later than the walk does. It goes out after breakfast and comes back just before lunch."

They were stuck with it now. As he walked off Suzanna looked over at Sally, trying to keep the disappointment out of her face. Sally had one eyebrow raised.

"Were you hoping he would take the boat trip out tomorrow?"

"I didn't think that far, but, yes, I hoped he would," Suzanna replied. "Still, it will be lovely out on the river, so perhaps we'll just stick to it now?"

"That's fine by me." Sally pushed her chair back. "Come on, let's see who's in the bar."

Pete, Steve and a few others immediately pulled up more high stools and made space for the girls to join their circle. Sally settled herself next to Pete while Steve bought them a couple of drinks. Suzanna noted that Rachel was elegantly perched on a stool further down the counter and was deep in conversation with a blonde haired man who hung onto every one of her words. As she talked she waved her hands to emphasize a point and the neck of her dress gaped slightly—more on purpose than by accident, Suzanna thought. She exchanged a glance with Sally. The vibes that Rachel was putting out were strong and flirtatious. It was evident what her plans were for the night.

The conversation ebbed and flowed around the two girls and the day's events were discussed. Gregg came in for a few minutes but he wouldn't accept a drink or stay and chat, much to Suzanna's disappointment.

"You work too hard, mate," someone called out. "Just have one for the road."

"Maybe another time," Gregg laughed. She couldn't take her eyes off him. It was incredible how expressive his face was. His laugh was so infectious you couldn't help but smile with him. He put one boot on the foot rail and leaned an elbow on the bar top while he shared a few words with a bloke standing further down. Suzanna admired the length of his leg and the way the material of his shirt pulled across his back to show the width of his shoulders.

Just as he turned to leave the bar, Rachel inclined her head at the blonde haired man and slipped off her stool to stop Gregg in the doorway. She put her hand on his arm and tilted her head, her eyelids half lowered and her full lips pouted provocatively. Suzanna couldn't hear what she was saying, but the body language spoke volumes. For all the world she appeared to be blatantly propositioning Gregg. A shaft of jealousy burnt a hole in her chest and sent a hot flush up her neck and into her cheeks. What sort of nerve did Rachel possess?

"Isn't that right, Suzanna?" Sally's voice distracted her.

"Er—sorry, what did you say?"

"Pete suggested he come along tomorrow morning and we all try a bit of tiger fishing off the boat. Sounds like fun to me."

"Oh! Yes." Suzanna battled to get her thoughts under control. "It would be great to see someone in action who knows what they're doing."

When she looked round again, Gregg had gone. But Rachel was back on her stool. Obviously her charms had not worked on Gregg—not tonight at least. Suzanna relaxed her shoulders, relief washing over her. 'So much for your efforts, my girl,' she thought.

Someone else bought a round of drinks, and then Sally and she bought one as their shout, and the laughter swelled as the conversation got louder.

Steve sat very close and directed most of his stories directly at Suzanna. When at last she stood up to head back to the room she staggered very slightly and held on to the back of her stool.

"Oops, this floor's not level," she giggled.

Steve immediately stood up and put out his hand. "I'll walk you back to your room, young lady. We don't want anything untoward happening to you on the way."

"No, no, I'll be fine." Suzanna waved his hand off, but he gripped her arm more firmly, and she let him lead her out of the bar as they all sang cheery good-nights to each other. Rachel had departed earlier, hanging onto the arm of the blonde man, and Suzanna had been happy to see her go.

The cooler night air cleared her head. The path and surrounds were deserted—no animals prowling out and about tonight.

They walked down the dimly lit path, neither of them quite sure how to break the silence. Suzanna kept her arms crossed with her hands holding onto her elbows to deter Steve from making any move to touch her. But now he stood between her and the door and she sensed he was deciding how to say goodnight. Trying to be subtle she stepped away from him.

"Thanks for walking me back Steve. It is quite a dark night, isn't it? I would have been nervous on my own."

His eyes glinted in the darkness and he took a step towards her.

"You're most welcome, Suzanna," he murmured softly. And then he added, "Suzanna? You must know that I'm getting more and more drawn to you. You're lovely, you know."

"Oh, um, well, thank you. I had a great evening. It was fun."

He stepped in closer, and reached out to take her into his arms.

A murmur of voices, a gentle laugh and footfalls on the path behind them made him hesitate. Sally and Pete were approaching and he waited, not sure how to proceed with the others there. Why had they come along at this precise moment? He had been conniving all night to get Suzanna alone, and now his moment had been spoilt. His hands closed into fists of frustration, and he hunched his shoulders forwards. Suzanna took advantage of the distraction. She had no wish to offend Steve, but neither did she want to be hugged by him.

"Thanks again," she said quickly. "Good night." She slipped through the door and left him to exchange a few words with the others.

Steve's words and actions filled her with dismay and she wasn't quite sure what to do without appearing hard and callous. He had misconstrued things. He was pleasant enough, and pretty good company, but she certainly didn't want him to think she had been leading him on. This was a very awkward situation.

Sally's hair was more dishevelled than usual when she finally came in, and she looked rosy cheeked and jubilant.

"Ooh—that man can kiss!" she sang, arms out in a wide gesture.

"It was lucky you came along when you did," Suzanna told her. "Things might have turned a little difficult with Steve."

"He's got his eye on you, that's for sure." Sally gave a twitch of her hips and did a couple of dance steps across the room.

"Well, I don't want him to have an eye on me. Not in any way. I hope he's booked for something else tomorrow. I don't want to spend the whole week looking over my shoulder trying to avoid him, and feeling on edge that he is going to try to grab me."

Sally laughed. "I'll take care of you. If he gets too much I'll ask Pete to give him a gentle word to back off."

Chapter 9

IN THE DEAD of the night the girls were woken by a noise immediately outside their room.

"Are you awake Sally? Did you hear that? What was it?" Suzanna whispered, clutching the sheet to her chin like a child's comfort blanket.

"I don't know. I thought it sounded like a rumbling noise—sort of like someone's stomach gurgling." Sally replied. "Let's go and look."

"Don't be crazy, Sally. Anything could be out there. Oh God. Listen! It's coming closer."

A distinct rustling, flowed by the sharp crack of a breaking branch and then a loud rasping sound, had the girls wide-eyed and fully awake.

Sally eased cautiously out of bed and crept on bare feet to the front veranda, carefully skirting the dark outlines of the furniture. Keeping well back, she peered round the edge of the door frame and then hissed at Suzanna.

"Come and look. Quick!"

Suzanna forgot her fear, eased out of bed and tip-toed after her cousin. Both heads craned round the door to see the looming shape of a huge elephant, contentedly rubbing his rump back and forth against the edge of the thatch. He was almost groaning in pleasure. His tusks glinted white in the dappled moonlight and the restless tip of his trunk stretched out for succulent leaves even while he scratched. The girls were entranced. The giant was no more than a few paces away from them, unaware of their rapt presence. His wrinkled hide, the hollow under his jawbone and one large round eye framed by amazingly long eyelashes, were clearly visible. As they watched, the bull walked a few paces, spread his back legs, lifted his tail and deposited an enormous pile of steaming, pungent smelling dung onto the grass.

Sally stifled a giggle. "No wonder his stomach was grumbling."

"Shh, you'll frighten him." Suzanna breathed. "Isn't he magnificent? He's so huge. Our own elephant. Compare the height of his back to that branch and then we'll see tomorrow how tall he is."

Feeding quietly, the bull moved on through the dark bush, heading towards the river. The girls watched until he'd gone and then padded back to bed, each filled with a sense of excitement and wonder, a brand new and unique experience burned into their memory cards.

They enjoyed lying in the next morning and, once they were ready, they wandered along for a delicious breakfast before heading down to the river.

Stanley was waiting at the boat and Pete sat on the jetty sorting out a confused pile of fishing tackle as the girls walked up. Both men greeted them and Pete stood up to give Sally's hand a squeeze. Thankfully Steve was no-where to be seen and the only other person due to go out was a rotund, pleasant faced man whom they'd met before. He was also fiddling with fishing gear.

"Hi Nick. You look all set to give it a go." He smiled at Sally's words.

"Fisherman are forever hopeful—the optimists of the world," he replied.

Once again the river was beautiful. They drove upstream for a short way and then, as the men lowered lines and bait into the water, Stanley allowed the boat to drift downstream with the current. Suzanna leaned back against the seat, feet up on the rails, tanning her legs and shoulders. The sun climbed higher and higher and a few white clouds drifted lazily above. The binoculars lay on her lap. When something caught her eye she focused on it, hoping to catch sight of the lioness once again. She was content to watch the passing scenery, but Sally was keen to try her hand at fishing. Pete showed her how to hold the rod and what to do if a tigerfish took the bait. Their hands touched and they sat close together.

On the fourth drift downriver Nick had a strike. He yelled with excitement as his rod bowed down and the line screamed off his reel. Everyone cheered him on, watching the water to see when the fish would break the surface. Slowly he wound in line, then let it out again as the fish ran once more, playing the tiger with care.

"Uh-oh, he's shaking his head. I hope he doesn't spit the hook." Nick's words made no sense to Suzanna. As the fish approached the surface, gleaming silver, it suddenly shot up and jumped a few feet into the air, showering droplets of water. Skilfully, Nick tightened the line and managed to keep it hooked. Deftly he played it in to the edge of the boat and Pete leaned over with a large landing net to scoop it out of the water. Everyone cheered as he held aloft a sizeable prize.

Carefully, using a pair of long-nosed pliers, Nick removed the hook from the fish's jaw. He showed them the row of razor sharp pointed teeth that meshed perfectly when the tiger closed it's mouth, and they admired the iridescent blue and silver of it's shiny scales and the round black eyes.

"Tigerfish are the best fresh water game fish," Nick declared. "People travel from all over the world to catch one of these. They have very bony mouths so it's not always easy to hook them. See those teeth—you don't want to get a finger in the way of that lot, I can tell you. Once you've caught a tiger, you want to do it again and again." His voice was full of pride and love for the strong, sleek fish. He lowered it carefully into the water and held it for a second just above the tail, waiting for it to regain it's balance in the water. Then, with a fluid swirl, the animal disappeared into the depths.

"Well done! That calls for a drink." Stanley handed out cold beers all round. He did several more runs up and down river. Pete managed to hook a smaller tiger and he quickly passed the rod to Sally. Her eyes shone as he stood close behind her, steadying her as she played the fish. She was thrilled when it was brought safely up on deck, and laughed happily into the lens of Pete's camera, holding it high.

The morning flew by and they were reluctant to go in for lunch. However, the sun had caught Suaznna's shoulders and she felt quite burnt. The midday heat pressed down, scorching the landscape.

Sally headed off to the pool after lunch, but Suzanna decided to read her book, curled into the deep armchair. Her eyelids drooped, the camp was quiet and still, and she nodded peacefully off.

The girls decided against going out on any other trip for the rest of the day, and instead sat in the shade of the trees by the pool, sipping tea and chatting idly. Suzanna kept an eye on the office door, hoping to see Gregg. Sure enough, he emerged a while later and raised a hand in greeting as he walked by.

"How was the river this morning?"

"As beautiful as ever," she replied. "Nick caught a big tiger, and Sally managed to land her first fish, so we had fun. We also had our very own elephant feeding right outside our room last night. It was magic." Slow down Suzanna! She took a calming breath. "How was the walk?"

Gregg smiled. "It was good, thanks. Do you think you'll come out tomorrow morning?"

What a dilemma! Of course she wanted to go, but only if he was in charge. She didn't want to make the same mistake twice and miss going out with him again. She glanced at Sally, willing her to help out here. The pulse started to beat in the side of her neck as he glanced from one to the other of them, waiting for a reply.

"Which trip will you be taking?" Suzanna had hoped Sally would be a little more subtle, but no—she just asked him straight out.

He seemed to be considering his reply. She forced herself to sit still and not yell out—please take us out—I promise not to trip over or embarrass myself—please take the walk.

"Um—tomorrow is actually my turn to take the boat out, but nothing has been decided yet."

She felt her face fall. Typical! That would be Murphy's Law alright. She pasted on a false smile. "The walk would be great to do. I'm sure there would be heaps we could learn from your knowledge of the bush."

Even to her own ears she sounded forced and false. She took a deep breath and fiddled with her tea cup, trying to appear unconcerned. Before he could answer, one of the scouts called to him, and with nothing having been resolved Gregg left them to return to the office. Suzanna's spirits dropped. She wanted to call him back, to keep him here talking to them and once again she marvelled at the effect he had on her. There was nothing to be done—she'd have to wait till tomorrow and see who would take the walk out.

Chapter 10

THE TABLES HAD been arranged in a different pattern for dinner that evening. Two had been pushed together allowing for six people to sit at each.

Pete was waiting at one of the tables, watching the entrance, and he stood up to pull Sally's chair out as the girls approached. Steve was already seated at another table, but he looked Suzanna's way and waved his hand. It wasn't clear if he was inviting her to sit with him, but she smiled back and quickly sat down with Pete and Sally.

Once again Gregg did the rounds of the tables, speaking to all the guests and booking everyone on trips for the next day. When he reached their table, he stood for a while chatting to Pete. Suzanna was anxious to ask if he'd decided to take the walk, but she held her tongue. She willed Pete to keep him talking just so that he'd stay close and she could openly watch and admire his handsome face.

Sally came to her rescue. She smiled up at Gregg and said, "We've finished eating. Why don't you join us for a night-cap at the bar? If we have to be up early for the walk we'll need to turn in soon. By the way, will it be you or Stanley who takes us out tomorrow?"

Gregg grinned back. His glance flicked from her to Suzanna, and she wondered if he could read the silent appeal in her wide brown eyes.

"I haven't spoken to Stanley yet, but, thanks, a night-cap would be good. I have to close up the office first so I'll join you as soon as I can."

Sally and Suzanna tidied their makeup in the ladies room, and then made their way to the bar. Suzanna's heart was fluttering and a thrill ran up and down her spine. They walked up to Pete and a few other guests, and were quickly offered a drink and drawn into the conversation. Suzanna watched the door, waiting for Gregg to finish his chores and join them, hardly able to concentrate or listen to what was being said.

Steve walked over and took the floor with a tale of his own. He stood close to Suzanna, leaning slightly forward to make his point, and although he was talking to the whole group, it was evident he was directing his story at her. His body language towards her was strong, almost possessive. He looked right into her eyes, trying to hold her gaze with an intimate smile. Suzanna smiled back at him but her eyes wandered, on the lookout for Gregg. What could be keeping him? Her attention wandered and she tuned out of Steve's monologue. She imagined Gregg at the desk in the office. Had he had a late phone call, or just doing general tidying up? She shifted restlessly on her bar stool, anxious for him to join them.

Her hair swung forwards and she put up a hand to brush a stray lock off her forehead. Steve bent towards her, taking her gesture to mean she was reaching out to touch him. He draped his arm round her shoulders and hugged her in to his side, laughing at the joke he had just cracked. Startled, Suzanna glanced up at his face, and then away to the door.

Gregg stood framed there, watching Steve's action.

Suzanna gasped, instantly furious with Steve. She moved sharply backwards, but it was too late. A deep frown furrowed Gregg's forehead and his eyes seemed to pierce right through her. He stopped where he was, spun abruptly on his heel and left the bar in a couple of long strides.

A flush rose from Suzanna's toes to her neck. She wanted to scream, 'Now see what you've done.' She stepped away from Steve and turned to whisper in Sally's ear.

"I've got a sudden headache. I'm just going to get a tablet from the room."

Sally had had her back to the door and hadn't seen Gregg enter and then leave.

She raised an eyebrow, "Are you OK? What's happened? Shall I come with you? Don't you want to wait for . . ."

"No!" Suzanna interrupted her quickly. "You stay here for a while longer. I'll be fine."

She pushed past several people in her haste to get to the door and try to see which way Gregg had gone. She felt panicked and flustered, and couldn't think straight. He'd thought the worst about Steve and herself, there was no doubt about that.

His tall figure disappeared down the path to the staff quarters, and she stopped in confusion. She couldn't just follow him. How would it look to go flying after him in the darkness? She wasn't even sure which his quarters were. What if she ended up at the wrong door? How would she explain to anyone else what had happened and what she was doing so late in the evening down in that part of the camp?

Tears of desperation welled into her eyes and she turned and made her way back down the softly lit path to the quiet solitude of the bedroom. She certainly had no intention of returning to the bar. Gregg's angry face returned again and again to her mind. Just when she felt she had made a slight break-through with him, this had had to happen. Damn Steve!

She paced back and forth, too restless to go to bed. The laundry had been returned, neatly folded and ironed and placed squarely on the end of the bed. She went over to sort it and put it into the wardrobe, and her gaze fell on a folded white square sitting right on the top of the pile.

Gregg's handkerchief!

The blood sang in her veins and she wanted to shout, "YES!"

Tears forgotten, and without a second thought, she snatched it up, raced back out onto the path, and walking quickly, but trying to look as though she wasn't hurrying, she made her way back down to the staff quarters. Her heart was hammering and she had no plan in her head about what she would say. Her feet carried her along, leaving her mind behind her.

She hoped she would see his light on. She gave not a thought to what else may have been out on the path at that time of night and luckily no animals were out to present any nasty surprises.

And, there he was. Sitting at his desk, clearly visible through the screened window. After her headlong rush, Suzanna's resolve suddenly weakened, and she hesitated and then stopped. What had she been thinking? Her heart was directing her head, and at that moment her head seemed to be totally blank and empty.

He'd heard her approach, though, and turned to listen better. He got to his feet and before she could change her mind and run, he opened the door to investigate the sound.

She was caught in the pool of light, and for an eternity she stood frozen to the spot, not able to say a word. His figure filled the whole door frame making her feel small and vulnerable, like a child facing an imposing parent.

They stared at each other in silence. At last she managed to drag her senses together, and she stuck out her hand clutching his crunched up handkerchief.

"I came to—um, I just wanted to return this," she stammered. "It's been laundered and was returned to our room, instead of yours."

He stared at her in silence and didn't move.

"Thanks for lending it to me, and I'm sorry I sneezed on the game drive. I messed it up for everyone. I have this huge sneeze that I can't control. Well—I try to—but generally without success."

Silence.

"Well, OK. Thanks then. I'd better be getting back. Here's your hanky." This was awful, and getting worse by the second.

She almost leapt backwards when he suddenly reached out his hand, and with a gesture that made her knees go weak, he gently wiped a drop of moisture off her cheek with the ball of his thumb.

"You've been crying." His deep voice could have melted a glacier ten miles deep. "Are you alright? Thanks for the hanky." He paused, considering his words. "Would you like to come in for a moment?"

'Of course I want to come in. That's exactly what I want.' For a second she was afraid she had she spoken out loud.

"No, I have to get back." Suzanna hesitated. "Um, well, yes, perhaps I could. Just for a minute."

God, woman, get a grip!

"Is it OK if I do? I mean aren't there camp rules about visiting the staff in their quarters?"

His answer was to hold the door wider and step back to let her pass him. The room had a similar layout to hers, but it was much smaller and was neatly equipped with the bare necessities. A well made bed, a desk covered in an assortment of papers, screened windows, one armchair, tidily stacked clothing on shelves, veranda to the front and bathroom to the rear.

He reached out and dimmed the overhead lights to a flattering glow. Then he turned back and stood regarding her solemnly. His eyes were dark and half his face was in shadow. Suzanna stood stock still, a few feet into the room, wishing he would say something. Her eyes were locked onto his mouth and she was sure he could see the sledge-hammer beat of her heart in her chest.

"It wasn't what you thought. Back there in the bar. With Steve. He shouldn't have put his arm round me. I'm not sure why he did it . . ." Her voice tailed off into silence, matching the silence emanating from him.

She couldn't read his expression, and she started to panic. Should she leave? Should she sit down or walk away from him? She was like a statue, hands clutched together in front of her chest, and eyes huge. She ran her tongue over her lips to moisten them, trying to decide what else to say.

Then, slowly, he reached out his arm and his hand wrapped itself round her wrist. It's warmth seared her skin. His touch was firm and his fingers met right round her flesh. Slowly he drew her towards him. For long seconds they stood absolutely still, facing each other only inches apart.

"God, you're beautiful!" His voice was low and intense.

She trembled as his hands moved down her arms and slid round her back. His touch was so electric that she felt certain there would be raised welts on her skin. His hold tightened. His arms were like two steel bands and his face was millimetres above hers.

She tilted her head backwards, silently offering to meet the lips she had admired so often. Her eyelashes lowered and she couldn't breathe.

His mouth descended, slowly, oh so slowly, onto hers. Unlike the strength of his hold, his kiss was gentle and soft. His lips explored the edges of her mouth. They moved over her face, dropping butterfly kisses onto the edges of her eyes, sweet petal kisses onto her temples, soft caresses under her ears and down onto her exposed throat. His hand was like a solid bar supporting her neck. His lips moved back to her mouth and the tip of his tongue flicked against the soft inside edges, inviting her to kiss him in return. Her arms stole more firmly round his waist and she gloried in the solid feel of his body as she moved in closer.

He drew in a deep, shuddering breath, lifted his head and gazed deeply into her eyes. She could feel his body locked against hers. His manhood pressed against her belly sending rivers of fire through her entire being. Her legs were like jelly. If his hold hadn't been so strong she would surely have fallen to the ground.

She slipped her hand round the back of his head and gripped a fist-full of thick hair, pulling his mouth down. She needed that mouth, wanted to feel it's strength. She longed to be consumed by it, and to consume in return.

He dropped his head and their lips crushed together. His mouth opened against hers, sweet, hot and demanding. His tongue explored the edges of her mouth, and then probed deeper, and still deeper. She responded, wanting more, wanting him to suck the very life out of her. She strained against him, her breasts pulsing into his chest, his arms holding her ever tighter, his hands moving up and down her back. His body felt like a pillar of rock. She was bent backwards, melding into him.

His mouth became more and more demanding. His hands moved over her shoulders, across her chest and tantalizingly close to her breasts. They were both panting as though they'd run a marathon. She strained against him, the emotions ripping through her. Never before had she felt this intensity, this incredible, all consuming desire. Her whole body felt white-hot.

She wanted him to strip off all her clothes and explore her body. Touch her burning skin. Run his hands down her legs, up her legs. Send his tongue into each and every secret fold. Crush her with his weight and make violent passionate love to her. She felt as though her senses had long since departed and would never return.

But, as though he read her thoughts, he lifted his head. She could feel the effort he made to silence his body, to make it relax and force his mind to unwind. He gave a deep shuddering sigh into her hair, lifted a handful of long strands, wound them round his fingers and put his nose into the curls, breathing deeply.

In all this time neither of them had spoken a word. Now they stood locked together, but quieter, as though they both knew that they had been only a second away from total abandonment. She rested her cheek against his chest, her arms still round his body, and felt his arms squeeze her tight once more in a fierce hug. She could feel his heart thudding as rapidly and loudly as hers was.

Then he took another deep breath and gently released her, although his hand stayed at the small of her back as though he sensed she might fall if he let her go too quickly.

"I should walk you back to your room," he murmured against her hair. "It's getting late."

"No. No—I'll be fine. Don't come. I'll be alright. I'll go straight there. You stay here."

He didn't want her to go alone, but she slid out of his grasp and stood back, staring at his face. The air almost crackled between them. Suzanna knew she had to leave, and leave right then. If she had taken one step back towards him, or he towards her, there would have been no stopping either of them.

She had no recollection of the walk back to her room. Her feet floated on air, her head was in the clouds and her spirit soared in the heavens.

Her senses returned somewhat when she saw her anxious cousin pacing up and down the path.

"Suzanna! Where on earth have you been? I was worried sick. I was about to call for help . . . ." She stopped as she caught sight of Suzanna's ruffled hair, her bruised and swollen mouth and her huge Cheshire cat grin. She smiled as Suzanna lifted her arms to the dark glittering night sky, and swung her skirts in a circle, twirling round like a forest nymph at a fairy ball.

"Oh, Sal. He's so gorgeous. He kissed me. I went to return his hanky and he kissed me. I don't think I'll ever be the same." She caught hold of Sally's hands and spun her about. "Let's race through the bush naked. Let's fly to the moon. Or better yet, let's go for a midnight swim. Skinny dipping. I'm so high right now, I'll never sleep. Come on,

Sal. It's hot enough to swim. There's no-one around. Let's do it."

Sally caught Suzanna's fizzing mood and laughed. "OK. But you have to promise to give me a full BBD on what happened."

"I will," she promised.

BBD was their private 'speak' for Blow By Blow Description. Suzanna grabbed Sally's hand as they kicked off their shoes and ran giggling towards the pool, like two schoolgirls on a midnight raid of the tuck-shop. The moon had just sailed above the dark line of the trees, bathing the whole area in glowing golden beams of gentle light. The girls stood on the damp grass at the edge of the pool and peered all round, checking for either human or animal company.

"Can't see anyone or anything," Suzanna whispered. "Come on, I'll race you in."

They stepped out of their skirts and lifted their tops over their heads. The cool night air touched their bare skins. They felt wicked and daring. They felt young and beautiful.

"It's all or nothing," Sally whispered back. "Off with the undies."

Filled with daring and pure excitement, they dropped panties and bras to the ground and stood for a second glorying in the delicious touch of fingers of air feathering against their total nakedness.

Suzanna ran her hands up her body, feeling the taught skin of her flat belly, the firmness of her neck. She lifted her hair and let the heaviness drop down her back. Her breasts felt tight and firm, the nipples were dark, perky and erect in the night air. She raised her arms up to the sky and slowly pivoted round. Sally followed her lead and they circled each other like two ancient priestesses performing a secret ritual dance. The moonlight glowed pale on their outstretched arms, caressing their breasts and shoulders, highlighting their long and supple legs. The curly triangles at the base of their stomachs formed a dark contrast. Sally's was a lighter brown, whereas Suzanna's was almost black in the darkness.

They paused dramatically at the edge of the pool, posing with legs spread wide, and then, one dramatic step at a time they descended down into the water. It was totally delicious.

Suzanna hadn't swum naked since she was a child. She floated on her back, revelling in the sheer intimacy of the refreshing water lapping at every pore of her body. Her hair spread out in a fluid dark cloud, swaying and rippling. Her breasts bobbed and floated in the small wavelets that she created, two islands of soft flesh capped with a dark tip, raised and hard. She spread her legs wide, feeling the silky water licking into the tender dewy hidden surfaces, caressing and erotic. She lifted a leg and pointed her toes to the dark heavens, admiring the silver droplets that ran down the smooth skin. Sally turned and dived under her, the moonlight glistening on the smooth roundness of her pale bottom and the back of her thighs. She surfaced, blowing water at Suzanna, and they giggled as they swam leisurely around, stretching their arms upwards, arching their backs, pushing their breasts up and rolling over in the clear water.

The chill eventually made them climb out of the pool. They posed on the edge and couldn't resist a few twirls—arms open, wet hair showering drops of water, faces lifted to the sparkling stars above, droplets gleaming on their triangular bushes. Slight goose bumps prickled their skins, making their nipples stand up.

At last they gathered up their clothes and swung them round like banners of the dance. Then, shivering in the cool night air, they ran on bare feet back to their room, breasts jiggling as they went.

They thought they had gotten away with not being seen. They thought they'd had the night to themselves, the moonlit pool belonging only to them, to their goddess like, glistening dances, silver droplets adorning smooth limbs and upturned faces.

Neither of them noticed the tall figure that stepped hastily back into the shadows so as not to be seen. He was attired in swimming trunks, towel over one broad shoulder. His plans for a quiet midnight swim had been destroyed, and he drew back, mesmerized by the sight of two mermaids in the pool in the dead of night. They didn't know that he had stood watching them, unable to tear himself away, transfixed by their antics, and seen their return down the path, naked wet bodies shining and moving in the moonlight. They didn't hear the low moan that escaped his lips, or the surreptitious adjustment he made to the growing bulge in the front of his swimming trunks, his mind on a passionate kiss that he had shared with one of the mermaids earlier.

Neither Sally nor Suzanna bothered to put on any nightclothes as they crawled under their respective mosquito nets, murmuring goodnight to each other.

The sheets felt soft and warm and Suzanna turned on her side, hugging her arms around her middle. Her mind returned to Gregg and she re-lived every passionate moment of his kisses, felt his incredible mouth on hers, his arms strong at her back, his tongue exploring and seeking. She arched her back, wondering what would have happened if she had stayed—knowing full well what would have happened.

The blood was high in her veins, throbbing and pulsing. Her fingers stole to her nipples, gently rotating and pulling, nails softly digging in. The fire burned through her body. Her hands stroked down her belly, fingers finding and working at the moist intimacy between her thighs. She imagined Gregg's hands doing the same. She pictured him lying next to her, his weight pressing her down, his body joining with hers, hot and demanding.

She rolled forward onto her stomach and tightened her fist to form a hard tight knot under her mound and moved against it, rocking and building, seeking satisfaction, until she felt the waves flood through her, pulsing, releasing, and yet so frustrating because it wasn't what she desperately craved.

Chapter 11

SHE WOKE THE next morning feeling heavy and lethargic. The loud and persistent grunting of hippo jousting and fighting down at the river had woken her several times during the night. A lion had also sent it's roar echoing through the landscape—the personification of wild Africa—a hollow echoing, resonant call that travels for miles in the still silence of the night—thrilling, and yet terrifying at the same time. Suzanna hoped their lioness was safe with her new cubs. A nightjar had called insistently from a thicket, it's repetitive song boring into her brain. Each time she had woken, thoughts of Gregg crowded her mind, sending mixed waves of pleasure and longing down her limbs. She had curled into a ball and hugged her pillow, tasting his kisses and trying to recapture his smell.

Once again coffee was delivered with tasty muffins wrapped in a crisp white serviette. Sally and Suzanna managed to shower, dress and present themselves at the office ahead of any of the other guests. A few minutes later, though, Alan and Diana Spain walked up, a pleasant couple that the girls had met the day before. It seemed the walking groups were kept to a minimum of people. They greeted each other and discussed the weather, plus the night sounds they'd all heard, waiting for the guide to arrive.

Suzanna's heart seemed to have done it's share of over beating, but it was at it again! She was almost hyperventilating wondering if Gregg would take them on the walk, and if he did, how should she handle what had happened the night before. Sally had discussed it with her and decided she should try to look aloof and casual . . . . all very easy for Sally to say!

Suzanna needn't have worried. Although it was Gregg who emerged from the office he looked remote and professional as he greeted the waiting guests, and then handed out binoculars to those without their own. He didn't so much as catch Suzanna's eye, and she could have sworn he'd forgotten the whole incident.

'Maybe it didn't meant as much to him as it did to you,' the sneaky voice in her head suggested.

He addressed the group, explaining how they should walk quietly along the sandy paths by slightly rolling on the outside of their feet, adding that he would do most of the talking using hand signals, so they should keep an eye on him as much as possible.

'No problem there,' Suzanna thought.

He showed them what the danger signal was, and if he moved his hand sharply downwards they were to drop to the ground without hesitation or question. Finally he said that if they wished to talk between themselves they could do so, but to keep their voices as low as possible, and limit the conversation.

"Just remember that you are about to enter the domain of the animals, and they are not pets. In general they will flee rather than attack, but there is no definite pattern. If they feel threatened in any way, their behaviour could be violent. So keep alert, keep your eyes skinned, and try to make as little noise as possible."

His gaze skimmed over them, checking footwear. Suzanna was glad she had worn her heavy hikers with Sally's socks to cushion them. Everyone had dressed in varying shades of green or khaki, and a satisfied gleam of approval crossed his face.

"Oh, and make sure you keep up and don't lag behind," he added. "If you have any questions, I will be happy to answer them."

Suzanna felt intimidated and nervous, sure she would do something wrong. She shot Sally a worried glance, but a blue eye winked back, encouraging and cheerful. Gregg handed Alan a couple of water canisters hanging on a leather belt, while he swung an alarmingly large rifle onto his own shoulder and checked that his hunting knife was securely snug in his belt pouch. The gun looked heavy but reassuring. Suzanna admired his strength for having to carry such a weight.

The first part of the walk took the small party along the high riverbank. They wound through huge trees—the same ones they had observed from the boat—and Gregg named each and every one of them. He showed them the apple-ring shaped pods of the acacias that the elephant loved to eat, and broke apart a fresh round ball of elephant dung to show them the seeds contained therein. They studied with awe the huge circular footprints left from the previous nights feeding, and were fairly relieved not to see the owners of the feet that had left the prints.

Gregg halted the guests and they stopped to watch a small troupe of baboons that were on the far side of a gully, earnestly turning over stones, seeking here and there with their human-like fingers, and popping delicacies into their mouths. Two of the females had tiny babies clinging like little limpets to the underside of their soft furry bellies. The added burdens did not impede the mothers in any way and the little babies watched the upside-down world go by with large black eyes.

A huge male jumped lithely up onto a fallen tree trunk, sat himself down with his elbows on his knees, and studied the party of people intently, all the while scratching at various parts of his anatomy. His actions were amazingly human-like. He opened his mouth in a yawning display of strength, showing frightening four-inch canines, while the playful youngsters rough and tumbled at his feet, as entertaining as children in a playground.

Suddenly the big dog stiffened, dropped onto all fours and uttered a loud bark—Buh-hoo! Several of the youngsters scattered and ran for cover, squealing in fright. Startled and worried Suzanna looked around to see what had alarmed him. The surrounding bush appeared calm and quiet.

"Possibly thought we've been here long enough," Gregg suggested. "Let's walk on."

Gregg pointed out several different species of birds and, without appearing to lecture, described interesting details on their habits. Everyone managed to find them in the binoculars for a close-up look. They agreed that they had never seen any of them before, and Sally and Suzanna were thrilled to learn more about them. The colours were radiant.

They stopped to study footprints of all kinds, both of animals and of birds that had crossed the dusty ground in the last few hours. Some were easy to identify, but others had the party foxed. Gregg, however, knew them all and could describe not only the creature, but the approximate time it had passed that way. The round pug-mark of a lion, as large as a man's spread hand, struck them with awe and fear and the girls looked fearfully about in case the animal was still close by, and even then preparing to attack. Gregg reassured them that the mark was several days old, but the chill of the evidence of the animal's passage stayed with them.

They also studied dung! Never before had any of them seen so many different kinds of dung. There were the small round pellets left by impala, neatly piled in communal middens, droppings of the bigger buck that were larger and shinier and resembled chocolate coated nuts, hard dry dog-like turds left by hyena that were a chalky white from the high bone content, and of course a great deal of cow-like pads deposited by passing herds of buffalo. The most impressive, of course, were the huge round balls dropped by elephant, the half digested grass and seeds plainly evident.

Gregg explained that one of the ways to check on the closeness of an animal, was to stick a finger deep into the dung to check for warmth. The warmer the dung, the closer the animal that had left it behind.

"It's a trick that hunters use, to ascertain how close their quarry is," he grinned. "I don't suppose anyone will volunteer and give it a try? Oh, great, look here." He drew them over to study a large beetle. It's large smooth and shiny back was half the size of a human palm.

"What on earth is it doing? Oh, I know. It's a dung beetle, isn't it?" Sally said.

The busy creature was digging energetically in a mound of soft elephant dung, clawing out the fresh material and rolling up an ever growing, perfectly round ball. It then turned to balance on it's front legs and deftly pushed the ball with it's hind legs backwards across the ground, heading instinctively towards a soft patch of composted soil and leaves.

"Once it finds the right spot it will lay an egg into the ball of dung, then bury the ball. Then when the larva hatches it will feed on the dung before emerging above ground. Dung beetles form an essential part of the African bushveld. They consume and move vast amounts of animal droppings. Without them the dung would build up into intolerable levels."

The guests watched the beetle for a while longer. It appeared to have no sense of direction and pushed it's precious ball in an erratic line, searching for a good place to start digging.

"Right—we should press on and leave this little fellow to it's business." Gregg straightened and swung the gun back onto his shoulder.

Suzanna began to feel more and more confident, and less worried about drawing attention to herself. The pace that he set was fast enough to cover the distance, but because he kept stopping to point out things of interest, no-one felt fatigued. He made them drink sips of water from the lid of Alan's canisters, and periodically asked if everyone was doing alright.

Suzanna revelled in the fact that she could walk behind him and blatantly watch the swing of his long legs and the way his back moved with each step. Her eyes traced the ripple of shoulder muscle down to the steady movement of his buttocks, the way his feet fell on the path, and the pull and stretch of the bush green uniform right down his body. She caught his scent—a heady mix of manly sweat mingled with traces of shaving cream and soap, and she had to drag her thoughts back to the present time and time again to avoid missing some of the interesting facts he shared. A shiver ran down her spine when she looked at his mouth as he spoke, and her thoughts returned to their passionate kiss, that wonderful mouth hot and devouring on hers.

From time to time they approached the banks of the mighty river following it's eternal course. As the sun steadily rose in the morning sky, the light became brighter and hotter. They longed to be able to indulge in a quick dip, but the sight of a grey croc changed their minds. It wasn't a very long one, but where there were little ones, bigger ones were sure to be as well.

The party rested briefly in the shade of a huge kigelia tree, enormous sausage like fruits hanging from the branches, and admired the beautiful scenery in both directions up and down river. A pod of hippo was lazing on a sand bank, their immobile and enormous round backs looking like weather-worn smooth black boulders.

Several smaller riverbeds cut through the dry landscape, snaking ever downwards from the distant mountains. During the rains the flood waters gushed through the gullies, racing down to swell the flow of the Zambezi on it's journey to the sea. Most of these smaller tributaries were dry, waiting for the rains to wash through them once again.

Gregg suggested they follow the course of one of them on their return to camp.

"I reckon you are all up to the challenge," he announced. "However, since the animals also use these dry gullies as paths and feeding areas, we have to be extra vigilant. Walk quietly and watch my hand signals. We should see some interesting and different things along the way."

The bush grew thickly along the banks, and since the bed was winding and sometimes stony, extra caution had to be taken not to stumble across an animal unexpectedly.

"We'll just look over this rise before we head back," he continued quietly. "Down on all fours everyone, and move with caution."

Silently they dropped to their hands and knees and crawled the last few meters to peer over the summit. Their stealth was rewarded. In the small valley on the other side lay one of the pools they had passed on their first day. They gasped with delight and it was hard not to exclaim out loud.

A charming little family of warthogs were scuffling in the mud, their bristly backs humped as they trotted about, busily digging with sharp hooves. Their skinny pencil like tails stuck straight up into the air as soon as they put on any burst of speed. One of the males chased off a younger rival, threatening him with a set of impressive yellowed tusks that curled round his upper lip. Several baboons strolled along the water's edge, daintily picking morsels from underneath overturned stones and occasionally pausing to stoop down to drink. A flock of Sacred Ibises clustered near the far reeds and a few of them adorned a dried dead tree. Their striking black and white feathers were taken straight off the animal cat-walk of fashion.

But best of all was the delicate form of a bushbuck. He had stepped out of the bush and was standing, head held high, ears pricked, alert and ready to flee at the slightest sound. They hardly dared to breathe in case he detected their presence. Once he had satisfied himself that all was safe, he picked his way delicately down to the life-giving water, spread his front legs wide, and lowered his head to drink. His gently twisted horns laid back against his neck, and the white stripe just under his eyes looked as though it had been painted on. He was a picture of beauty, with his rippled reflection showing off the rich dappled browns of his smooth hide.

Suzanna had managed to place herself next to Gregg on the way up the rise, and now she was lying flat on her stomach with her shoulder almost touching his side. She absorbed his scent, and it was all she could do not to wriggle closer and tuck herself up against him.

After a while, he quietly indicated that it was time to move on, and, reluctantly, they eased back down the slope, leaving the animals to drink and feed in their natural surroundings.

Gregg stood up, then turned towards Suzanna and put his hand out to grip hers to help her to her feet. She glanced up at him in surprise, and for the first time since they'd set out that morning, they looked into each other's eyes. For a long second they stood, her hand in his, their gazes locked together. A shaft of sunlight lit up the side of his face and turned his eyes a greenish brown. His expression was unreadable. He seemed to be asking her a silent question but she couldn't decipher what it was. She licked her dry lips, and they stepped away from each other. The others had taken a few paces down the slope and she hoped none of them had noticed the silent exchange. Suzanna pressed a hand to her middle to calm the fluttering inside, and bent to brush the grass and dirt off the front of her clothes. Then, not knowing if she felt happy or sad, she trailed along in the rear.

The walk back to camp along the dry streambed was uneventful, but they walked with great caution and fully expected to see an animal round every corner. A few meters further on Gregg drew their attention to a roughly dug hole in the firmer sand.

"This is interesting," he said. "Elephant dig these holes. The great animals can smell water way below the surface, and they swing one foot backwards and forwards, loosening the sand which they blow out with their trunks. They can dig down for several feet, slowly widening the hole until a trickle seeps in at the bottom. During the dry season a whole range of other animals, from tiny rodents to various types of antelope, rely completely on the elephant holes for life giving water."

Huge boulders littered the streambed—rolled and washed and left behind by years of flash floods. Suzanna bent and picked up a perfectly round black stone almost the size of a cricket ball. It had been shaped by hundreds of years of wear against larger and harder rock, spun and rolled this way and that and finally left to lie in the sand. She studied her treasure and dropped it into a pocket to keep forever as a reminder and talisman of the trip.

If an animal was ahead of them, or in the bush along the dry stream banks, they saw no sign of it, although the sandy bed was pitted with hundreds of footprints and strewn with dung. Clouds of black midgies descended on the walkers from time to time, buzzing irritatingly round their eyes, seeking moisture. The movement of air in the gully was restricted by the high banks and the heat slowly built up, pressing around them. Their shirts were stained dark with sweat by the time they finally emerged onto the higher ground near the camp where the slight breeze was a welcome relief.

Gregg was friendly and at ease, and answered Suzanna's questions in a pleasant professional manner, pleased that she was taking such an interest. The party walked back into camp with the camaraderie of a great shared experience. The outing had taken slightly over a couple of hours, and everyone was ready for a drink and something to eat.

Suzanna turned to Gregg.

"Thank you for being such a good host and guide. I was really nervous that I'd fall over or do something silly, but I loved every moment. Thank you."

He grinned down at her. "Thank you. I'm really glad that you enjoyed it."

"Please—won't you call me Suzanna? Especially after . . . well . . ." She took a breath. "Just make it Suzanna." Her cheeks flushed and she turned to hurry after Sally, who was waiting ahead on the path.

"Suzanna," he murmured under his breath, almost as though saying it out loud for the first time. And then louder. "Suzanna?"

She turned to face his half serious, half mocking expression.

Almost under his breath he said, "Your name is as beautiful as you are."

The moment hung in the air between them and she had to restrain herself from returning to fling herself into his arms and grab him in a bear hug. She glanced up from under her lashes, giving him a burning, sideways look and her lips lifted in her most seductive smile.

"Thanks Gregg."

His eyes bored a hole in her back as she walked away. If she had turned back again she would have been surprised by the aching look of longing that creased his forehead. The beads of sweat shone along his eyebrows, uncomfortable and hot.

Feeling his eyes on her back, Suzanna put a tiny bit of extra swagger into her stride, swinging her neat bottom and shoulders like a model on a cat-walk. She considered doing a little skip with a sideways click of the heels, but managed to keep her step long and elegant despite the singing in her heart and the weakness in her knees.

Chapter 12

THE GIRLS RETIRED to the pool for the rest of the morning, enjoying the clear sky and the cool water. Suzanna decided to flaunt her figure and tan her stomach. Her maroon bikini with white trimming was nothing more than four small triangles, and better suited to a beach frequented by the rich and famous, but, daringly, she decided to wear it. She grinned at her reflection in the mirror, and swivelled round to see all angles. She tied on a pale rose sarong to walk down the path, and hitched her bag over her shoulder.

Sally and she settled themselves as before, spreading suncream, and joked and giggled about their midnight swim of the night before, remembering how erotic it had felt to be totally naked in the intimacy of the silky water. They laughed about how they would have looked trotting back to the room, breasts and bottoms jiggling and bouncing, clothing trailing behind, and they congratulated themselves on getting away without being seen.

Once again Rachel strolled up to join them. She looked as lovely as ever as she laid out her towel and other gear.

Suzanna's smile was strained, thinking about Rachel's attempt to waylay Gregg last night.

'You don't know what followed later, though, do you?' She hugged the delicious feelings close and said out loud. "Hi Rachel. Have you had a good day so far?"

"You sounded happy, both of you. What were you laughing at? Did you enjoy the walk?"

Sally and Suzanna described several of the things they'd seen and then told her about their mid-night swim. Rachel's lower lip pouted forwards and she lowered her sunglasses to peer over the top rim.

"I don't want to burst your bubble, but I hope none of the staff saw you. They often come down for a late night swim when they know the guests have gone to bed. I know for sure that Gregg often does that. He feels more comfortable doing his workout when no-one is around."

Suzanna sat bolt upright. "You're kidding! Gregg comes to the pool at night? What workout?" She was immediately sent into a dither of emotions. If he'd come to the pool last night he'd have seen them for sure. The moon was bright enough to see clearly, and he would have had no difficulty in identifying the mermaids.

Rachel continued smoothly, "He spends so much time in the office that he likes to get a good workout at night, and he'll often do an hour or so just swimming up and down as fast as he can."

She looked at the pair with half closed eyes and added, "The pool is wonderful at night, isn't it?"

The thoughts were tumbling through Suzanna's brain, but she didn't want to discuss what she was thinking in front of Rachel. From the way she'd spoken, there was a clear message that she had spent time in the pool at night with someone else. Suzanna wondered if Rachel had been entirely honest the day before about her relationship with Gregg. How come she knew so much about him all the time?

"I'm sure we'd have seen him if he'd been here last night," Sally chipped in. "The moon was as bright as day. He probably would have mentioned it on the walk this morning, if he'd seen us."

She'd noticed Suzanna's shocked expression and tried to change the subject.

"What did you do this morning, Rachel?" Her voice was smooth. "We loved going out on our walk—it was wonderful. Thankfully no big animals, but plenty of other interesting things."

Rachel launched into her account of the game drive, relating how they'd come across a pack of wild dog on the side of the road, and how they'd sat and watched them for at least an hour. Suzanna squirmed, green with envy. Rachel always seemed to be one up on them. She was so self-possessed all the time, so poised, so confident of her beauty. She always seemed to have done something better, or seen something more exciting, than anyone else. If there was one animal both Suzanna and Sally would dearly love to see, it was a wild dog. They had read several articles on them and just loved their painted coats, intelligent eyes and large round ears.

"There were several puppies in the pack, so Stanley thought they could be in the same area this evening. He plans to take the evening drive back there to try and spot them again. Of course they are officially called painted dogs now, and you can see why. I got some fabulous shots of them and I've already booked a place to go out again this evening."

Suzanna forgot her anxiety on being seen last night, and pushed the less charitable thoughts about Rachel to the back of her mind. She grabbed her wrap and stood up.

"Come on, Sal. Let's go to the office right now and let them know we'd like to go out this evening if there's room. If we leave it too late, we may miss out on a place."

Sally was delighted with her enthusiasm.

"I swear, if you don't look out this place will get under your skin, and you won't want to leave," she grinned. "And not just for the wild life," she added teasingly.

Suzanna scowled at her. Naturally she had told Sally about Gregg holding her hand out on the walk, and she had been given a miss-know-all look and a click of her tongue.

"The plot thickens," she'd said. "I told you he was smitten with you."

They wrapped their sarongs over their swimming costumes and walked down to the office. As luck would have it, Gregg was sitting behind the desk working on the computer. He looked up as they entered the office, and there was no mistaking the involuntary glance that ran up and down their scantily clad bodies. Suzanna thought she caught a gleam of something cross his handsome features, and the blood rose to her cheeks, wondering if he had actually seen them naked in the pool, or not. She suddenly felt embarrassed standing there in her clinging sarong, which was almost totally see-through anyway. But he stood up and greeted them in a friendly manner with one lifted eyebrow and a smile that melted her bones.

"Um, oh! Hi!" she stuttered. "Er—we were at the pool, and um, Rachel said they'd seen wild dog this morning, so we came straight away to book, for this evening, that is, if there's a place. Um... I mean on the game drive."

Her voice died, but her pulse didn't. It was knocking like a steam engine against her rib cage. She lifted a hand to press to her chest and her fingers fiddled with the knot of her sarong.

Once again Sally came to her rescue, and took over the explanation. Gregg's grin spread even wider.

"Of course you'll both be welcome to join the drive. We'll leave just after 5.30 as usual and we'll probably take two vehicles again. And certainly, we will head back to the area where the painted dogs were seen earlier. It's very likely they'll still be there. They're pretty territorial, especially if there are pups amongst the pack."

He put up a hand to brush back a lock of hair and then spread his hands on the desk, wide shoulders forwards. The overhead fan whirled cool air and a chill ran down Suzanna's spine. Hastily she tried to cross her arms to hide the fact that her nipples had reacted once again, but, too late, she noted Gregg's glance flick in that direction, and the muscle in the side of his jaw clenched.

His tongue moved behind his teeth and the very tip of it touched the inside centre of his top lip. There was a wicked gleam in his eyes, and the side of his mouth lifted in a lopsided grin.

"I'm glad you enjoyed the walk this morning. It was a pleasure taking you out. You seem a little more settled in the camp today, Miss Scott. That's great to see."

He was openly and blatantly teasing her. Now her cheeks felt steaming hot. She knew he was referring to their kiss, but she wasn't sure how to respond. A million retorts flashed through her mind. What was he inferring? Should she acknowledge his comment?

Nothing brilliant or witty came into her mind but instead she mumbled, "Thank you. It is a lovely camp." She looked straight into his eyes and added, "and there are certainly plenty of attractions in it." 'There, read that how you like,' she thought.

"Well, OK—see you later then." Sally breezed.

They turned to go and Gregg walked round the counter to open the door for them.

"I'll look forward to it."

Suzanna still felt uncertain of him and, as she followed Sally out of the office, she kept to the other side of the doorway so that there was no possibility of brushing against him. Head held high, she swished through the doorway, took two steps and felt her sarong being tugged from behind and pulled off her body!

"Omigawd! Help!"

She whirled round with a cry of dismay, suspecting the worst and instantly ready to verbally attack Gregg. She looked back and realized the fine material had caught on a large splinter of wood sticking out from the doorframe. Without realizing it, she must have loosened the knot when she fiddled with it. The fine material had billowed out, hooked on the splinter and there it had remained as she stalked through the door. She turned back and grabbed at the silky stuff with both hands but only succeeded in making things worse. It turned into a big soft ball in her fumbling hands and she couldn't find the end of it.

There she stood, clad only in her itsy-witsy bikini, in the doorway of his office, desperately trying to spread out the sarong so that she could wind it back in place. Sally was no help either. She turned to see what the problem was, and let out a snort of laughter at her cousin's dilemma.

"Suze, what are you doing?"

"Don't just stand there, Sally. Do something."

Gregg stepped forward. His expression was studiously serious.

"Allow me to help you."

Gently he took the sarong out of her hands, shook it out and began to unfurl the silky mess. It seemed to take him a little while to find the edge and her discomfort increased with each second. Then he stretched it out, towel fashion, to hand back to her. He was standing very close—too close—and this time he made no secret of the fact that his eyes were thoroughly enjoying their trip up and down her body. She was close enough to see a pulse beating at the side of the Adam's apple in his throat, and she felt her composure slip further out of control. His keen gaze worked upwards and his eyes came to rest staring into hers, alive and sparkling with humour.

"Thank you." She took it from him and wrapped it back round herself. Her fingers shook and seemed unnaturally stiff, so she held the knot firmly to avoid losing it once more. She turned, and with Sally following, she fled headlong back to the pool. At the corner of the path she stopped with a backward glance.

Gregg was leaning on the inside of the doorframe, doubled over and shaking with silent laughter.

There wasn't a breath of breeze and the midday heat settled around them, thick and oppressive. Even the insects were quiet, and nothing stirred. Heat waves shimmered over the landscape and the white light reflecting off the river seared the eyes. Everything was caught in the torpor of hot waves of air and burning sun.

Sally and Suzanna relaxed in the shade by the pool. No sooner had they climbed out of the cool water than their skins dried off in the stifling heat and they had to get back in again. After a light lunch washed down with an ice-cold beer, they staggered to the room and collapsed onto their beds for a midday sleep. The fan stirred the air, but the temperature remained high.

They emerged later for a cup of tea on the lawn, looking forward to the cooler evening air. Suzanna made sure she had her dark glasses plus a handkerchief, and the girls wandered across to the office. As usual the vehicles were parked out the front, but this time Gregg and Stanley were already seated and waiting for the guests to arrive.

Suzanna threw a look at Sally, and sucked in her cheeks. Rachel had arrived early and was sitting in the passenger's seat right next to Gregg. She leaned in towards him, smiling intimately and murmuring in a low voice. Suzanna wondered again if she was trying to make a play for him and a stab of something very close to jealousy shot through her.

"She's a natural predator, I reckon," Sally whispered. "But I also feel she won't fool a man like Gregg."

"Who could say—but I hope you're right." Suzanna replied. "I wonder how things are going with his girl back at home? All this could get complicated."

"Well, keep that strongly in mind at all times," Sally warned. "You've only just recovered from Dave, remember. I don't need to deal with another bout of depression from you."

Suzanna stuck the tip of her tongue out. "Miss know-all!"

The second row of seats was still empty in his vehicle, so without another word between them, the cousins greeted Gregg and Rachel and clambered up. Suzanna deliberately chose the centre seat this time—confident that she could hide behind her dark glasses and yet watch Gregg's eyes in the rear-view mirror, plus admire the spread of his shoulders and the curl of his hair. She could watch the way his strong fingers held the steering wheel, and remember how those same hands had felt on her body.

She hid a smug grin—Rachel thought she had chosen the best seat in the vehicle, but in actual fact it was Suzanna that had it. She pressed her lips together when Gregg looked straight in the mirror and gave her the tiniest suspicion of a wink.

"Evening ladies. Er—do you have everything you need? OK, Miss Scott?"

She knew he was teasing her. A laugh bubbled out of her throat, making Rachel spin round to study her face.

"I hope so. Thank-you Gregg," she answered.

Sally's eyebrows shot upwards at her use of his name, but she ignored her, ignored Rachel as well, and busied herself in adjusting the binoculars lying on the seat. Both vehicles filled up with guests keen to see the painted dogs, and they set off. Suzanna kept one eye on Rachel while she admired the passing landscape. It wouldn't be beyond her to hotch over the seat on any pretext to sit right up against Gregg's side.

The sky was streaked with delicate wispy clouds, and the setting sun decided to show them a true African sunset. The clouds nearest to the sun were lit up in brilliant yellow streaks, edged in flaming white gold splashed from a celestial artist's palette. The lines spread in fingers across the sky, the colour deepening on the far side to a warmer glow of bronzes and deeper golds. As they watched, the sun slowly sank, seeming to grow larger and turn into a fiery red ball that hovered just above the horizon, reluctant to disappear and let the night commence. The colours in the sky softened into hues of pinks and reds, then deepened into a mauve light that spread across the landscape, and transformed the harshness of the bushveld into a wonderland of shadows, gentle purple rays, and a promise of the coolth of darkness.

They struck it lucky.

The dogs had moved into a slightly different area, but Stanley's vehicle found them a little further down the road, and Gregg followed. It was perfect viewing and there was enough light left in the day to see the animals clearly.

There were a couple of adults and six pups, all tussling and playing together, just as a pack of domestic dogs would do. Their large rounded ears and intelligent faces turned inquisitively to regard the vehicles and humans as they drove slowly closer. Each dog had it's own individual coat markings of mottled blacks, tans and yellows that blended incredibly well with their surroundings. Each of them had a beautiful white tip to the end of their tail, and this seemed to be what was drawing the attention of the pups as they tried to catch and bite the illusive waving flags.

None of the animals showed any concern at the presence of the vehicles, and they made no move to run away into the bush. In fact one of the inquisitive pups trotted right up to the side of the vehicle and posed for photographs as he stared silently upwards. His bright eyes took the people in and he showed no fear at all.

"On occasion I've been able to get out of the vehicle and approach to within a few meters of a pack without spooking them," Gregg said quietly. "They can be very trusting."

"He's so skinny," Sally breathed. "Look at his sunken belly and long thin legs."

"Makes you want to take him home and feed him up," Suzanna agreed. "But his coat is good and he doesn't look in bad condition. None of them do."

"They live a pretty hard life," Gregg continued. "I can't say I've ever seen a truly fat painted dog. Look to your left, here come some more adults," he added quietly. "They could possibly be bringing dinner to the pack."

Sure enough, the pups went into a frenzy, twittering and jumping at the newly arrived adults who trotted up, heavy and ungainly with huge round bellies. Everyone watched in total fascination as they disgorged chunks of slimy meat onto the ground, only to have the pups grab the offerings and gobble them up. The adults who had been left to guard the pups also managed to snatch a few morsels. Every regurgitated scrap was consumed, covered in dirt and leaves or not. Two pups grabbed the same piece of dirty meat and neither would let go. They pulled backwards and forwards until the piece tore into two and each convulsively swallowed a chunk.

"They don't seem to bark or make a noise," Rachel observed.

"You're right," Gregg replied. "They make a strange chirping, yipping sound, completely unlike any other canine. Sadly they are high on the endangered list, so it is a real privilege to see them interacting like this."

By this time Gregg had switched the headlights of the vehicle on, clearly lighting up the pack. But even having the bright lights turned on them didn't appear to worry the intelligent animals. However, once the meat was finished, and the last scrap fought over and swallowed, the dogs collapsed down in a close group to do some serious digesting.

"Dinner's over for another day. They will lie like that and sleep for at least and hour or so now, so I suggest we take a different route back to camp and see what else is out and about tonight."

"Great idea." They were all keen on Gregg's suggestion. He signalled to Stanley and his vehicle went one way while Gregg went another.

They drove slowly along, keeping to the open sandy roads. Suzanna was relieved to see that Rachel appeared to be engrossed with spotting game and stayed over on her side of the bench seat. Gregg held a spotlight that he directed from side to side trying to pick up the gleam of eyes. They stopped to watch a herd of impala held in the beam, skittish and alert, and jostling each other to decide which direction to run in. Suzanna's heart went out to them.

"They are so delicate and beautiful but they spend their lives on the edge of fear—both fear of man, and fear of being eaten at any moment by one of the big predators," she said. "One of them could even have just been dinner for the pack of painted dogs."

Talking of predators, they gasped with excitement as a leopard suddenly took a few steps out onto the road ahead of the Land Rover. Gregg immediately stopped, and they sat in entranced silence as the magnificent animal posed for a few moments, tail twitching and showing off his glorious spotted coat. He was a young adult in his prime, vigorous and proud. He was half crouched, showing muscles that spoke of pent-up power waiting to explode into devastating action. His eyes gleamed golden in the beam of light and the intricacy of the black markings on his face was rich and vibrant. The cameras clicked again and again, capturing his wonderful beauty before he disappeared with one huge bound into the dark bush.

They let out a collective sigh, and it was hard to keep their voices low as they discussed how lucky they had been to see him. They knew Stanley's vehicle wouldn't have had such luck. Gregg drove on, but nothing else stepped out onto the road until they reached the edge of camp. The hump-backed shape of a hyena slunk off into the darkness looking furtive and guilty, as though it had been up to no good.

"Hyenas can be a real menace round camp," Gregg said. "They smell out meat and food, and will even bite at cold boxes and deep freezes to try and get at the contents. They can be quite aggressive as well. They are the scavengers of the bush and are drawn to the bone-yards on the edges of the hunting camps."

"Did you say bone-yards? What's a bone-yard?" Suzanna asked.

"The site where the carcasses of the animals are thrown after the hunters have stripped off all the meat," he replied. "Scavengers gather there for a meal, from the smaller jackals and vultures to the larger animals such as hyena. Even lion will go past on occasion to see if they can pick up a morsel. You can sometimes have good game viewing at the bone-yards."

She shivered, hating the thought of people shooting game for any reason at all. Leaving the bones in an abandoned pile for other animals to pick over sounded perfectly ghoulish.

Chapter 13

A HIVE OF activity was taking place in the camp. A huge fire had been lit in the barbeque pit not far from the pool, and the staff was bustling about organising the evening meal outdoors.

The heart of the fire crackled and glowed with an intense red heat that lit up the surroundings and flickered over the people standing nearby. Red sparks from the blazing mopani logs flew up into the night sky looking like dancing fireflies. Moths were drawn to the light and heat, and flew crazily into the flames only to vaporise in an instant.

Candles shaded in brown paper bags lined the pool area and more were set out on long trestle tables. Guests mingled around, holding drinks and nibbling at the array of snacks and eats. A tantalising smell drifted to greet the new arrivals.

Since the meal was to be outdoors, Sally and Suzanna didn't bother to change, but headed to the bar to get a glass of wine. They joined a group standing near the pool and were soon discussing who had had the best viewing of the day. The painted dogs were on top of the list and everyone agreed it had been the cherry on top to have seen the leopard. When Suzanna mentioned the hyena, and asked about the hunting camps, Pete told them that hunters have to pay large amounts of money for the privilege to shoot animals in the Zambezi Valley, and the killing program, plus the areas in which the hunting was done, were strictly controlled and regulated. If an animal was wounded it had to be followed until found, and duly dispatched.

"Every hunter, from the first time out guys to the really experienced and skilled shooters, have to be accompanied by a back-up armed Park ranger and at least one or two scouts. The scouts can track animals even over rocky ground, and if an animal is wounded they can follow the blood spoor until the beast is found. It is against the law for an animal to be left to bleed to death, and heavy fines and penalties can be invoked against the hunter if the animal is not followed up and eventually killed. At times the hunting party lay themselves open to finding wounded buffalo in thick bush—a very dangerous and difficult business. The buffalo will deliberately hide and wait to attack his attackers. More than one hunter has been badly gored by mis-reading the signs and not being careful enough."

Pete's explanation didn't make her feel better about any of these fabulous animals being shot for their horns, or their tusks or skins. It was hard to understand how anyone would want to do it. She shivered and tried to change the subject, but several of the men standing around had stories of their own about encounters with wounded animals. Steve related a tale of three hunters who had surprised a bull elephant grazing on the far side of a giant anthill. The hunters had approached without due caution, not expecting to see him, and the elephant had immediately attacked, killing one of the men and very badly wounding the other before swinging away into the dense bush.

"Where were the scouts? Wouldn't they have known it was there?" Suzanna was horrified.

"The story is a little fuzzy about the presence of scouts at all," Steve replied. "Some chaps get too confident about their skills and wind up in trouble. Being trampled and knelt on by an angry elephant is not how you would wish even your worst enemy to die. A man on foot doesn't stand a chance against that mighty body and flailing trunk. But, I suppose accidents will happen, even with the best laid plans."

"Enough of the gories, let's head towards dinner. I could eat a dead horse," Pete declared, and was relieved to have his weak joke make the ladies smile.

A wide range of barbequed food and salads were laid out on the tables, and the guests sat around on the loungers and chairs with plates balanced on their laps. The romantic setting under the canopy of brilliant stars, with the fire still flickering and drawing their gazes, could have been taken from a top level travel advert.

Pete settled himself close to Sally but when Steve sat down near to Suzanna she gently found an excuse to get up for a little more food, and then managed to move her chair backwards a bit. She didn't want to offend him, but she didn't want him to get any more ideas either.

Steve had already had a couple of drinks, and confidently held the floor with his tales, delivering the punch lines with humour and leading the laughter. Suzanna had already noticed that Gregg and Stanley had finished their meal and were doing the rounds of the guests, laughing and sharing stories—popular and perfect hosts. The cover of darkness allowed her to follow Gregg with her eyes while carrying on a conversation with everyone sitting around.

They were in for another treat. Once the meal was over and the long tables had been cleared, a group of waiters dragged out a selection of tom-toms, one almost waist height, tucked them between their knees and, with flashing smiles and flying hands, they sent the driving, pulsing rhythms out into the night. This was more than the brief call for dinner. It was the sound of ancient, primitive Africa. The throbbing heart beat of the oldest land on earth, with the power to conjure up visions of brutal rites and traditional dances. It was mesmerising.

And then the guests gasped to see a ghastly man-creature shuffle out of the shadows. The figure was adorned with a conglomeration of trailing bits of animal skin and strips of bright cotton materials. A grass skirt hung around his waist, rattles made from seed-pods were tied round the bony ankles and wrists, and a hideous black and white wooden mask covered his face. He held a long spear in one hand and a stick that ended in a heavy round knob in the other—both fearsome weapons. The bare feet began stamping and leaping in time to the driving beat of the drums. The skinny body jumped and twisted, sending the skirt and skins flying, dancing and stamping in a frenzied display, lost in the compelling rhythm that ebbed and flowed, holding both performer and audience captive.

The beat echoed out into the night, louder and then more gentle, building up into a crescendo and then dropping to a whisper, only to build up once again. The gyrating figure was the lone representative of ancient and historic rituals, of painted and adorned tribes performing dances and songs that dated back through primitive time.

The fascinated guests were reluctant to let them finish, clapping and shouting encouragement. When the beat finally died away for the last time and the figure had melted back into the darkness, the night seemed to breathe a quiet sigh—and then as though pre-rehearsed, the wailing and slightly insane laugh of a hyena split the silence. The eerie 'Oooo-oop, oooo-oop, hee, hee, hee,' raised goose bumps on flesh. An answering call from another indicated that the pack was out hunting, and once again Suzanna wondered how their lioness was faring with her new cubs. She hadn't been sighted recently, so no-one knew if the cubs were safe.

One by one the guests finished their drink and got up to leave and head off to bed. The circle of chairs grew smaller as the remainder drew up round the fire, sipping from refreshed glasses and enjoying the wonderful ambiance of the night. There was the slightest stirring of a breeze, and the air was caressing, sultry and warm.

Gregg had stayed on after dinner, and he seemed relaxed as he talked and laughed. Suzanna watched him, and from time to time she caught his glance and sent him a smile.

Rachel sat very close to him, making a flicker of envy pinch at Suzanna's throat. Once or twice she touched his knee as she laughed gaily, self assured and elegant even in this informal setting. Silently Suzanna willed her to go to bed, but it seemed she was determined to stick it out to the end. It was quite clear that she had set her sights on Gregg, and it seemed he was happy to enjoy her attention. Suzanna frowned, trying to ignore the hot knife that pierced her innards. Was he drawn to her? Was it Rachel he actually preferred? Had he kissed Rachel like he had kissed her? Had their few intimate moments been just a whim, snatched up because the opportunity had presented itself? She wished she knew. One moment she was up and the next she was down. This sea-saw of emotions was hard to cope with.

Rachel was in the middle of an animated story, hands waving to emphasize her point, when the duty officer appeared at Gregg's side and quietly called him to the phone. Several of the guests automatically glanced at their watches to check the time—it was late.

He looked startled and immediately stood up to go to the office. He was away for quite a while, and when he returned his face was set into hard lines and he looked grim and strained. He had obviously received bad news of some sort. Suzanna stared up, trying to catch his eye, but he was pre-occupied and tense and just flicked a glance over the whole party.

"Excuse me everyone. I think I'll turn in. Goodnight."

Her heart twisted as he excused himself. She wanted to jump up and go after him, but she had to sit still and watch him stride away down the path to his room. She longed to go to him, share his burden and comfort him, but she had no cause to do so.

Rachel obviously didn't feel the same way, though. With a quiet, "Excuse me," she rose and followed Gregg. The dagger twisted even deeper, and Suzanna hugged her arms round her body and hunched over in actual physical pain.

The conversation resumed. Several people tried to guess what news Gregg had received.

"I reckon Rachel thinks she can be of some assistance to Gregg anyway."

The snide remark to her left drew sniggers from a couple of the women and Suzanna wanted to scream at them to shut-up. That it was none of their business.

She wanted to pummel her fists into the ground with frustration. She stuck it out and managed to remain in her chair for a little while longer, but the restlessness eventually made her get to her feet and say goodnight. Steve stood up and offered to escort her back to the room, but she firmly declined his offer and he didn't press the point.

She walked away from the rest of the guests, but had no intention of going back to the bedroom. She was possessed by a burning compulsion to sneak past Gregg's room and see if Rachel was there. For a second she stopped, undecided, resisting the impulse, telling herself it had nothing to do with her. Silently she argued that she had no rights as far as Gregg was concerned—that one passionate and wonderful kiss did not mean any kind of commitment, from either of them.

The other voice in her head replied, 'But what about the secret looks he's given you, and holding your hand? I reckon that should count for something.'

'Perhaps he didn't mean them like we thought he did,' she answered.

'Well, you can't go to his room, it's far too late at night.'

'I know, I know—it would be too awkward if Rachel was there anyway.'

While the thoughts flowed through her brain, her treacherous feet took her to the edge of the office from where she could see down the path towards his room. A loud laugh from the bar made her jump and look guiltily around to see if she was about to be discovered. No-one came along.

And then, her hand flew over her mouth and she had to struggle not to cry out loud.

Gregg walked out of his room—and he had Rachel at his side.

He had his arm round her shoulders and their heads were turned towards each other, deep in conversation. Their low voices didn't carry to Suzanna, but she cringed when Rachel gave a soft chuckle. They stopped, facing each other, clearly outlined. His hands were on her shoulders, and hers were tucked against his sides. Suzanna was rooted to the spot, terrified of what she would see but unable to tear her glance away. What else had Rachel managed to achieve in the time she had been away from the fire? Had she seduced him? He bent his head down slightly—was he going to kiss her?

She didn't wait to see any more, terrified they would discover her and know she had been spying on them. She ducked back behind the office and, trying to stifle the instant tears, she fled round the back of the dining room.

'So—there's your answer,' the mocking voice told her. 'You should have known that a man like him, as gorgeous and hunky, would have all the women chasing after him. OK—so he kissed you. What does one kiss mean? It's evident that Rachel is out to get him—girlfriend or no girlfriend back at home. And it's evident that he's quite happy to be with her. You made a plan to keep away from him, now stick to it before you get your heart broken once again. Whatever he heard on the phone changes nothing. He has a girl already, and, by the looks of it, possibly another one right here in camp as well.'

She flung open the bedroom door, noting that Sally hadn't returned, and flung herself onto the bed, tears dripping down her face. She felt angry with herself for re-acting like this, but she just couldn't help it. It was almost as if some internal fabric had been torn, leaking pain and emotion into her system. It was difficult to understand—after all she didn't even know the man properly. All she knew was that he created instant effects that no-one else had ever had on her, and for a while she had dared to hope he felt the same way.

Impatiently she brushed the tears away, but her heart was heavy and she felt totally flat. She wondered if Sally was spending the night with Pete. Good for her, lucky girl. She imagined Gregg and Rachel together, and her body writhed in torment. It should have been her with him, not Rachel. Despite all her sympathy and fond gestures, Suzanna couldn't squash the impression that Rachel would just pin Gregg's scalp to her belt if she managed to share his bed.

The warm night air defied the steady rotation of the fan, and Suzanna's limbs stuck to the sheets. She got up, changed into a soft cotton nightie, and then, on the spur of the moment walked outside and stood for a while listening intently to the sounds of the night. The stars had disappeared and it was darker than usual with clouds covering the moon. The heavy air was sultry with the promise of a storm building beyond the hills. No rain would fall for several weeks yet, but the pressure would continue to gather force until the rain fell in deluging sheets that would instantly transform the dry bush, fill the gullies and turn the deep layer of dust into a quagmire of sticky mud.

Suzanna gathered up her courage and tip-toed a little way towards the pool. The shadows moved and rustled with a life of their own and she didn't dare go too far. She was desperate to see if Gregg was there, doing his late night work-out, but no obvious idea of what she would say or do if she saw him came into her mind. Would she ask him about Rachel—ask if anything had happened between them? Ask him about the phone call? She had no right to do either—no right to claim his attention at all, actually.

But the pool area was quiet. There was no sight or sound of anyone splashing or swimming. The disappointment washed over her and she realized she had been counting on seeing him there. Once again her emotions sank leaving her deflated and miserable. Her shoulders drooped and all the energy drained out of her like sand out of a bucket.

A sudden rustle in the bushes was startling and she stared hard in the direction it had come from, terrified something would emerge. The sound came again. There was definitely an animal scuffling around and heading towards the pool.

She decided to retreat—and quickly.

Chapter 14

ONCE AGAIN THE girls had booked to go out on the morning flat-boat trip up the river. Of course Suzanna hoped that Gregg would be on duty, but it was Stanley who was waiting at the jetty. There was no sign of either Rachel or Gregg, and the whole camp seemed quiet.

Neither Sally nor Suzanna had had much sleep, but for quite different reasons. Sally was wearing a smug look and hummed under her breath, unable to take the smile off her face or the sparkle out of her eyes. Suzannna looked and felt tired and did her best to squash the comments that leapt to her lips. When she quizzed Sally about Pete, her cousin giggled in her most irritating way, and subtly changed the subject—no BBD from her—but Suzanna gathered that they'd had a good night together.

The boat trip was as lovely as before. Early sunlight sparkled and danced off the surface of the restless moving water, and the day promised to be hot. A crowd of local women were clustered on the Zambian side of the huge river and were busily washing a colourful collection of clothes, while their naked children splashed and played at the water's edge. The kids jumped about and waved at the boat, as happy and carefree as a bunch of baby brown seals. They called and beckoned, trying to get the people to land on their shore, but Stanley continued on upstream, laughing and waving in return.

"Aren't those women worried that their children will be taken by crocs?" Suzanna asked Stanley.

"They do get taken from time to time." His matter-of-fact reply was shocking. "But it doesn't seem to stop them playing in the water. They have a pretty fatalistic approach to life. Most of them have lived for generations in villages next to the Zambezi River and they know all it's moods, and the habits of all the animals that live here. They only clash when elephants raid their crops, or there's a problem lion around—mostly they all exist in harmony."

It appeared to be a simple, carefree way of life, but none of them could imagine how they would feel if a child of theirs was dragged into the water by a large croc, never to be seen again—a chilling and terrible thought that sent shivers down all of their spines.

Further upstream two elephant were just beginning to cross from an island in the middle of the river over to the far mainland. They stepped determinedly into the water, and keeping close together they waded into the deeper and faster running current. Everyone watched them nervously, worried the animals would be washed downstream. At times the smaller one disappeared completely under the surface, just the tip of his trunk sticking up like a living periscope to show where he was. Their heads and the round curve of their backs rose and fell as they worked against the strong current. Stanley scanned anxiously for crocs, not knowing what they would do if one of the gentle giants were to be attacked. Everyone willed them to swim quicker.

They made it safely across, and managed to haul their bulks up the steep slope of the far bank. Their age-old wrinkled hides were shiny and washed clean, black against the dusty surroundings. They headed straight for the shade of the outstretched boughs of an acacia tree, and spend the next half an hour or so feeding on the apple-ring seedpods that littered the ground. Their dexterous trunks reached out, scooped up several pods at once and then deposited them into the open pink mouths waiting above. Their large leathery ears never stopped gently fanning backwards and forwards, the softly hanging edges moving the air and keeping the great bodies cool.

It was a wonderfully peaceful scene.

Once again several pods of hippo watched the passage of the flat-bottomed boat, looking like giant inflated balls with bristly noses above huge mouths. They stayed bunched together, eyes bulging and ears twitching, watching with great interest. A huge male opened his cavernous pink mouth in a vast yawn. His long yellowed canine tusks stuck up prominently from his lower jaw, sharpened by constant slicing against the upper teeth. One by one, as their courage failed, they vanished amidst a swirling wash of water.

As before, Stanley stepped out and anchored the boat on the sand of the island at the turnaround point. The water was so clear everyone decided to get out of the boat to paddle and cool off in the shallows. The current had deposited more sand onto the island, which had increased considerably in size, so they all felt quite safe. Even so, they kept a sharp eye out for any passing lurkers. Suzanna grinned to herself, realizing how much she had changed in the short time she had been at the camp. She would never have dreamed of doing this on her first day, but now she was aware of a deep attachment to this wonderful place, and it twisted her up to realize they didn't have many more days to enjoy.

She looked around her, loving the peaceful scenery up and down the river—the contrasting browns, blues and greens of the water against the khaki and deeper hues of the riverine vegetation. The secret promise of the alleys and hidden pools beckoned one to look around the next bend and the next corner. The harshness of the dry landscape inland had it's own beauty, and Suzanna wished she could come back during the rains to see how it would magically spring into life-giving greenery with the first soaking. The changing light and sounds of each different time of day seemed to top up her soul with a feeling that left her mystified. Even the pressing heat of the middle of the day was part of it all, a vital piece of the intricate puzzle and complexities of the whole area.

It would be hard to get back to work next week.

Her thoughts strayed back to Gregg and her spirits sank to realize there was a possibility that, once she had left this magical place, she might not see him again. Her stomach knotted into a cramp and she felt quite sick for a few moments. How was he feeling, and what news had he received? Was Rachel with him? Fussing and fluttering around him like an exotic butterfly? As soon as she got the chance she spoke as casually as she could.

"Um, Stanley? Gregg seemed a little upset after his phone call last night. Not bad news I hope?"

"I don't know," he replied. "I didn't see Gregg for long enough to chat this morning. He seemed a tad quiet though."

Suzanna desperately wanted to find out, but it wasn't fair to quiz Stanley any further. She would have to decide whether to try and speak to Gregg himself or, if the opportunity arose, find something out from Rachel first.

She and Sally headed straight for lunch when they got in from the boat, enjoying the cool dining-room and sipping at the freshly ground coffee, so the sun was high by the time they stripped off their sarongs and lay out on the loungers. Suzanna wore her sheer blue one-piece again, hugging a smile when she thought of Gregg's reaction to her little cat-stretching scene.

Rachel walked up to join them, looking as though she had just stepped out of a woman's magazine once again. Suzanna's tight smile didn't quite reach her eyes, and she stared at Rachel trying to read her expression and see into her mind. It occurred to Suzanna that she couldn't possibly ask her about Gregg's phone call. There was no way that she could, or would, discuss him with her. She would just have to bottle it up, and see if Rachel broached the subject by herself.

She needn't have worried. Rachel couldn't wait to tell them. She was hardly settled before she started to chatter, happy to be so important with the latest update.

"Did you hear about Gregg's girlfriend?" she asked.

Suzanna's heart did a sudden plummet, and she reached for her drink to hide her concern. The girls stayed silent, but Rachel wasn't to be put off.

"She phoned him late last night to break things off. That was the phone call he got while we were all at the barbeque. It was quite dramatic, apparently."

Suzanna squirmed inside and hated the fact that the elegant beauty made out she knew so much about the call, as if she'd been right there at Gregg's side when it came through. But Suzanna needed to hear the rest and she didn't stop Rachel.

"I think I told you before what a good looking girl she is, like a model. Very vibrant and alive. Well, she's met someone else." Rachel's lovely eyes were wide. "I know," she said, as though one of the girls had spoken, "It's unbelievable, isn't it? Who would do that to a man like Gregg? It seems she's been going out with him for a while, unbeknown to Gregg, and now she's pregnant. She was in floods of tears, apparently, and apologising like mad, but she's broken up with Gregg and plans to marry this bloke. Gregg was quite upset, I can tell you. It came right out of the blue for him. Personally, I wonder if he'd had his suspicions that she was two-timing him, but of course he would never tell you that. He was certainly not expecting news of this sort, poor thing."

"Shame, that's too bad," Sally murmured. "Anyone would be knocked sideways hearing something like that."

"He's considering going back to the city to see her, to talk things over," Rachel continued. "But I told him I didn't think it would achieve much since the whole thing is a 'fait-accompli' so to speak. Plus this is the height of their season here, so he wouldn't be able to get away for a few weeks anyway."

All sorts of scenarios had run through Suzanna's mind, but she hadn't covered this one. Poor Gregg. No wonder he had been so upset. However, she couldn't quite squash a tiny but traitorous quiver of happiness deep in her heart, or silence the minute voice that whispered messages of hope in the back of her head.

Rachel chattered on, "I was glad to help him talk through it all last night. He needed someone to off-load onto and I was glad to be there. I even offered to stay the night—just to be near at hand if he needed a friend, of course . . . not that I wouldn't have gone further if he'd wanted to . . ."

Suzanna froze, hanging on Rachel's next words. The sleek dark head tipped forwards, drawing out the moment for dramatic effect. She paused to adjust the front of her swimming costume and fiddled with her dark glasses, looking at both girls from under her lashes.

"But he wanted to be alone, poor darling." She gave a light laugh. "It was quite a serious let-down, really. I would have loved to stay the whole night with him. She's a fool to lose a man like that. A lot of women will be happy to know he's back on the market. I may even stick around myself."

Suzanna couldn't take any more. Rachel was so sure of herself—advising Gregg what to do and what not to do, and making such sweeping assumptions. She muttered an excuse and got up to walk to the steps of the pool. As she leaned down to hold the rail she glanced towards the office and was startled to see Gregg walking out of the door. He paused for a moment and their eyes met. The moment stretched on, drawing out and holding them captive. She felt almost guilty, hearing about his girlfriend like that. He was perfectly able to see Rachel there, and she felt sure he knew what the topic of her conversation had been.

Suzanna managed to half raise her hand in greeting, and, as he walked on, she descended the steps into the cool water, all fluttery inside. Why was it that a single glance had this effect on her? If only she had the courage to follow him and talk to him, use any pretence as an opening. But the moment passed and the opportunity was lost.

Later she and Sally changed to go out on the evening drive. Her mouth pinched at the corners to see that it was Stanley and not Gregg at the wheel of the vehicle. The second Land Rover was still parked by the office and obviously not scheduled to go out. There was no sign of

Gregg. She glanced through the door of the office but he wasn't there. A little ache beat inside her—where could he be? She wished she had spoken to him earlier, but she had been put off by Rachel's gossip, and hadn't had the confidence to approach him. She had hoped he would take them out on the drive, and perhaps she'd have had a chance to say something, but all the words she had been practicing in her mind now vaporized like smoke.

Once they were settled, Stanley drove down the road leading out of camp. It had become familiar over the last few days—a nice comfortable feeling.

The sunset was just as spectacular as it had been for the last couple of evenings—fingers of gold intermingled with soft yellow puffs, and long flaming streaks painted the sky. They turned from fiery molten brilliance into orange and pink hues, before giving way to the purple tones that gently settled over the landscape. One moment the scenery was bright and alive, and a few moments later it softened with the encroaching darkness that held the promise of the mysterious awakenings of the night.

A large herd of buffalo trotted across the road right in front of the vehicle. Two huge bulls stopped, front legs spread wide, in the middle of the track, heads lowered menacingly. Their horns began in a wide bosse on top of a broad forehead and then swept in a curve to end in vicious points, seeming to push their ears downwards out of alignment. Powerful neck, shoulder and loin muscles bunched under their smooth dark brown hides. Their overall attitude was one of 'don't mess with me or you'll be sorry.'

The whole herd stopped, staring at the Land Rover. They formed a tight group, with the calves tucked against protective adult legs. People and animals regarded each other solemnly. Then one of the huge males lowered his head, scooped a hoof-full of sand backwards and grunted loudly, pausing and gathering himself to charge the vehicle. He walked another pace forwards, tossed his head, stared hard at the intruders—and turned away to trot smartly into the bush. This was the signal for the whole herd to move. As one, they galloped off after him, noses up, heads tilted backwards and tails swishing, disappearing in a cloud of dust that hung on the still air.

"Whew! For a moment it looked like he might come at us," Sally said. "What an amazingly powerful animal. He was solid muscle from head to tail."

They drove on for several more kilometres, but, apart from the ubiquitous impala, nothing else was to be seen that evening. The night had wrapped it's soft veils around the landscape, velvety and mysterious, darkening the shadows. Suzanna took a deep breath, trying to absorb every last smell and listen for each last sound. She couldn't believe how deeply the magic of the bush had seeped into her soul.

She told herself that this brand new feeling had nothing to do with Gregg—that she had discovered a bond that she never suspected existed, a tie as strong as rope that attached her by the roots to this land of her birth, and to the animals that shared this remote area.

She tried to ignore the inner voice asking, 'Do you think it would mean as much if you were to cut Gregg out of the picture?'

'Shut up!' she replied. 'Don't ask me stupid questions.'

Pete, Sally and Suzanna joined Alan and Diana Spain for dinner. They discussed the walk they had been on and the camp in general. It transpired that Alan owned and operated a tobacco farm and he was full of interesting stories. He had a great way of describing the local people who worked for him and the incidences that were a part of their daily existence. It seemed there was never a dull moment on a tobacco farm. Diana described her life too. She was kept very busy doing the books, keeping the accounts, taking care of the workers and paying their wages, plus helping to sort out all their day-to-day problems. Suzanna admired them both.

During the whole of dinner her eyes strayed round the dining room keeping a watch out for Gregg. But tonight it was Stanley who did the rounds of the guests, politely enquiring how they were, and what trip they would like to join the next day.

There was no sign of Gregg, and even late into the evening he didn't make an appearance.

Rachel sat across the other side of the room, animatedly talking to a couple of blokes, who hung on her every word and couldn't take their eyes off her. Suzanna had to admit, she looked very striking in a blue dress that drooped off one shoulder, exposing her long neck. As far Suzanna was concerned, if Rachel was here in the dining room she couldn't possibly be with Gregg. If there had been no sign of her, as well as no sign of Gregg, it could have only meant that they were together.

Her eyes kept straying towards Rachel. She was afraid that the dark headed beauty would get up and leave and go in search of him. As though sensing she was under scrutiny, Rachel turned and caught Suzanna's eye. She smiled—a fat-cat smile that screamed, see how popular I am, the men just love me. Suzanna smiled back. She didn't give a toss, just as long as Rachel stayed where she was.

Steve had also been trying to catch Suzanna's eye across the room. Now he walked over, pulled up a chair and placed it next to hers. As he lowered himself down into it, he draped his arm across the back of her chair, giving out the impression that they were beginning to establish something serious. It was very awkward but it was impossible for Suzanna to move her chair away without making an obvious statement. At the same time a slight cold sweat prickled at her skin. She had tried to tell Steve that she wasn't interested in him. Why did he persist in trying to get close to her, and making such blatant moves and remarks towards her? Why didn't Gregg appear so that she could manufacture an excuse to get up and change places.

She breathed deeply and tried to steady her thoughts. Perhaps she was reading more into the situation with Steve than was necessary. She tried to force her mind off Gregg, to relax and join the conversation.

Someone bought another round of drinks and the party soon developed. Steve sat back a little, giving Suzanna more space, and she decided she had misread his intentions earlier. She beckoned to Rachel, inviting her table to come and join theirs, and, when they walked over she was more than happy to scoot over and make space for everyone. Suzanna needed to keep Rachel close by, where she could see her.

As usual Steve was in good form and related a very funny story about a retirement home where his aged aunt lived. The old people had been given beef olives for dinner, which had been so tough that the unfortunate oldies with false teeth hadn't been able to eat them. Finally, in frustration, one of the men had taken the teeth out of his mouth and laid them carefully on the plate, clamped up against the offending roll of beef. He then called the orderly in charge and asked if he could assist his teeth to chew the meat as he himself had been totally unable to make any headway with them.

Suzanna sipped her wine, laughing and enjoying the company. Steve reached over and put his hand on her arm a few times. His gestures were easy and friendly, and his dark eyes caressed her with their lowered lids. The wine eased Suzanna's resistance, sliding fingers of false security into her system, increasing her confidence. For a change she felt as though it was she and not Rachel who was the centre of attention. She did nothing to encourage Steve, but at the same time she didn't draw away.

'He's not such a bad bloke, and he has a good sense of humour.' The sneaky voice was at it again. 'And where's Gregg anyway? You may as well have a good time tonight. Steve thinks you're beautiful and sexy. He's harmless, so enjoy yourself.' The wine was lowering her defences, weakening her resolve to refuse his advances.

Finally someone stood up and declared that they had an early start the next morning. That was the cue for several of the others to leave as well. Pete and Sally had spent the whole evening murmuring sweet secrets and hadn't been able to take their eyes off each other all night. They excused themselves and Sally directed a private wink at Suzanna.

"I might not be in tonight," she whispered. "Don't be worried if I'm not."

Suzanna smiled and nodded, and found herself stuck in a difficult situation—she wanted to leave as well, but if she left now she wouldn't know what Rachel got up to. She was reluctant to let Rachel out of her sight without knowing where she went, and at the same time she didn't want Steve to offer to walk her back to her room. He had been drinking steadily, and hanging over her more and more as the evening had progressed. She had been happy to put up with his attention while it remained on a light level, but his remarks had become increasingly pointed and flirtatious and it was pretty obvious that he was becoming more intent on charming her. She tried to move away from him, but he wasn't allowing that, and kept touching her and smiling into her eyes.

At last Rachel stood up. She gave a tiny delicate stretch that instantly drew all the men's glances. Looking directly at Suzanna she said, "Well, good night everyone. I think I'll call it a night. See you all tomorrow."

Suzanna wondered if Rachel had sensed she had been waiting for her to move.

"Perhaps I'll walk back with you?" Suzanna smiled, getting up as well and hoping to thwart any ideas Rachel may have had about going to Gregg's room.

Her plan didn't go as it should have. Steve leapt to his feet and stood beside her.

"I'll walk you back Suzanna. I'm heading in roughly the same direction and it would be my pleasure. You don't know what may be out and about at this time of night." He had used the same line before, but in a way he was right. Anything could have been roaming around the camp in the darkness.

However, the hesitation must have been evident on her face.

"Oh, don't worry." She tried to sound casual but firm. "I'll go back with Rachel."

"Ah—I'll walk Rachel back." It seemed everyone had something to say. Bill, one of the blokes who had been hanging over her all night stood at Rachel's side and took her arm. He was rewarded with a smug smile of encouragement.

"Thank you kind Sir. I would really appreciate that. Who knows what dangers I may face out there." Rachel's low voice was loaded with suggestions.

Suzanna looked from one to the other of them and heaved an inward sigh. Drat! That meant she couldn't refuse Steve.

They walked along in silence, listening to the quiet stillness of the night. Suzanna hugged her arms to her chest, trying to keep a space between them. But Steve moved closer and placed his hand at the back of her neck, holding her hair. She felt his eyes while his fingers twisted into the soft curls. He tightened his hold, and her neck bent sideways as he gently pulled her towards him, lowering his arm to wrap it round her shoulders.

Suzanna stiffened. "Um, Steve. I don't think—that is—I don't want you to think . . . ."

He chuckled. "Just let the romance of this wonderful African night pour into you, Suzanna. Have you ever felt air so heavy and filled with the promise of rain?"

They stopped at the door. Steve had his arm around her and he drew her closer, holding her firmly. Suzanna tried to wriggle out of his grasp. She put her hands on his chest and pressed him back, but his grip tightened and he bent his head and leaned in to kiss her.

"Steve—no! I'm sorry, I didn't mean to give you the impression that . . ."

"Suzanna, you are so lovely. You've been on my mind so much, I can't stop thinking about you. Can't we get to know each other better? Can I come in for a few minutes?"

She leaned away from him, bending backwards with her head turned to the side. But his mouth found the side of her neck, kissing upwards towards her ear, and he held her fast.

"Steve. Please. Let me go. You're hurting me."

"Don't do this to me Suzanna. You're tormenting me. I can't think about anything else. Please let me love you."

His hold tightened further, squeezing the breath out of her. She grunted as his lips and tongue worked over her collar-bone, and her alarm increased. His whole attitude had changed. A little while ago he had been a charming entertainer, lightly flirting and teasing and having a good time. And now he was imposing and threatening, intent on trying to kiss her. The blood was pounding in his veins, and Suzanna's words were not getting through to him.

Instead of pushing against him, she suddenly relaxed her whole body and went limp in his arms. The gesture surprised him and his grip relaxed slightly, wondering if she was giving in to him. She tried to step back, but he quickly caught on to what she was doing and his hands held her shoulders, fingers digging into the flesh.

"Don't tease me, Suzanna. I'm serious about wanting you. Let me love you. I need you."

She winced, trying not to show the pain, sensing that she should keep him calm.

"Steve, I'm sorry," she said again, "this is not a good time for me." Her mind raced, one part stunned into thinking that this was not happening, and the other desperately whirling to find a way out of it all. What should she tell him? How could she defuse the situation? Make him back off. He seemed to have lost all reason and was like a completely different person, driven by his desire.

"I've—er—I've recently broken up with my boyfriend." She struggled to keep her voice calm and steady, "and I'm just not ready to get involved so soon. Please Steve. Don't."

Her voice rose and she pushed at his chest. But he pulled her towards him, pinned her arms under his and bent his head down to her mouth, breathing heavily.

"I want you Suzanna. You're driving me crazy. I need you."

She twisted sideways, but he gripped her jaw and turned her face back towards his. His breath smelled strongly of beer as he crushed his mouth against hers, his fingers digging into her cheeks.

She struggled in his hold, but her efforts were completely ineffectual. His desire gave him extra strength and he took no notice of the mewing noises as she struggled against him. He pushed her back against the wall of the room, stepping on her foot to make her move, and pressed his body against hers. His knee thumped into her thigh, forcing her legs apart. There was no mistaking his intentions as he thrust and ground his pelvis against her, his body hot and hard. He pulled at the neckline of her dress, rough fingers feeling for her breast. She managed to force her arm in the way so he lowered his hand and dragged at her skirt, pulling it up while his mouth suffocated hers. His fingers groped, grabbing at her flesh, seeking and probing.

Serious panic ripped through her. Sally had gone with Pete and his room was a little apart from the others. There was no-one near by to hear her or come to her aid. Steve hussled her towards the door, kicking at it with his foot and fumbling for the handle. Her breath stuttered in her throat and she wrenched her head to the side.

"Help! Help me. Stop it Steve. Let me go."

He twisted his hand into her hair and pulled her head backwards. His panting breath puffed into her face, reeking of beer. His fingers caught the side of her panties, ripping and dragging them away. Then his hand returned to his own pants, desperate to free his burning desire. He was so intent on what he was doing that he didn't hear the voice behind him.

"What the devil . . . . !"

A strong hand gripped his shoulder and swung him round. Suzanna stumbled and almost fell as he was forced to let her go. Her knees threatened to give way and her hand flew up as a fist crashed into Steve's jaw sending him sprawling down onto the paving stones.

She shrank back against the wall, quivering and crying with reaction. Stanley stood over Steve, fists bunched and expression furious. Steve lay awkwardly spread-eagled on the ground, unsure of what had happened to him. Stanley took two strides, leaned down and grabbed the back of his shirt, hauled him to his feet and shoved him violently in the direction of the pool.

"What the bloody hell d'you think you're doing? Get the blazes out of here. Get away before I belt you again." Stanley turned. "Are you alright Suzanna? Has he hurt you?"

Her hand was tight against her mouth, trying to wipe away Steve's saliva and the overpowering feel of him. Eyes huge, she nodded wordlessly.

Stanley turned back to Steve, "We'll deal with you tomorrow, mate. Meantime I suggest you get the hell away from here and go and cool off."

Steve hunched over and took a few staggering steps. A slight trail of blood darkened the edge of his mouth and his shirt hung out at the waist. He gripped his jaw, turned threateningly towards Stanley with his fists bunched, and the two men faced each other. They were much of a size and build, but Stanley didn't give an inch of ground. He faced Steve with his hands hanging loosely at his sides, ready and waiting for an excuse to take him on.

"Come on then, give me another reason to take you apart. Because I can assure you, I will."

"Oh, what the hell." Steve ran his hand through his hair and wiped at this mouth. He swung round and, unsteady on his feet, he walked away. Suzanna watched him go, shaking uncontrollably and fighting to remain upright. Stanley gently took her elbow and helped her into the room. He settled her into the armchair, handing her the box of tissues from the side-table. His face showed his concern.

"Are you alright, Suzanna? I had to go back to check that the office had been closed up when I heard you cry out. Thank goodness I did. I couldn't work out what the noise was. I wouldn't normally have been at the office at this time of night, but I was worried that it hadn't been locked properly. Dear God—how lucky that I came back to check it. Are you sure you're alright?"

Suzanna took a deep breath, hanging onto her self control with every ounce of her strength. She clenched her hands together, trying to stop the shaking.

"Thanks Stanley. I was really frightened. I don't know what came over him. I think he'd had too much to drink." She sniffed and wiped the tears off her cheeks. "As long as he's gone I'll be fine now. Thanks for helping me. I'll be OK now."

"I'll make doubly sure he won't come back, don't you worry," Stanley's expression was grim. Once he was satisfied that she was calmer he left her alone, closing the door firmly behind him.

Suzanna curled into the pillows, hugging her knees. Her body trembled and shuddered, the muscles juddering and quivering, and gulps of air shook her chest. She longed for the comfort of Auntie Ann's loving hug and a cup of her hot sweet tea. She would comfort her niece, and sympathise, and say the words to make everything better.

When she could finally drag herself to her feet, she ran the shower, stripped off and threw her clothes into the waste bin and then stood letting the water pour it's soothing heat over her. The tears had stopped but the inner quaking remained. She shivered to think of what Steve would have done if Stanley hadn't heard her cries. She couldn't believe the amazing transformation that had come over Steve. How had he changed so radically in the space of a few minutes?

Surely he hadn't seriously thought she was giving him 'come-on' signals. She thought back over each moment of the evening, re-speaking the conversation in her head, attempting to work out if she had encouraged Steve and lead him to think she wanted him in any way at all.

Exhausted and drained, she crawled into bed and buried her head under the covers, hugging her arms tight round her body. Her mind spun off into conflicting orbits, not able to leave it all alone, endlessly re-hashing and re-living it again and again.

Finally she drifted into a half dreaming state where Steve was reaching for her, laughing as he grasped her hair and ripped open her top, while Rachel leaned towards her and confidentially whispered she was about to have Gregg's baby.

"He's mine," she giggled. "He's not on the market at all, because he loves me. He wants me and he has done all along. See, here are his shoes under my bed. Give up Suzanna, he'll never be yours."

Chapter 15

SALLY'S BED WAS empty and undisturbed the next morning. Suzanna turned over and gingerly stretched her limbs out, grimacing at muscles that felt stiff and sore, as though she had fought several rounds in a boxing ring.

The events of the night before crashed back into her mind, and she lay still, recalling each awful moment and realizing again how lucky she had been to have Stanley come to her rescue when he did. Slowly she eased out of bed and poured a coffee from the tray that magically and silently arrived each morning. Her body was achingly heavy, and her head felt fuzzy with the trails of the dreams still twirling and echoing in her mind.

She hunched over her knees, sipping the hot liquid and wondering what she would say to Steve when she saw him later. How could he have lost it so badly? Like a switch had flicked on in his mind, sending him into a sphere of savage intent. He had taken no notice of anything she had tried to say, and hadn't listened to her pleas for him to stop. She wondered how much more brutal he might have become had

Stanley not appeared. Rape was something that happened to other girls—Suzanna had never thought she would ever be subjected to such a demeaning experience. She could understand why victims stated that they didn't feel clean for ages afterwards.

She folded into the chair, pleased she hadn't booked to go on any of the early morning trips. It had been well after half past three in the morning, and two sleeping tablets later, that she'd finally stilled her mind and had some decent sleep.

Slowly, though, the beautiful peace of the early morning eased into her consciousness. A bird hopped on the outside of the thatch, chirping happily to it's mate and picking amongst the grasses looking for insects. A hippo grunted, and a fish eagle screamed from a lofty perch down by the river.

The sounds comforted her and yet filled her with sadness. She and Sally were due to leave tomorrow, and she may never return to this lovely camp. It had been a perfect time filled with so many new experiences. If it hadn't been for the incident with Steve, that is. Sadly, it had tainted the end of her stay.

The more she thought about the feel of his hands and arms grabbing at her, the press of his hot body and mouth against hers, the angrier she became. How dare he ruin it for her? She wanted to go out and punch her fist into his face—not so much for what he had tried to do to her, but for spoiling her precious time in this magical place. What right did he think he had to force himself on her body and her time? He was nothing but a shabby ally cat, and his friendly approaches just a guise to get into her pants.

The anger built up in her mind until it became rage, and swelled into a red mist that hung over her, blinding her to the early morning sights and sounds. It hammered in the back of her ears and head. She wanted to leap up and go in search of Steve and rip into him, wreck his day like he had wrecked her night. She found that she was clutching at the arms of the chair, breathing in gasps, gulping in air like a drowning person with no-one at hand to haul her up out of the murky water. The panicky waves threatened to overcome her, swamping her with a violence equal to that which Steve had shown towards her.

A sweat broke out on her forehead, drenching her back and making her heart race. She mopped at her face with the edge of the serviette, fighting the panic that threatened to overwhelm her. Waves of nausea rose into the back of her throat and her hand closed over her mouth trying to quell the spasms that heaved at her chest, threatening to make her vomit.

And then—one tiny part of her mind recognised that this was just a reaction to her awful experience, and slowly, very slowly, the recognition grew into a conscious thought. Desperately she took a long slow breath. Why was she wasting her energy fretting about a no-good waster like Steve? She was just lucky that he hadn't managed to force himself on her, and more than that, hadn't hit her or become violent. He had been incredibly strong and could easily have used his fists to get her to submit to him. A cold shiver ran down her spine—maybe he would have resorted to violence if Stanley hadn't appeared when he did. She pondered this thought for a while—recognising the "what if" syndrome.

With a huge effort of will she channelled her thoughts into calmer routes, leaning heavily on her yoga lessons and concentrating on the memory of the quiet and sincere voice of her yoga master encouraging the class to relax, breathe,

and absorb the stillness of the moment. At last she got it all
into perspective and managed to settle her trembling hands
and steady her breathless body. She leaned her head back
and closed her eyes, working her thoughts downwards from
her jaw and the back of her neck through her shoulders,
arms, torso and legs, forcing herself to relax, devoting every
fibre into pushing away the anger and tension. Her last day
was way too precious to let a rat-bag like Steve consume her
emotions like this.

At last she swung her legs off the chair, biting her lip
at the sudden stretching of sore muscles, but determined to
shove him out of her mind and enjoy her last day in camp.
With all her strength she hung onto the quieter thoughts,
determinedly keeping away from the destructive anger as
she walked slowly to the edge of the veranda and leaned on
the rail, absorbing the sounds once more and memorizing
the intricate patterns of the million different greens of the
bushes and trees.

Breathing slowly and calmly once more, she felt proud
of herself for getting her perspective back. An inner smile
spread outwards until it encompassed her whole face, and
she looked about her with a renewed spirit. She realized
she hadn't even explored the whole perimeter of the camp
properly and had no idea what lay beyond the dining room,
or behind the kitchen area.

On an impulse, she decided to go for a walk before
breakfast, while it was still cool, and then possibly even have
a quick swim afterwards. Hopefully most of the other guests
would be out on one or other of the drives. Despite her
determined control, the last thing she wanted was to meet
Steve—or anyone else for that matter. She wanted to be alone
to absorb as many of the last impressions of the camp as she
could. Company was definitely not what she needed.

She ran a hot shower and checked herself over carefully again. There were no marks apart from the bruise on her arm and a large one on her inner thigh. Determinedly she squashed the sinking feelings that swept over her when she thought of last night. She would not let it spoil her last precious day here. If she bumped into Steve—well, she'd have to play it by ear. She would not creep around the corners or stay indoors for her last day just because of him.

She swept her hair up in a pony tail, flung on a pair of khaki shorts and a bottle green shirt and stepped out of the room. The day promised to be warm, with a clear sky that spread above the endless grey green bush stretching beyond the boundaries of the camp.

The pool area was deserted. Thankfully.

She walked past the dining room and nodded politely to one of the guests who was having an early coffee, and waved to one of the waiters busily laying out cutlery. Through the office window she saw another of the orderlies working at the desk and she presumed that Gregg and Stanley were out on the drives. No-one else was around and she was hugely relieved not to see Steve lurking somewhere.

The path wound beyond the last of the buildings, but the bush wasn't dense and she felt quite safe exploring further on her own. Through the trees to her right, the river glittered on it's eternal journey, but there was no sign of any animals along the banks. She walked quietly on, heading towards a series of outhouses a hundred meters or so further on.

A large machine was housed in a lean-to shed with no door. The ground was stained with spillings of old oil and a couple of bits of metal lay forgotten in the dust. A selection of rusty vehicle parts was stacked up against one of the walls, and several fuel drums stood in a line under the tree. A strong smell of diesel fuel hung in the warmth of the morning. Suzanna caught a glimpse of someone bent over in the shed, tinkering with a spanner on the big machine housed there. Her curiosity drew her closer, but she stopped abruptly when he straightened and she realized that it was Gregg.

He had on an old pair of dirty jeans, his army style boots, and that was all.

His torso was bare and for long moments she stood transfixed, admiring the browned muscles running down his back, and the way they stood up in ridges as he bent over the machine. Her eyes enjoyed the spread of his broad tanned shoulders and strong forearms. His pants had slipped slightly downwards showing the very tantalising swell of the top of his buttocks, a white strip beneath the deep tan of his back. He emanated pure male power and sex appeal.

He was unaware of her presence, but she couldn't move without giving herself away. He reached for another tool and bent over the engine again. The tool slipped out of his hand and fell with a clatter underneath a round metal cowling.

"Shit!" His loud expletive smacked of frustration.

She clamped her hand over her mouth to stop an instant giggle—too late! He started at the sound, turned round and bumped his head on a metal rod, biting off another swear word when he saw her standing out in the sun, watching him. His hand went up to rub the spot on his head, further ruffling his already tousled hair.

Now that he was facing Suzanna she could admire the ripple of the muscles spanning his chest. Her eyes traced the spread of dark hair and the athletic ridges that ran down his belly, ending at the belt of his pants, which now hung dangerously and enticingly low on his hips.

God, he was gorgeous! Following the direction of her eyes, Gregg hooked his fingers into the back of his pants and yanked them up. An uncomfortable sweat broke over his torso and he stood motionless under her scrutiny.

For a while neither of them spoke.

Frantically Suzanna tried to drag a sensible thought into her mind.

"Do you have a problem?" She cleared her throat and gave it another go. "Sorry, I didn't mean to creep up on you. Is your head alright?"

"That's OK," he grinned. "I was so involved with the wretched generator, I didn't hear you coming. Why didn't you go out on a drive this morning?"

"I forgot to book anything," she replied, while her mind sang, 'And now I'm ecstatic that I didn't.' What an amazing bit of luck to find him here and have him all to herself.

She continued out loud, "Um, we missed you at dinner last night." It was hard to control her wandering gaze and keep the grin off her face.

He frowned and scratched at the back of his neck.

"Yeah. It was my night off and I decided to take it for a change. Usually I don't worry about it, but I had some calls plus a few big decisions to make."

He paused as if considering whether to go on, and then lifted the side of his mouth and said,

"I wouldn't have been very good company anyway." He waved a hand at the generator. "And then this problem developed this morning so I asked Stanley to take the morning drive out while I attempted to fix it. I think I've found the problem so that's half the battle, I guess."

"That's good." Her fingers fiddled with the buttons of her shirt, then smoothed and twisted her pony tail. She didn't dare ask about his phone call. If he wanted to tell her, he would, she decided. She wondered what excuse she could make to stay on and chat to him longer. He seemed to be thinking the same thing as he put the spanner down on the edge of the machine. Then he reached for his shirt and buttoned it back on, somewhat to her disappointment, and came towards her.

His expression was as severe as the first time she had seen him. He stopped a few paces in front of her, looking intently down into her face.

"Suzanna—Stanley told me what happened last night with Steve."

She flushed and looked away from him, not knowing how to answer.

"I think he'd had too much to drink." She knew she sounded lame, but she didn't want to make things any worse than they were. She wondered if he thought she'd been flirting with Steve and that was why he'd attacked her.

Gregg's voice was like steel. "How much he drank is entirely besides the point. He was way out of line and his behaviour was completely unacceptable. Thank God Stanley was there and heard you cry out."

A strange light had crept into his eyes and he took another half a pace closer. "If he'd hurt you, I would have . . . ." He looked up at the tree above and then back at her face. "Well, let's just say that Steve and I had a little chat in the wee hours last night, and he decided to catch the early mail boat going past this morning. He's left camp."

"Oh! That's such a huge relief. Thank you." Suzanna's cry came straight from her heart.

A slow smile softened his features, and left a weak spot at the base of her spine.

"Thank goodness you're alright." His hair tipped forward as he tilted his head at her.

She smiled up at him, shading her eyes with her hand against a ray of sun.

"I didn't sleep very well, and I had to battle against huge anger, but yes, I am fine. Thank you."

Another silence fell between them. Then he looked beyond her to the river.

"Uh, have you looked out over the river this morning? It's very pretty from here."

Side by side they walked together to the edge of the bank, and were surprised to see four long canoes silently floating downstream on the far side of the sun streaked dappled water. Each was being paddled by two people, and a pile of gear was heaped in the back of each boat, almost looking too heavy to manage.

"Wow! Where would they have come from?" Suzanna gasped. "Surely it's dangerous for them to paddle down this river. What about the hippo? Won't they attack the canoes?" She remembered reading an horrific account of a guide who had been killed when his canoe had been overturned, and a client had been badly mauled in the same incident.

"They have to be very careful," Gregg relied, "but if they take proper care and stick to the faster channels, it's safe enough."

It was a colourful sight. They watched the occupants manoeuvre their long crafts into a narrow channel that would afford them a safe passage past a pod of basking hippo. One of the huge males had been watching their approach and he launched himself off the bank, heading alarmingly quickly towards the fragile boats, while the rest of the pod raised their heads to watch his foaming wake streak through the water, and then lost their nerve to crash into the water behind him, sending waves of water sparkling and showering against the bright morning light.

"Oh, they're in danger. He'll get them." Suzanna's pony tail swung and brushed his face as she turned impulsively to Gregg.

"Shout at them—let them know the hippo is after them. He'll tip a canoe over."

"Don't worry. The boats are in deep water—it's unlikely that he'll attack them there. And the guides will have seen the hippo, so if I yell it will only distract them from paddling clear. I'm sure they'll be OK."

With bated breath they watched as the occupants worked frantically to clear the channel and escape into the relative safety of the water beyond.

Gregg stood just behind Suzanna's shoulder and she felt the heat radiating off him. The slight scent of manly sweat and the tenseness of the moment sent her senses reeling. She had to resist the urge to step backwards and lean against him. They watched as the canoeists cleared the narrow strip of water. Together they raised their paddles in a triumphant gesture. Suzanna waved back and hooted across the water. She shuddered in a mixture of relief and reaction and smoothed her hands down her arms. She kept her eyes on the boats, not daring to look round at Gregg, knowing that she desperately wanted to turn to him and see his expression. Why did her pulse always go up a notch like this when he was near?

She felt him step a pace closer behind her and the thumping beat in her chest increased even more when his broad hand moved over the skin of her shoulder and slipped under her hair. She glanced sideways at him and realized that for the last few moments he had been looking at her and not at the canoeists at all. Was it the sun that caused her cheeks to turn pink?

"You have such beautiful hair, Suzanna," he murmured. "It catches the sun and lights up in a hundred different colours." He lifted a handful of locks and twisted them round his fingers.

She laughed lightly to take the intensity out of his words.

"Why, thank you, kind Sir," she quipped, "but a hundred colours is hardly accurate. Perhaps three or four."

His eyes held an expression that was deep and unreadable as he gazed steadily down at her. Slowly he turned her round to face him Gently his fingers brushed a strand of hair away from the side of her face. His voice was deep and low.

"I'm so sorry that you had such a frightening experience last night. It was lucky for Steve that it was Stanley and not me that heard you calling for help."

His mouth—that enticing mouth—was only inches away. The memory of their warmth on hers sent a shiver down her spine. Her eyes were locked onto his and his hand seemed to burn the skin on her neck. Her hands reached out and settled themselves on the solid chest in front of her nose, wanting to pull him close and yet not daring to move too quickly.

The canoeists and whatever other picturesque scene was laid out before them faded into oblivion as he lowered his lips gently, so gently, and kissed her.

All the breath ceased in her lungs and time hung endlessly as she raised up on tiptoe and clung to him. She pressed against him, loving the feeling of him holding her, comforting her, squeezing her slender frame tight against his body. His hands moved up and down her back while his kisses became deeper and more intimate. Her mouth was warm, soft and moist as she kissed him back, opening her lips against his. He tasted salty and delectable.

Oh, how she wanted the moment to last forever. His hair wound through her fingers, her hand held his head down to hers. The heat rippled through both of their bodies, arousing and urgent, demanding more. The tips of his fingers reached inside the neck of her shirt, stroking the soft skin under her collarbone and sliding round to hold her shoulder—skin to skin. His touch was electrifying. She pressed closer, edging deeper into his arms, returning kiss for kiss, silently encouraging him to take more, give more, delve deeper into her emotions.

A discreet cough behind him made both of them leap apart as though they had been shot.

One of the camp orderlies stood on the path looking very sheepish and embarrassed—which was nothing in comparison to the way Suzanna felt right then. She was hot all over, flustered and off balance. Perspiration popped out onto her brow and a drop trickled uncomfortably down her back. She put up her hand and attempted to smooth her escaped pony tail into some sort of order.

The orderly's involuntary glance dropped to her chest, and to her horror she glanced downwards and saw that the top button of her shirt had popped out of it's button hole. The neck had pulled wide and the swell of one creamy breast, cupped in it's black bra, was exposed for all to see. Gregg's fascinated gaze was also fixed on the voluptuous softness. Hastily Suzanna dragged her shirt back into place, face flaming crimson.

The orderly cleared his throat. "I'm sorry Sir, but the chef wants to know if the generator is repaired. He will have to cook breakfast on the barbeque if it is not."

"Oh!" Gregg took a deep breath. "I almost have it sorted out. Tell the chef to start cooking on the barbeque for now. It shouldn't take too much longer to fix."

His eyes flashed vividly. Suzanna wasn't sure if it was in anger at being caught red handed kissing one of the guests, or in amusement at the whole situation.

It was clear that the confused orderly wasn't sure either, and he hurriedly left with a quick, "Thank you Sir."

Suzanna battled to keep her face straight. "I'm sorry! I should go. Perhaps I'll see you later?"

Before Gregg could move or say anything else she turned and started back along the path to the camp. He stood still, watching her for a moment, and then returned to the generator hut and picked up the spanner once again.

Just before she turned the corner in the path she glanced backwards, caught his eyes, and they shared a long moment. She considered blowing him a kiss—'No, Suzanna, don't be so frivolous.' Instead she sent him a wide grin and fluttered her fingers at him. He smiled a broad white smile, raised a hand in return and bent back to his work.

Suzanna's heart sang, and she found it hard not to jump into the air with a sideways kick.

As she entered the room, Sally emerged from the shower with her hair wringing wet. She threw her arms round her cousin.

"Zannie! Where have you been? Stanley told me about last night—well he gave me the gist of it. What on earth happened? Thank God you're OK. What a bastard that Steve turned out to be."

"Yes, well, he's left camp now. Gregg saw to that."

The girls sat in the deep armchairs discussing their recent events. Sally was horrified to think she had abandoned Suzanna and left her alone to face Steve.

"I go cold all over when I think about it. If he had—well, if he had . . ." she stopped, unable to say the ghastly words.

"Oh, Suzie, I'm so sorry. It would have been all my fault. I would never have been able to forgive myself. Ever."

"Don't be silly." Suzanna hugged Sally. "I was pleased that you left with Pete. Who could have anticipated what Steve would do. I've managed to get it into perspective, and I guess I've leant a lesson as well. The main thing is that I'm fine, and this is our last day and we have to make sure it's a good one. And I have just had the most amazing few moments with Gregg which has wiped Steve and his sleazy intentions completely out of my mind."

She knew this wasn't quite true, but she didn't want to discuss him a minute longer. Sally's attention was successfully diverted.

"You devious Minx! Tell me everything."

The confidences that they had always shared eased them and had them smiling once again. When Sally spoke about Pete her lovely face lit up with remembered precious moments. There was no doubt that things were progressing well between them. Suzanna squashed a shaft of envy—perhaps things were progressing well between Gregg and herself, as well. She had been so down when he hadn't come to dinner last night. Thoughts of Rachel being in his arms and perhaps his bed had tortured her, thanks to Rachel's confident attitude that she would get him if she chose to try. Now things had swung in Suzanna's favour again, and she was as high as a kite taking off on a summer breeze.

"Well, I reckon we should relax up for the day. Enjoy our last few hours at the pool. We've missed all the morning drives anyway. I'm all for sipping a few long cold beers and working on my tan," Sally declared.

"Sounds good to me. I'm going to miss this place. Who would have thought so much could happen in a week."

Sally smirked with pleasure.

"Perhaps we should make this an annual trip, dear Cuz of mine?" She studied Suzanna from lowered lashes. "Bring back a few sweet memories if nothing else, hey?"

Then she leaned forward and took Suzanna's hands in hers.

"Zannie, I know that I've met someone who will always be a very important part of my life. For the first time I truly think I'm in love. Pete is the most wonderful person. I'm mad about him and I think he feels the same way about me, too." She clasped her hands together and her smile contrasted to the sparkle of tears in the corner of her eyes. She put up a finger and brushed them away. "But I'm a little worried about you, Suze. I know you've fallen pretty heavily for Gregg—have you any idea how he feels and what you'll do after we leave the camp?"

"I don't know how I feel, Sal," Suzanna replied. "And I just don't know what he's thinking. It's too soon to tell. One moment I think he may have feelings for me, and the next I have no idea. I've decided to try not to get too intense about it."

Who was she kidding? Her stomach turned to water if she let herself think about tomorrow and the possibility of never seeing Gregg again.

She tossed her hair back, "We're getting too serious. Let's head for breakfast, I'm starving." She tried hard to smile. "Plus I want to see if Gregg managed to fix the generator."

Several of the other guests were at the pool and there was quite a crowd when they pulled up loungers to join them. For a change Rachel was already there, and Suzanna was delighted to note that Bill was sitting close to her, applying suncream to her flawless skin and generally hanging over her. She looked like the cat that had finished the cream. Her whole attitude was one of pure self-satisfaction. Perhaps now she would concentrate on seducing Bill and keep away from Gregg.

Sally and Suzanna were quickly drawn into the group and the conversation. Pete settled himself next to Sally and, trying not to be too obvious, Suzanna ran her eyes over his long frame—he was certainly a good-looking bloke. Sally only had eyes for him and almost purred when he spread sunblock over her shoulders. Suzanna looked around at the group and realized they had made some good friends among this bunch of people. Idly she wondered if they would keep in contact.

She had her back to the office so she gulped and flushed hotly when she heard Gregg's deep voice right behind her. She turned and the sun reflected in her brown eyes and set fire to her hair as she looked up at him.

"Hi everyone. Apologies for interrupting." He looked around and grinned at the guests. "The lists for the drives for the rest of the day seem to have been mislaid. Sorry about that. Please could you all confirm what you'd like to do later?"

He described the trips and noted everyone's choices on his clipboard, courteous and thorough. Suzanna reached for her dark glasses and secretly watched his handsome face, re-living their incident by the generator hut. Her fingers twisted together, and the heat spread through her stomach once again.

But he had his official face on and was businesslike and efficient, recording all the details, his glance moving from one guest to the next.

Eventually he turned to Pete, Sally and Suzanna. Was his hand trembling slightly? No—surely not. She must have imagined it.

"Which drive do you want to go on—river trip or bush drive?" he asked.

She was thrown into an instant dilemma. Which drive would he be taking out? She didn't dare to ask out loud in front of the other guests. Instead she hesitated, chewing the edge of her nail.

Pete and Sally shared a look.

"Perhaps the bush drive," Sally eventually said. "Do you have three places in the vehicle still? We'd like to go out together if possible."

"Yep, that's fine." Gregg's expression was unreadable as he marked them down. He read out the times that each drive would be departing and turned to go back to the office.

Suzanna's eyes hadn't left his face for an instant, and she got her reward. Just as he spun on his heel he flicked a glance at her and one eyelid dropped in a wink directed straight, and only, at her. It was a delicious private moment, made all the more special because it was in front of all the other guests but none of them appeared to have noticed. Suzanna clamped her hand over her mouth to stifle the laugh that threatened to bubble out of her throat, and she could have leapt up and danced a wild fandango on the spot.

Somehow she managed to get through the remainder of the day. She didn't want the time to hurry by, but she was in a fever to go out on the drive. Suzanna was totally certain that it would be Gregg who took them out. Pete and Sally spent the whole day together—who could blame them? Suzanna read her book and even dozed for a few moments in the comfort of the armchair.

Earlier she and Sally had seen a notice on the board outside the dining room telling everyone that live music and a dance were scheduled for the evening's entertainment. Suzanna picked through her clothing, trying to decide what to wear so that it would be ready on their return from the drive. She chose a three quarter length white dress with spaghetti straps, a fitted waist and a ragged handkerchief hemline. The back hung in a soft cowl that dipped almost to the waist and would show off her golden tan. She shook the dress out and laid it on the bed.

Then she half packed her case, trying hard to squash the sad feelings that threatened to swamp her. They were scheduled to leave soon after breakfast the next day. Suzanna sat down on the edge of the bed, her head spinning round and round—how would she be able to contact Gregg once they had left? If only she knew his feelings and what he was thinking. Was she just a temporary romance—someone to fill the gap left by the break-up with his girl? She wished she knew. It seemed he liked being near her, and he obviously thought she was beautiful. But was that as far as it went? There was no doubt in her mind that she was falling more heavily for him and the thought scared her. All her resolve to keep away from him and rein in her emotions had counted for nothing in the end.

She wandered onto the veranda and stood looking out at the landscape. She made a mental note to ask Sally if she had taken enough photos of the camp. Suzanna drank in the radiant blues reflecting off the river, edged by all the greens, browns and every shade in between, of the surrounding vegetation. The long rays of the afternoon sun began to deepen the folds of the hills, sending dust laden rays of light stretching to the horizon and lengthening enticing shadows, adding a mystery that called to one's spirit to get out and explore.

At the moment nothing moved. It was as though everything was waiting for the onset of dusk before venturing out into the cooler air. It was a magical scene, peaceful and calming and totally African.

Chapter 16

THE GIRLS WANDERED across to the office well before departure time and they clambered up into the far vehicle. A secret smile lifted Suzanna's heart when Gregg paced up with his long stride and climbed into the driver's seat. She pinched her lips together to stop the grin of satisfaction. She was seated in the first bench row as before, but this time she was on the outside. Sally sat in the middle with Pete on her right. Suzanna had chosen the left hand side because she reasoned that Gregg would see her with just a slight turn of his head, and she could watch his profile as he drove.

But sitting on the outside seat meant there would be nothing between her and any wild animal that they may encounter. It was certainly a vulnerable feeling and Suzanna felt more than a little nervous. She had made sure to take a hanky, although the dust hadn't worried her so badly during the last few outings. Which was just as well, as the ground was very dry and the dust was as bad as ever, billowing up in clouds behind the vehicle.

One of the scouts climbed up into the front beside Gregg. He leaned down to check a rifle lying at his feet and he fiddled with the spotlight, making sure it was working properly by flicking it on and off a couple of times.

Gregg headed out of camp in a different direction and very soon the bush closed in on both sides of the road. They drove slowly past a couple of pans, one of which was no bigger than the swimming pool back at camp. But either they were too early or the animals had passed that way already and had vanished into the grey-green of the spiky, leafy surrounds. Or they had yet to emerge—but all the water holes were deserted and there was nothing to see on the sandy roads except the ubiquitous tracks of all the game that had passed that way.

Suddenly they were surprised by a small herd of impala that pronked and leapt over the road ahead of the vehicle, kicking their pointed hooves high, as nervous and skittish as ever. They disappeared as quickly as they had arrived. Gregg stopped on a high rise and spent a little while scanning the area below. The landscape stretched out, rolling away to the hills, immense, silent and apparently devoid of life. Then, through his binoculars, Pete picked up an elephant browsing way off in the distance below, and everyone directed their glasses until they found him as well. He looked like a lone toy lost in the vastness of the Valley.

They drove on, slowly eating up the miles and Suzanna's eyes began to ache with the effort of staring into the bush. In one place the sharp rotten stink of dead animal flesh tainted the air like a heavy pocket of noxious gas and they strained their eyes to catch sight of any kill. But nothing could be seen—no sign of either the dead carcass or the reason for it's death. Darkness was descending and it wasn't easy to see for any distance beyond the first line of trees.

"Whew! That's a strong smell. I wonder if there's a kill somewhere close by."

The scout fiddled with the spotlight, but Gregg told him to wait a while longer before switching it on to scan the bush.

"Isn't it funny that there are no animals out tonight?" Suzanna queried. "We've had such good viewing that it seems strange not to see anything. I guess we've just been lucky."

"Sometimes it goes like that," Gregg's words floated backwards over his shoulder. "The game just possibly happens to be in the thicker bush off the main roads."

No sooner were the words out of his mouth than he rapidly stepped on the brakes and the Land Rover shuddered to a halt. Dead ahead of them in the middle of the road stood an enormous bull elephant.

He was about two hundred meters from the vehicle, but he was so huge that his bulk filled the narrow track. The height of his head and curved spine were immense. His dark grey leathery hide was coated along the back with a thick layer of dust and his legs were the size of tree trunks. But it was his impressive tusks they noticed most. Gleaming white in the gathering dusk, the left one was as straight as an arrow while the other curved inwards towards it.

"What an incredible tusker," Pete breathed. "I didn't think there were any left in this area."

The enormous bull had emerged from a thicket and was about to cross to the dense bush on the other side of the road. It seemed he was as surprised to see the tourists as they were to see him. The huge animal hesitated, looked ahead to the far side, hesitated again, then swung his enormous head back in their direction. Suddenly his whole body pivoted and he stood facing them, threatening and aggressive.

There was a collective gasp. They hadn't done anything to aggravate him but the bull presented a seriously hostile attitude towards the vehicle and it's occupants.

"Something is not right here everyone. This bull is not happy to have us here. You'd better hang on, this could get nasty." Gregg spoke quietly but there was no mistaking the urgency, plus a note of worry, in his voice.

He murmured something in a quiet undertone to the scout in the front seat. The scout reached down, lifted his rifle and held it upright with the barrel pointing heavenwards. He also made sure the spotlight was near to hand on the seat next to him.

"Keep absolutely quiet, no matter what happens," Gregg warned everyone. "And duck down behind if I have to reverse in a hurry, so that I can see the road."

All their eyes were wide with fright as they waited to see what the awesome animal ahead of them was about to do. His long white tusks were raised and pointing straight at the vehicle. The end of his trunk lifted and pointed towards them, waving in the air as he breathed in their scent. His huge ears fanned out sideways and the width of his forehead was frightening. There was a distinct click from the back row of seats as one of the men took a photograph.

"Easy with the photos," Gregg warned in a low voice. "We don't want to spook him. Only take them if your camera is quiet."

By this time Suzanna's heart was pounding in her chest and her knuckles were white as she gripped onto the handrail in front of her with one hand and clutched Sally's knee with the other. Sally looked as scared as Suzanna felt and that served to unnerve her even more. Sally never panicked about anything, and on the odd occasion when she did, it blew Suzanna away completely. Pete took Sally's hand and gripped it hard, speaking softly to reassure both girls.

"Keep calm. He's just showing us who's boss. We took him by surprise a little and he's trying to decide if we pose a threat to him in any way. He's giving us a show of strength, that's all."

The scout spoke in quiet tones, "See his shoulder? There's a cut across it and blood is still oozing from the wound. That could be why he's so angry."

Gregg agreed with him. "Not much can penetrate an elephant's skin. He could have been fighting with another bull, but it looks more like he has been shot at—probably by poachers. It looks like the bullet has grazed the skin, which is lucky for him. If it had penetrated into the shoulder it would have had very serious consequences. No wonder he's on edge if he's been shot at. And if there are poachers around it could explain why there are no other animals to be seen."

He spoke quietly over his shoulder so that everyone could hear him clearly. "He's not giving way, so it's time we left him alone."

The huge animal remained tense and rigid, afraid of the people and yet not willing to give way. He hadn't dropped his tusks or relaxed his stance in any way. Now they all gasped once again as he shook his enormous head, sending dust flying in a cloud. He flung his trunk upwards and split the air with a terrifying trumpet of sound.

Gregg gripped the gear lever to ease the Land Rover into reverse gear, and, with everyone still staring anxiously at the huge bull, he turned in his seat to see the road behind.

"Look out Boss. Here he comes!" The scout's voice was sharp and urgent.

The elephant's nerve had given way. With a sudden movement he tucked his head down, furled his trunk towards his chest and with his huge forehead prominent, tusks pointing straight at them, he charged towards the vehicle.

"Oh my God!" They were all petrified with fear.

Suzanna couldn't believe how fast such a big animal could run. His straight thick legs covered the ground at an alarming pace. His shoulders seemed hunched forwards and his ears flapped like huge sails, giving him an immensely huge profile.

"Down!" Gregg shouted.

Everyone ducked sideways like skittles felled in a bowling alley. He half raised himself in his seat, gripped the handrail behind him, revved the engine and sent the Land Rover rocketing in reverse down the track.

The scout kept up a running shouted commentary, telling Gregg what the elephant was doing.

"He's still coming! Keep going Boss. He's not giving up. Move it, Boss, he's gaining on us."

Everyone kept low behind Gregg. He was twisted round, balancing on one hip with his right leg stretched fully out to reach the accelerator. He stepped hard on the pedal and steered the vehicle backwards in a remarkable display of controlled driving. The engine screamed in protest, but he didn't dare let up on it. The enraged elephant was coming at speed and if Gregg hesitated or stopped, he would attack and kill them all.

They were terrified.

All of a sudden the Land Rover hit a soft patch of sand and swerved sideways. The sweat gleamed on Gregg's brow as he fought with just one hand to control the swaying vehicle.

As the open truck bucked in the sand, the side of it brushed past the slender branch of a thorny scrub bush. Suzanna's head was tucked down and she didn't seen it coming, but the swerve threw her sideways and she felt the sharp sting as a vicious three inch thorn caught at the shoulder of her shirt and ripped open a long slash.

In an eternity of slow motion she lost her hold on the handrail and, to her horror, felt herself falling out of the vehicle. Instantly she knew that not only would she likely be crushed under the wheels, but the angry elephant would make mince-meat of her in a few seconds as he trampled her under his huge circular feet.

She cried out in panic as she was thrown back with the next swerve. Unconsciously she flung her arm up to grab the handrail but her flailing fingers closed on air and she knew she was gone.

"Suzanna!" Gregg yelled. He almost lost control of the vehicle completely as he made an attempt to grab Suzanna's hand. All his strength was concentrated on driving them backwards to safety and he struggled to keep his balance and not let the bucking Land Rover swerve again. He was powerless to help her.

Suzanna screamed again, sure she would be killed.

At the last second, when more of her body weight was outside the vehicle than in, she felt an excruciating pain in the back of her head, and she was jerked sideways and dragged back onto the seat.

Pete saved her life.

His hypnotized gaze had been fixed on the charging bull. Suzanna's cry and Gregg's shout broke the spell. In a split second he saw her plight and instinctively lunged across the seat behind Sally. The only thing his outstretched hand could make contact with was a substantial handful of hair. His fist closed and he hung on with all his strength, jerking her back into the safety of the vehicle.

Sally managed to regain her own balance and clutched at her cousin as well, pulling her inwards. She sprawled across Sally's lap, whimpering with fright and the extreme pain in her head.

"He's turned, Boss! The elephant is going into the bush."

The scout's triumphant yell brought them all back to reality. He had kept up his running account of the actions of the approaching animal, taking the place of Gregg's eyes to the front. All his attention had been focused on giving exact details of what was happening, and how close the bull was getting.

"He's going!" the scout yelled again.

Sure enough, the mighty bulk veered off to the side of the track and crashed through the undergrowth, only meters from the front mudguard. An ear shattering trumpeting split the air once again, and he disappeared—swallowed up in a second by the dense cover.

Gregg continued to steer the vehicle backwards for another hundred meters or so, and when he deemed it safe to stop, he braked and brought the vehicle to a halt in the middle of the track. Everyone sat in silence, shocked and stunned, listening to the sounds of the enraged bull as he crashed his way into the distance.

Then Gregg turned, his face pale and concerned.

"Are you alright, Suzanna? You gave me a nasty fright back there. I thought for a second that I was going to roll the truck."

Pete's expression was also worried. "I'm so sorry, Suzanna. Are you OK? I reacted without thinking and the only thing I could reach was your hair. Lucky it's so thick and long."

"Thank goodness you did," Suzanna stammered through chattering teeth. "I thought I would fall out of the truck and be crushed. I was terrified. Thank you Pete."

Gregg and the scout listened intently to the retreating sounds of the angry bull.

"Will he come back?" Sally voiced everyone's fears.

"No, he's going into the thick bush now," Gregg replied. "He'll try to get as far away from any contact with humans as he can."

One of the men in the back seat drew in a deep breath and said in a sardonic tone, "Bloody good driving, Mate."

The reaction set in and Sally gave a tiny hysterical giggle, which set Suzanna off and they leaned together while the tears ran down their faces and the laughter shook their shoulders. Actually, they weren't sure if they were laughing or crying. Suzanna flinched when Sally put an arm round her shoulder, and they were both suddenly silent when she drew her hand away and saw that it was covered in blood.

"Crikey, Suze! You're pouring blood. Look your whole sleeve is soaked."

Suzanna looked down and her head reeled dizzily. In the pressure of the moment she hadn't felt a thing, but the thorn had not only torn her sleeve.

Gregg spun round and took in the situation at a glance.

"Squeeze your hand over the wound," he ordered. "I'm going to get us onto the main road just to be sure we're safe. Hang on now, it's not far." His calm, authoritative words gave the girls confidence, and Suzanna tightened her hand over the deep cut. It was incredible that she had only felt the impact of the thorn and not realized how badly it had slashed her skin as well as her shirt.

The engine restarted with a roar, Gregg turned the vehicle round, and once again they bumped and rocked in the open Land Rover, this time racing towards the main road. The headlights picked out long deep shadows and if anything had been on the track a collision would have been unavoidable. Gregg's worried eyes sought Suzanna's in the mirror, and she tried to smile to reassure him that she was fine. Sally held her and the other guests leaned forward to voice their concerns.

Once the road widened and it was safe to stop, the scout held the spotlight while Gregg dug under the front seat and pulled out a large first-aid box. He walked rapidly round the vehicle.

"Are you OK?" he asked again. "Did that bush catch you? You gave me more of a fright than the elephant did—I thought . . ." His words trailed off. In a gesture that poured honey through her heart, he stared into Suzanna's eyes and brushed a strand of hair back from her face.

He insisted that she relax against the seat while he gently cut the sleeve of her shirt off at the shoulder.

"Sorry about your shirt," he grinned, "but it had pretty well had it anyway."

He frowned when he looked at the gash, and with hands as gentle and efficient as any medic he cleaned up the blood, and applied a soothing ointment. Suzanna's hands were trembling and she felt faint, but she clenched her teeth, determined not to wince or grimace.

Instead she made the most of being so close to him. His hands were large and yet so gentle, the fingers long with a slight fuzz of hair on the back of the first joints. The muscles moved under the skin of his tanned forearms. She watched the way his brow creased between his eyes, the slight lift at the corner of his mouth and the way he occasionally pinched his lips together. His hair fell forwards over one side of his forehead, almost touching the dark eyebrow. The slight stubble on his chin gave him a rugged look. Her gaze wandered over his face, drinking in every detail. But it was his mouth that made her yearn to lean forward and sample another sweet kiss.

He sensed her scrutiny and glanced up. Their eyes met—his filled with concern and hers large and adoring.

"OK?" He murmured.

"Mmmm." She replied.

He stripped off narrow plasters and stuck them across the wound in a neat series of butterfly stitches. Then he deftly bound a bandage round her upper arm and secured it with a safety pin.

"There, that should sort it out," he grunted in satisfaction. "Does it feel comfortable?"

"It feels fine. Thanks very much, Gregg." There were a million other things she wanted to say, and several million she wanted to do to this extraordinary man. She smiled at him and thanked him again.

"Right everyone." He packed the first-aid box and stood up. "We'd better get back to camp and get spruced up for that party tonight. And I reckon we could all do with a cold beer."

Amidst a general cheer of agreement, he once again started the engine and they set off, more than happy to be returning to the comfort of camp.

Chapter 17

SUZANNA PINNED HER hair up at the sides, and left it to tumble down in the usual waves. She massaged her scalp gingerly with the tips of her fingers, wincing at the tenderness, and thanked her lucky stars, convinced that Pete and her hair had saved her life. What with both Stanley and then Pete dashing to her rescue—well, she could do with less drama in her life at the moment.

She decided to stick to her choice of dress, despite the bandage on her upper arm. Somehow it was a memento of their trip—a war wound of sorts.

As she studied her reflection in the mirror she thought again of Gregg's words. 'He was lucky it was Stanley and not me . . . . If he'd hurt you . . . God, you're beautiful!' She hugged them and rolled them round in her mind like precious gems. Well, she didn't know about beautiful, but she was sure going to do her best with her appearance for the last night. She pictured his hands cleaning and dressing her cut and the tender way he had asked if she was alright.

The heat trickled through her body and she grinned to her image. She had a feeling tonight would be a good night.

Her heavy gold chain was cool round her neck, and tinkly bracelets adorned her slim wrist. Sally wore her draped yellow dress, fluffed out her blonde curls, and they both took time over their makeup. Both girls agreed that they felt quite glamorous as they walked to the dining room.

Instead of the usual layout the tables had been joined into a long horseshoe shape and place names had been set out next to each gleaming glass. Candles burned brightly in a line down the centre of the tables, giving off a soft and flattering light, while strings of coloured fairy lights draped from the beams above. In one corner a band had been set up, and the single guitarist was already strumming and singing a Country and Western ballad. His foot operated a set of drums, and his synthesizer played the background music. The tune was catchy and his voice deep and melodious.

Suzanna was pleased to see that Ray was seated to her left. His wife Sheila was a few places down the table and she smiled and waved her hand. Nick, the fisherman, was on Suzanna's right. He stood up as she and Sally approached, and gave a low wolf whistle.

"Wow, ladies, you look superb tonight," he commented. "I heard about the incident out on the drive—hope your arm is OK, Suzanna? That was a bit of a close call all round."

News certainly travelled fast round this camp. Perhaps they knew why Steve had left as well?

The flickering candles picked up the auburn lights in Suzanna's hair, making her eyes sparkle and her skin glow. The temperature had dropped slightly and a soft cool breeze played with the tiny flames, making them dance. And dance was what Suzanna wanted to do. The rhythmic beat of the music had her foot tapping.

She cast a glance down the table and disappointment washed over her to see that Rachel was seated next to Gregg. He had just walked into the dining room, looking devastating in a white shirt that opened at his throat. His sleeves were rolled up to the middle of his forearms, and his black jeans fitted to perfection. His hair was neatly brushed back and he was clean-shaven, but Suzanna thought she detected faint shadows under his eyes. She drew in a steadying breath.

He flicked a glance in her direction, inclined his head with a smile, spoke to a hovering waiter and then seated himself next to Rachel. Rachel, of course, leaned towards him and beamed brilliantly into his eyes—the mouse who had won the cheese.

She looked stunning in a black dress that hugged her figure but left her shoulders bare and set off her dark hair and large eyes. Suzanna strained to hang onto her smile. How did Rachel get seated next to Gregg? She toyed with her fork, trying to get her emotions under control. She wondered how things were progressing with Rachel and Bill. He had been all over her at the pool, and she had certainly appeared to encourage and enjoy his attention. But Suzanna didn't know her well enough to discern whether she was taking him seriously or not. Now he was seated across the room, and although he was talking to a lady on his left, his eyes drifted constantly back to Rachel. Suzanna hoped she wasn't leading him on for nothing—not that it was any of her business.

She clenched her teeth and decided that she would have a good evening—no matter what! She was determined to enjoy these romantic and lovely surroundings for the last night, and she made herself chatter happily to Nick and the others near by. They discussed the enraged elephant and her accident, agreeing that Gregg had done an excellent job driving the vehicle, and his passengers, to safety in such difficult circumstances.

The first course arrived—half a baby avocado stuffed with shrimps, drizzled with a light white wine dressing and set on a leaf of crisp lettuce. It was the perfect starter.

Once everyone had finished and the waiters had cleared for the next course, the music man surprised the party by addressing everyone over his microphone, causing laughter and general confusion.

"Welcome, Ladies and Gentlemen! On behalf of the Manager and staff of Nkuni Camp we are sure you'll enjoy your evening. I will endeavour to entice you all onto the dance floor later, but for now we hope you enjoy your meal. In the spirit of good fun, would all the ladies please stand up and move two places to their left for the next course." He looked around at them all, chuckled and continued. "We hope you don't encounter anyone's false teeth left behind, and if you need help identifying your left hand, please don't hesitate to give me a call. It's the one you *don't* wave out of the window when you're driving! Oh, and please take your drinks with you."

Several men stood up to pull out and hold chairs for the women, and amidst giggles and plenty of ribald comments, the ladies did as he asked. Suzanna noted that she was now closer to Gregg, and she wondered if they would be asked to move again after the next course. She quickly calculated that it would take two more moves. Rachel rather reluctantly moved two places down the table, but wasted no time charming the next man she was seated by.

The second course was melt-in-the mouth steak, drizzled with a red wine sauce and accompanied by baby potatoes and green vegetables. Suzanna discussed the food with her present table-mates and they agreed that the meals had been superb all week. The wine flowed and no sooner had her glass reached the half way mark than it was instantly filled up again. She realized she would have to pace herself. Already she felt a little light-headed. But she also felt happy and carefree and the beat of the music continued to tease her feet. She ignored the throb in her arm, and kept reassuring everyone that it was not a life-threatening wound, and that she felt fine.

Sure enough, after the main course, the ladies were asked to move once again, and Suzanna's heart tilted to see she was within one move from being at Gregg's side. Sally would be seated next to Pete, and Suzanna wondered if the seating had been carefully worked out beforehand. She caught Sally's eye and they both got up to go to the ladies' room together.

"Do you think the seating has been planned? Have you noticed where we will both end up if we move again?"

Sally gave a low laugh, "Yes, I've noticed. We may not move again, though, so don't cross your bridges too soon."

"I've been dying to sit next to Gregg, but now I feel awkward. What should I do?"

"Just talk naturally, you silly girl. Oh, and try not to sneeze, or fall off your chair or anything. You've been rescued enough times already."

Suzanna grinned and gave her shoulder a push.

"Have I ever told you that you are completely impossible? Come on let's get back."

A fresh lemon sorbet dusted with icing sugar sat at each place. It was the perfect sweet to end the meal. But Suzanna needed one more course to be able to sit next to Gregg. It was all she could do to sit still and not keep looking down the table at him. She willed the music man to stop playing and announce the next move, but he was unaware of her plight and his deep voice continued in it's song.

Several couples were now getting up to dance. It was evident that no further move was scheduled. The dance floor became full of moving bodies, tapping, stepping and whirling to the catchy beat. Out of the corner of her eye Suzanna saw Nick walk across the floor towards her.

"Can I have this dance, Suzanna? I've been waiting to ask you, hoping to get in before you get besieged by all your admirers."

She forced a smile onto her face as she stood up. "What admirers?"

They walked onto the floor. Suzanna hesitated for a moment and touched her injured arm in an unconscious action of self defence, wary of allowing him to get too close. But he didn't press himself and was a fairly good dancer. He held her hand gently and turned her carefully across the floor and soon their steps matched while the beat swept them along. Suzanna occasionally glanced over at Gregg. He remained seated and his gaze took in the swinging crowd, flicking over her from time to time, but he made no move to get up and dance. Nick led Suzanna round and round, charming her with his conversation and his fluid movements. Her hair swung as she twirled, and her smile showed her enjoyment. It was good to dance for the sheer pleasure of dancing. Several people watched her, smiling with her and admiring her smooth and accomplished steps, the subtly sexy twitch of her slim bottom and the way her skirt spun round her legs. Both she and Nick were breathless when he escorted her back to the table for another drink.

And then, Suzanna's pulse did a double take. She had hardly been seated again when Gregg got to his feet, smiled at the lady on his far side and came to sit down next to her.

She held her breath and studied his face. His expression was serious but that glint was back in his green-brown eyes.

"Hello again. How are you feeling, Suzanna? I have to say, you are looking as gorgeous as ever, despite the bandage on your arm. You seem to be enjoying yourself too? You and Nick were having a good time there."

As usual Suzanna was caught slightly off balance by his comment. Could it be that he was jealous of her dancing with Nick? She smiled at the thought. Nothing like a little competition! Her evening had just been made two hundred percent better.

"You did a great job with my arm, Gregg. Thanks very much. It's not giving me much pain at all. I'm sorry I caused you more stress. We were all so impressed with the way you handled that whole situation. I don't know how you kept the Land Rover on the road going backwards at that speed."

He tipped his head back and laughed, recognising that she had avoided his question and was softening him with flattery. "Actually, we practice doing it so we know how to handle the vehicle in exactly those situations. Generally, if we are unlucky enough to be charged, the elephant will lose it's determination before actually attacking. I haven't had one actually hit the vehicle yet—hope I never do. We make it a point not to shoot into the air unless the animal really gets close."

"Golly, I thought he was close enough as it was," Suzanna replied. "He certainly gave us all a good fright. He was so big and looked so angry. Poor thing. Will his wound heal, do you think?"

"Animals have amazing powers of recovery. He'll be fine if infection doesn't set in. It is more difficult for big animals like elephant as they don't have the ability to lick wounds clean."

His tone lowered, "I hope you have enjoyed your stay here, Suzanna. I should apologise for being a bit short on occasion."

He sounded so formal that she had to answer in the same vein.

"I actually came on this week's holiday very reluctantly." She hoped her words weren't too harsh. "But I've been completely blown away by how much I've come to enjoy the camp, and the bush . . . and . . . everything else." She looked at him with lowered eyelashes, not sure how he would take her remark.

A slight grin lifted his mouth. "You've had some good game viewing. A lot of our visitors go home without seeing half of what you've seen. Have you taken many photos?"

"Um, I didn't bring a camera. I mean, I don't actually own one, but I know Sally has taken a lot on hers." She flushed. Who would come to a camp to view game and not bring a camera? His disapproval was tangible. He looked away at the dancers on the floor and the sudden silence unsettled Suzanna. She was afraid he would find an excuse to get up and go chat to someone else.

"I'm not looking forward to leaving tomorrow," she blustered. "The week seems to have flown, now that we're at the end of it."

"I expect you'll be glad to get back to your partner, and back to work, won't you?" His eyes were slightly shadowed, dark and unfathomable. "Do you work in an office?"

"Yes I do." Suzanna spent the next few moments describing her job and how she came to work in the advertising agency. "I'll have a heap to catch up on, but I enjoy the work and the others in my team. We all get on well together. But, um, well—I don't have a partner. Not any more, that is. I did have one—but, er, he decided he wanted some time alone and he ended things. It happened quite recently, actually. We'd been going out since school and—well, it's all history now, really." Suzanna swallowed, trying desperately hard not to come across as a jilted, heart broken lover—although that's exactly what she had been.

Gregg pinched his top lip with his thumb and forefinger and his hand muffled his reply.

"That's too bad. The man must be a fool."

"I'm sorry?" Suzanna queried. Her thoughts spun off back to their shared moments, and their incredible kisses. She smoothed her hand down her arm and, with an effort, dragged her gaze off his mouth.

He sat for a second, not answering her question, and then asked abruptly, "Would you care to dance?"

'Yes! Desperately! You have no idea how much.'

"Yes, thanks," she answered.

They moved out onto the floor. A tremor shot up her arm as he took hold of her hand, drew her into him and placed his hand on the bare skin of her back. It felt as though she had been touched by a charge of electricity and she almost gasped. Her right hand felt small in his and his shoulder was broad and firm under her touch. Her body moulded to his as they moved slowly to the beat of the music. Her face was inches from the V at the neck of the collar of his white shirt. Just the same as men will check out a woman's legs or breasts, Suzanna had always been drawn to, amongst other features of course, the strength of a man's neck and the base of his throat. Gregg's throat was tanned and strong, and she longed to plant a kiss right there. Secretly she breathed in the scent of his skin.

"About the other night—and when I was fixing the generator . . ." his lips were next to her ear.

"You don't have to apologize," she interrupted. "I should never have come to your room. And I didn't expect to see you down at the generator hut. I was exploring the camp."

His thumb moved against the skin on her back, making her want to arch her back and purr. The song was slow and sensual and he held her effortlessly against him.

She drew away slightly and looked up into his face.

"You don't have to apologize," she repeated, "it was my fault. I don't know what I was thinking."

"Actually, I wasn't going to apologize." He looked down with that unreadable spark in his eyes.

Suzanna wanted him to say more but the music changed to a loud, strong, driving beat, making speech difficult. For a while they danced apart, moving together and then away. He held her hands firmly, turning and guiding, pulling her in and then moving her out, turning again, the pulse and rhythm urging their feet to join in with enjoyment. Suzanna let her natural sense of rhythm and her love of music and dancing take over, and she abandoned herself to the tune and the beat. To be on the floor with a good partner who knew how to bring out the best in both, was heady stuff. Her smile was brilliant, her movements calculated to attract, and she could have flown to the moon with happiness.

The beat slowed once more and she moved back into the circle of his arms as though she belonged there. She didn't want the evening to end. She wanted to stay like this forever—held against him, feeling his hand on her back, the other enclosing hers, moving together to the music. She forgot about the others in the room. They could have been alone for all anyone else mattered. Suzanna wanted the dance to go on and on.

"You are so . . . ." His voice was intimate against her ear.

She looked up at him. "So . . . . what?"

She could almost see the thoughts tumbling around in his head as he decided what to say. The music was soft and embracing, and she revelled in the feel of his arms around her. Not once did she think of drawing away because of the slight pain in her arm. She could stand anything just to be near him like this.

"So slim. And so lovely. And you're a very good dancer."

"Well, you're not such a bad dancer yourself," she grinned back. "In fact you're a great partner and you lead very well."

He laughed, held her tight and spun them both round, and her spirits soared with elation.

"This is the night for compliments. Well, why not? I meant what I told you at the river about your hair. I can't say I've ever seen hair that holds so many beautiful colours. It's almost alive."

Now he was making her feel uncomfortable. She had been used to countering his abrasive side, and she wasn't quite sure how to answer his compliments without seeming too forward. Why did he always put her off balance—it was crazy. She made an effort to change the subject and get the limelight off herself.

"How long have you run this camp? You are obviously very good at it and enjoy what you do?"

"I've worked my way up the ranks, I guess. I started as a guide but I love the bush and managing a camp like this is the cherry on the cake."

"There must be heaps of different challenges every day—and not only from difficult guests?" She smiled. "Life must be interesting to say the least?"

Before he could answer, their private moment was shattered by a chirpy voice behind Suzanna's shoulder.

"So there you are Gregg! I've been looking for you. What about that dance you promised me?"

Suzanna could have killed her on the spot. Where Rachel thought Gregg had gone to, she couldn't imagine. She wanted to slap her for interrupting, to yell at her to go away and leave them alone. How could she be so selfish and thick-skinned? Instead, she glanced up at Gregg's face, noted the way he was smiling at Rachel, and her mind drained like water out of a bath.

"Excuse me, I need to visit the ladies room." She stepped away from him, turned and fled across the floor.

One second ago she had been ready to fly to the moon with elation, and now she felt so crushed there was no way she could return to the table and smile and make small talk as though everything was perfectly alright. It was obvious that he had promised to dance with Rachel, and that she had been watching and waiting for him, choosing her moment to step between Gregg and Suzanna. Ready to pounce like some sort of slinky predator. She had the power to turn men's heads and intoxicate them with a glance and a coy word. It wasn't enough that she had Bill under her thumb—it seemed she was determined to get Gregg as well. Once again Suzanna wondered if Rachel had seduced him after the barbeque.

She was upset and needed to be alone.

Sally was on the dance floor, hugged tight against Pete's rangy frame, so she scooped up her purse as she passed her seat, and slipped out into the darkness.

The glow of the lights around the pool beckoned to her. She sat down on the edge of one of the loungers and hugged her arms round her knees, swallowing tears and trying to reason with herself and persuade herself that she was just another 'girl in camp' as far as Gregg was concerned. Sure, he found her attractive, and he had certainly enjoyed dancing with her, but she was allowing herself to read too much into the things he said, and the looks he had given her. What had happened to her resolution to keep things light and friendly?

'Let's face it, we haven't handled this whole thing very well.' The inner voice mocked her. 'We've let the romance of this enchanting place affect us, that's for sure.'

The music carried across the lawn. The disco man was crooning a taunting ballad and the words echoed through Suzanna's brain . . . . 'How can I live without you, if you only knew . . .'

Her chest tightened in pain. She couldn't bear being out there any longer under the canopy of stars with the romantic setting calling to her. She grabbed her purse and stood up to return to her room, turned, and walked straight into Gregg's rock solid form. She let out a little cry of fright and stepped back. He had approached on silent feet, and had stood for a moment looking down at Suzanna's bent form with a concentrated frown on his brow. She was so lovely and her obvious distress touched him to the heart. He had been almost as startled as she was when she suddenly leapt up to her feet.

Now he reached out a hand but stopped short of touching her.

"I'm sorry, I didn't mean to startle you. I was just about to speak when you suddenly stood up. I really mean it, I'm sorry." The frown puckered his forehead.

"Uh, that's OK. I was miles away and didn't hear you coming." Suzanna scrambled for her composure, but she couldn't help adding, "Where's Rachel?"

"I think she's relating the story of her last adventure to another of the guests." He smiled to take the sarcasm out of his words.

"She's a beautiful girl. Anyone would be glad to listen to her stories." Was Suzanna fishing? Who me? She hung breathlessly on his reply.

"Beautiful?" He seemed slightly vague. "Yes, I suppose she could be considered beautiful. In a plastic sort of way. I don't think her character quite lives up to her looks, though. But I'm sorry you left so abruptly. I had no option but to dance with her since you'd left so quickly, and abandoned me in the middle of the floor."

Suzanna was almost stung into a sharp retort. 'You wanted to dance with her,' she thought silently. 'Don't make out you didn't.' She turned her back on him to hide her feelings, but he stepped up behind her and stood close. He ran his hand up her uninjured arm and she shivered violently at his touch.

"I'm only teasing you," he murmured. "Please don't be angry."

Gently he turned her back to face him and tucked her into his embrace. "Since we were so rudely interrupted before, may I have this dance, Miss Scott?"

How could she resist? What was the point in resisting when it was what she craved? She melted against him. They could hear the music quite clearly. Their steps were slow and their bodies moved together to the haunting tune. Suzanna thought she would die right then and there. She was consumed by the beauty of the moment—the soft lights around the pool, the darkness of the night with the brilliance of the stars above, the feel of his arms round her and his body pressed against hers.

His fingers moved over her shoulder, up her neck and tilted her chin to bring her mouth up to his. For a second that lasted several years, he looked down into her eyes and then brushed her lips with the softest feather of a kiss. His fingers sank into the thickness of her hair as he held her head in the palm of one hand, while the other slid around her back and caressed the skin inside the waistline of her dress.

His voice was deep and low. "I don't know what you've done to me, Suzanna. I've been bewitched by your beauty. I can't think straight. You are on my mind every minute of the day and night."

She reached up and held his face in both her hands. She didn't dare to breathe lest she shatter the magic of the moment. She drew his face down and their lips joined in a kiss that quickly became heated, more urgent, more demanding, more passionate. Their breathing quickened. His arms wrapped tightly round her. She felt his hips move against hers, felt him harden—and yet, felt him hesitate.

Suzanna's breath caught in her throat. She knew she would seriously and instantly die if he pulled away now and let her go. She drew back, and studied his face. His eyes seemed to smoulder and burn into hers. She knew without any doubt that he wanted her as badly as she wanted and needed him.

All reason left her and taking the initiative, she grasped his hand in hers and led him down the path, through the softly enfolding blanket of the night, towards his room.

Chapter 18

THE DOOR BANGED behind her as she burst through the doors of the office. She looked wildly around, searching for him, wondering where he was and why he hadn't been on the landing down at the river. Stanley stood behind the desk, with his hands poised in mid action and a look of surprised enquiry on his face.

"Hi Suzanna. What can I do for you? Is there a problem?"

She glanced about, hoping to see him somewhere. "I—er—I wondered where Gregg is?"

"I'm sorry, Suzanna, Gregg isn't here." Stanley regarded her solemnly, while the overhead fan whisked at the air. The smell of formaldehyde was suffocating. A pen with a life of it's own wove itself round and round Stanley fingers.

The words burst out of Suzanna's mouth. "Why? Where is he? Could you call him, please?"

"I'm sorry, he's gone out into the bush. They went on foot."

"Do you mean he's not in camp at all?" She hung onto the edge of the desk, feeling weak and almost dizzy. "He knows we're leaving today. He has to be here." She stopped as Stanley's words penetrated. "Did you say 'they'? Who's they?"

Stanley frowned. "One of the scouts reported that a kudu had been caught in a snare, so Gregg took a team of blokes to go out and try to release the animal before it's too late," he explained. "They went out at first light, and more than likely won't be back for a couple of hours."

"But he didn't say . . . that is, I wanted to thank him and say goodbye. I was sure he would be here today. Couldn't someone else have gone out to see to the kudu?"

Suzanna knew she sounded like a spoiled hysterical brat, but she couldn't help herself and it was a battle not to burst into tears. She was gutted that he wasn't here to say goodbye, to see her to the boat, to smile and hold her hand. To tell her he would see her again, and reassure her that everything would be wonderful. The panic spread through to the core of her being, and she considered refusing to get on the boat until he got back. A grey mist smothered her, almost closing out Stanley's words.

"Gregg takes the snaring of animals very seriously. We all do, but he's the one with the knowledge of how to dart them if it's necessary. Sometimes the larger animals have to be tranquillised in order to handle them. Being caught in a snare is a terrible way for them to die. The wire slowly tightens as they struggle. If it's around their necks they suffocate to death, and if they're caught by a leg, they cannot escape and slowly die of starvation and thirst. It's dreadfully cruel."

Suzanna dragged her wits together and tried to imagine how terrified the poor animal would be. She thought of the beauty and majesty of a kudu's curving spiralled horns, set high on it's head, the elegant turn of it's long neck, and the smooth lines of the graceful body and legs. How could anyone want to hurt or injure such a magnificent creature?

Stanley appeared to read her thoughts. "The snares are set by poachers and they use wire that is thick and heavy. Even an animal as powerful as a buffalo would be unable to break the death grip of the loop round it's neck before it succumbed. It's essential to find and help the animal as quickly as possible." He placed his hands squarely on the desk, leaning towards her. "Gregg suspects that this bunch of poachers are the same ones that shot at your elephant. We've reported both incidences, the wounded bull and the kudu, and hopefully the Anti Poaching Unit—the APU—will mop them up sooner rather than later."

Another of the guides put his head round the door. "Excuse me Miss Scott, the boat is waiting to depart."

Suzanna swallowed hard. A small part of her senses returned.

"Stanley, I need to thank you for—well, for helping me the other night. And for making this trip so enjoyable for me." She struggled to find the right words. "If it hadn't been for you—well—you brought everything to life for me, and showed me how much beauty there is out here."

He grinned and held out his hand. "It's been entirely my pleasure, Suzanna. I hope we'll see you in our camp again. Someday soon perhaps?" If he knew about she and Gregg, or if he suspected the true extent of her feelings, he didn't show it. The silent voice was at it again. 'He'll make a wonderful partner for some lucky girl. You should have fallen for him instead, Suzanna—much less complicated.'

Her throat constricted. "Uh, could you tell Gregg I said goodbye, please?"

"Yes, of course I will. I'm sure he'll be sorry to have missed you."

Her vision was blurred as she walked out of the office for the last time. On the door frame there was a red circle drawn round the splinter of wood that had caught her sarong. She wondered what the significance of it was, and why it hadn't been removed and the edge sand-papered properly.

Sally was pacing up and down the jetty, watching the office door for Suzanna to emerge. When Gregg hadn't been at the landing to see them off, she knew Suzanna had to go and look for him and find out why. Pete was at Sally's side, and when he noticed the slender brunette brush a tear off her cheek, he walked forward to give her a hug of reassurance.

"It must have been something important for him not to be here," he said kindly.

Suzanna realized Sally must have spilled the beans about her feelings for Gregg, but she didn't mind. Pete's understanding manner, rugged looks and long wiry body emanated trust and dependence. Sally was lucky to have met him. It was obvious that their relationship was going to continue. For now, though, he gave both girls another hug, kissed Sally deeply, and told her he would see her as soon as he could arrange it.

The cousins stepped into the boat and found a place amongst the luggage and other bits and pieces. As the driver started the engine they turned for a last look at the camp. Suzanna imagined Gregg running down to the jetty, just in time to catch and delay the boat. But the grassy slope remained empty except for the cheerful, waving figures of the camp staff. The girls lifted their hands in return, dabbing at tears, and watching long after they had disappeared behind the first bend in the river.

Suzanna hunched forwards and hugged her knees. Pain and longing sliced through her, cutting her open to leave her emotions bleeding and bare. She had been so reluctant to come on this trip, fought hard against Sally's persuasive wiles, and now leaving this magical place caused a deep physical, and very unexpected, ache inside.

The craft was travelling with the flow of the current, and they fairly flew over the water. It seemed a lifetime since they had come in on this same low red boat. Suzanna forced the lump out of her throat and watched the scenery unwind. Fortunately the noise of the boat and the rushing of the air made speech impossible. She couldn't be sure if it was entirely the wind making the tears fly backwards across her temples. She was glad of her dark glasses, and kept her head turned away towards the land, hoping against all vain hope that she might catch a glimpse of a khaki clad figure striding along the high bank. Her sympathies were with him. It had been hard enough to force herself out of bed this morning, but he had had as little sleep as she had, and now he had to walk who knows how far to rescue an animal in distress. Suzanna hoped he had a good team of blokes to help him.

With everything working in reverse, they drew into the main landing that they had departed from a week ago. The driver skilfully brought the boat up alongside, killed the engine and they all started to unload the baggage, cases and boxes. Everything that had to go back to the city, including the girls' luggage, was packed into the waiting dusty Land Rover.

The sun was high and the air was much hotter here than it had been in the shade of the huge trees of the camp. The hair stuck to Suzanna's forehead and neck, and the shirt clung to her back. Sally looked hot and uncomfortable too, and fanned herself ineffectually with her hand. They agreed that they would both like to be back lying by the pool, sipping a long cold beer, instead of standing around in this heat.

"When does Rachel leave camp?" A sudden thought popped into Suzanna's mind. Without her there she would have free access to Gregg. A dart shot into her heart, but after last night she felt confident that Rachel would be wasting her time, even if she tried her most sneaky of schemes on him.

"I think she goes out later today, when this boat gets back to camp," Sally read her cousin's mind like an open book. "Pete leaves tomorrow, so another boat must go out then as well."

"So why couldn't she have come on this trip—taken my place? Then I could have waited for Gregg to get back from helping the snared kudu." The back of her eyes pricked again.

"Don't ask me," Sally replied. "That's just the way everything was planned, I guess. Jeepers, it's hot and dry here. It's a shame they don't water this area like they do round the camp. It would make a huge difference and cool things off considerably." She strolled over to perch uncomfortably on a fallen log, checking carefully for ants and other insects before sitting down.

"Relax for a moment, Suze. This heat is enough to make you feel faint."

They seemed to wait around for ages before the Land Rover was packed and ready to go. As though their whole trip was being rewound backwards, they climbed in and set off down the awful corrugations of the inland road. Since time was on his hands, the African driver was not in a hurry, and he drove more carefully than he had on the inward trip down to the camp, managing to miss most of the potholes. The air that blew in was uncomfortably hot, and when he slowed to negotiate a dry storm gully, the tsetse flies swarmed in through the open windows. The girls hastily wound them up and spent the next few kilometres sweltering while they swatted at the illusive black insects before they had a chance to inflict their stinging bites on legs and arms.

Half the day had gone before they were once again in Sally's car, luggage intact, and heading back along the highway to town. Sally opted to drive for the first leg. Exhausted and depressed, Suzanna leaned her head back on the headrest, closed her eyes and at last allowed her mind to wander over those precious hours last night. To re-live each sweet and wonderful moment, to savour each sensation and to hug every memory close.

As they reached Gregg's door she was the one to hesitate. Perhaps she had been too hasty. He hadn't said a word while they were walking, neither had she, but she had no way of judging what he was thinking, other than that he didn't pull away or stop, or do anything to indicate he didn't want her to go to his room. Suzanna wished he had completed his sentence earlier about not apologising for their first kiss, and then she would know where she stood now. Perhaps she had been too pushy? Maybe he didn't want another relationship so early after breaking up with his girlfriend. Suzanna reminded herself that he had not said a word about her, and she only knew what Rachel had told them.

Now she turned to tell him that perhaps she should go back to her room, after all. He looked down, his hands on her shoulders, and his unspoken answer was to descend on her mouth once again.

"Please stay, Suzanna." His lips were against hers and she almost swallowed his words. He took her soft murmur as a yes. He bent and swung her up into his arms, carrying her weight as easily as a child. Her arms stole round his neck and she nuzzled into the masculine strength at the corner of his shoulder. Her pulse was beating hard as he pushed the door open with his foot.

The thatched room was dimly lit with just one corner lamp. The satisfied grunting of a hippo wafted in through the open veranda end. Suzanna smiled. It seemed the perfect background tune—that and the incessant trill of the myriad insects belonging to the African night.

He held her up against him, kissing her lips, her eyelids, the bridge of her nose. She dropped her head backwards and his lips found the base of her throat. Her hand stole inside the collar of his white shirt, and she thrilled to feel the skin of his neck and shoulder under her touch.

He lowered her gently to the ground. Her legs felt weak and unsteady and she hung on close to his solid frame. His arms wound themselves right around her body, and she felt his fingertips steal under the edge of her dress to gently stroke the slight bulge of her breast at the side of her rib-cage.

She leaned away from him and slowly unbuttoned his shirt. At last she could press her nose to the base of his throat, and plant the kisses she had yearned to do earlier. She slipped the shirt off his shoulders and gloried in the strong, tanned spread of his torso, running her hands over the muscles of his chest, curling her fingers through the light cover of hair, caressing and admiring the firmness of his slim stomach. She kissed his collar-bone, flicked her tongue along the firm ridges. He shuddered but didn't say anything.

Without speaking, they wanted the moments to draw out and to carry them along in the thick and sensual current.

Their movements were slow—an erotic dance that dated back into eternity.

He reached behind her, found the fastenings, unclipped them and then smoothed his hands across her shoulders, slowly pushing the clothing down. It fell in a circle at her feet and she stepped out of it. She stood before him, clad only in her brief panties.

He drew in a sharp breath as his gaze and his touch travelled down over her breasts, lingered at her nipples and smoothed down over her hips. He circled her waist with his hands—his fingers almost touching right round her. She could feel the slight roughness of his palms, gently scratching every place they roamed. He cupped her breast, rolled the ball of this thumb over the hardened point.

Now it was her turn to shudder. Once again he sucked in a breath.

"Oh God, Suzanna! You are so beautiful. You take my breath away."

Her entire being pulsed with a desire so strong, flooded with a feeling so heavy and completely encompassing, it was unlike anything she had experienced before. She stepped closer to him, gripped his shoulders and gently rubbed her nipples across his bare chest.

The switch flipped from slow and languorous to urgent and compelling.

He gave a low moan, swung her into his arms and in one motion deposited her onto the wide bed. He leaned over her, holding her in his arms, kissing, licking, stroking and exploring. She arched upwards against him, panting, wanting more and more. Her hands gripped his shoulders, ran down his back. His beautiful mouth found her mouth, her neck, then her nipples, drawing them proudly upwards, gently biting, sucking. She set her teeth into his shoulder, her fingernails into his skin. His fingers and his tongue inched downwards, kissing her belly, stroking her mound, finding the secret moist warmth hidden inside. She dropped her legs open, inviting him in, clutching at his shoulders, desperate to get more and more of him.

He lifted his head and moved up to gaze into her eyes, murmuring, "Suzanna, I don't have anything with me—we should stop."

"No. No. It's alright. Oh God, Gregg. I want you so badly. I have since the moment I saw you. Please don't stop. Hold me. Love me."

He fumbled with his belt, the zip of his pants, and at last she felt the whole of his body against hers. She ran her hands down his back and over the firmness of his buttocks, pulling him towards her. She gloried in the strength of his manhood pressed hard and long against her thigh.

He lay over her and kissed her deeply, their tongues meeting and entwining. She held his head and drew him deeper into her mouth, winding her arms round his neck, opening her body up to him, desperate to feel fulfilled. She felt him press gently against her, opening her like an exotic flower, and then he thrust more urgently. His length filled her, quenched the emotional burning thirst and wild desire that had consumed her thoughts.

At last their bodies were joined, and she was complete.

The blood sang in Suzanna's ears. For an instant Gregg lay still, savouring the moment like an exquisite jewel. Then he pushed more firmly and they moved together, giving and taking pleasure, building and receding and building again. Bucking and thrusting, panting, kissing. She arched upwards against him, crushed under his weight, loving his weight, needing to feel him press her down.

Then he rolled her over to lie on top of him and a whole new range of sensations burst through her. His hands were free to cup her breasts, tease her nipples, move down and hold her hips hard to his body. He filled her entire being, speared upwards through her core to touch her heart. He moved with a primal savagery that was, at the same time, tender and loving. She held onto him with all her strength, moving with him, bucking against him.

She threw her head backwards. Her hair tumbled freely down her back and over her shoulders, and her breasts strained towards his touch. She looked down. The darkness of their hair merged together and she admired the contrast of her smooth slim stomach against the strong tanned ridges of his lower belly.

The fire built in intolerable waves, consuming her, ripping her senses apart, flooding and roaring through every fibre, sending her brain reeling and her body into fabulous, shuddering spasms that went on and on, consuming and rocking her to the depths of her being. He grabbed her even closer and cried out as his senses spiralled with hers, out of control.

The moment joined their souls, hung between them like a fireball of intense colour and sensations, pulsing and shimmering with red-hot passion.

An eternity later she lay curled up in the curve of his body. She felt she had come home. She was totally spent and so was he. Their bodies were slick with sweat and moisture, and her hair clung in strands. He lifted himself onto one elbow and gazed deeply into her eyes. His hand smoothed the side of her face and caressed her cheek, traced a gentle pattern over one breast, stroked down her belly and came to rest holding the side of her hip. His thumb stroked the smooth skin inside her hip-bone and traced small circles on the edge of her dark triangle of hair.

"I'm not going to tell you how amazing that was," he grinned. "I think you probably know."

Suzanna lifted a finger and traced the line of his mouth, smoothed his eyebrows.

"You have the most tantalising mouth I have ever seen," she told him. "It is truly beautiful."

He tipped his head back and gave a deep-throated laugh. "Beautiful? I've never been told I'm beautiful. A few other less complimentary things, but not that." He rewarded her by kissing her long and tenderly with the subject of their discussion. Then a serious look passed over his features.

"Suzanna, I need to tell you—I had a girl—she lived in the city. We, er, we broke up. She phoned me. That was the call that came through the other night. But our break up is not the reason for me being here with you now. I want you to know that. I am not in the habit of seducing beautiful clients who visit this camp. Somehow, you have sent me into a spin. Affected my thinking and even crept into my dreams."

She smiled up at him. "Thank you for telling me that. I knew you'd been upset by the call, and I desperately wanted to come to you. But, um, Rachel rather beat me to it." What did she have to add that bit for? She could have bitten out her tongue.

A frown creased his forehead. "Rachel means well, I guess. She thinks she can sort out the problems of the world. She helped me talk through it, that's all. Nothing else happened. How did you know she had been here, anyway?"

Suzanna's eyes were large and luminous as she stared back at him. Her hair formed a soft jumbled pillow round her head. She knew she risked making him angry but she had to give him a straight, honest answer.

"I watched her leave the barbeque area and follow you. I wanted to trip her up, or rugby dive her onto the ground—anything to stop her going to you. Then a little later I saw you both walk down the path together, and—I didn't know what to think. You must know she is out to get you, don't you?"

Gregg gave a faint smile. "So you admit to spying on me?"

She relaxed. He understood after all. She didn't tell him that Rachel had told her and Sally all about his break-up. Rachel had also reluctantly said that nothing had happened between them. She wouldn't have been able to keep it to herself if it had been different.

"Talking of spying," she grinned at him, "I don't suppose you saw Sally and me in the pool the other night?"

A mischievous look settled over his handsome features, and his eyes held a wicked glint. Suzanna could see he was considering his answer, making her wait.

She giggled. "You rotter! You did see us, didn't you?"

"I have to admit that I did," he replied. "It was the most erotic sight I have ever witnessed. I was transfixed—literally couldn't move. You were lucky not be ravaged right there on the path to your room. You sure know how to rock a man to his core."

"No. We didn't mean it like that. We were just having fun and never expected that anyone would see us. It was very late, after all."

His thumb resumed it's circles, moved inwards, found the dewy oyster hidden in the thick hair, stroking persistently, working downwards and inwards, into the already wet channel. She writhed in rising ecstasy, the passion flaring again. Her hand stole down his ribs, over the ridges of his stomach to find and caress his manhood, stroking up and down, marvelling at the length and strength of him.

This time it was slow and sensuous. Deep and loving. They brought each other slowly to explosive heights, crying out with the intensity of their feelings, panting and drawing in air as though they had run a marathon. The emotion squeezed Suzanna's heart and gripped her throat. The tears dripped across her temples and into her hair, and Gregg leaned over her and kissed them away, holding her close. She wanted to pour her feelings out to him. Tell him she had never felt this way before. Her chest constricted with fierce emotion and she had to struggle against saying what was in her heart.

She held him fast, never wanting to let go. How could she leave tomorrow? How could she ever get up and walk back to her room? Even stand upright ever again? She wanted to curl up against his body and sleep. Wake up in his arms. Tomorrow and forever.

It was Gregg who gently reminded her that she had to move. He helped her dress, easing her clothes back on and kissing her shoulders and neck. He dragged on his own clothes and, arms round each other, they walked back to her room. They stopped several times to share a lingering kiss, but the words she wanted so badly to say remained unspoken.

The bar area and the pool were dark, quiet and empty. The party was over and even the waiters had gone. Thrillingly, the wonderful resonance of a lion's roar echoed from the far side of the river, sending palpable sound waves that completed the beauty of the still night. They stopped and he tightened his arm round her.

"Hear that?" Gregg asked. "Absorb that sound, Suzanna. Draw it into your very soul and keep it treasured there, because you are among the privileged few who have heard it. One day that sound could very well have vanished into extinction. Man's greed will one day ruin this wonderful land and probably most of the animals that exist here."

She shivered at his prediction of gloom, and realized how deeply he loved the bush and the wildlife. His intensity scared her a little, and yet made her fiercely proud of what he was trying to achieve by getting his guests to appreciate what he loved with all his heart.

At her door he kissed her long and deeply. Very reluctantly she let him go and tiptoed inside. Sally was in bed but not asleep. Suzanna supposed she had been with Pete and only recently returned herself.

"You OK, Suze?" she murmured sleepily.

"Oh God, Sal! More than OK. I am totally in love. He is fabulous. I have to find a way to be with him. I never would have thought I'd feel this way about anyone, especially in such a short space of time. He is just amazing."

She lay back and stretched her arms over her head. Like a cat she licked at the skin on her arm, tasting and smelling his scent that was still all over her. She thought she wouldn't be able to sleep, but in fact she dropped into a deeply relaxing and embracing velvety softness, and only woke when the coffee was brought to the door at first light the next morning.

Now, as she sat next to Sally and the scenery rolled past, the tears dripped under Suzanna's dark glasses and ran down her cheeks. She sniffed and dug for a tissue. Why had he not been there to say goodbye? How would she know when—and if—she would see him again? Had he been upset to be called out? She knew duty would come first, had to come first, especially an animal in distress, but she couldn't bear it that he hadn't been there to see her off.

Sally reached out her hand and squeezed Suzanna's.

"Don't worry, Suze. He'll call you. I know he will. You'll see him again."

"I didn't think it was possible to feel like this, Sal. I think I'll die if I don't see him again. I never felt like this with Dave—not even close. I feel as though I'm only complete with him next to me. How could this have happened so fast?"

"I feel a bit like that with Pete, but I don't think men like to commit themselves as quickly as we do. But I know what you're going through," she replied. "Pete has almost told me he feels the same way, so I have a little more to hang onto. He's coming into town next week and I'm counting the hours till I see him again."

"Oh, Sal. I've been so wrapped in myself I haven't even considered how you would be feeling. I'm really pleased for you. Pete is a great person and it's obvious how he feels about you. Imagine if we hadn't gone down to the camp, we would never have met Pete and Gregg. The thought makes me feel totally sick."

Sally laughed. "After all your moaning and groaning about going. I must have had a premonition that things would turn out well."

"Do you think they will? I don't know how I'll survive for the next few days. Would the camp have our phone number? Or an email address? Will Gregg know how to contact me? Do we have their address?"

"I'm sure I still have all the details at home. Try not to stress about it." She took her attention off the road for a few seconds while she flashed Suzanna a cheeky smile. "We'll get our double wedding yet, you'll see."

Chapter 19

BOTH GIRLS WENT back to work the next day. Suzanna was pleased to see her workmates and they were keen to hear how she had survived for the week in the primitive conditions of the bush camp. She did her best to describe how up-market it had been, and what a wonderful time they had had. But thoughts of Gregg made her throat close and she hurriedly changed the subject.

She struggled through two whole days. Sleep evaded her and she spent a large part of the night staring out of the window at the sparkling stars, remembering the same stars shining over the camp, wondering if Gregg was thinking of her, looking at the night sky too, missing her, planning to call her. How long would it take for him to contact her—should she take the bull by the horns and ring him? It was a battle to keep everything under control. The questions pummelled her brain and took a toll on her body. She felt listless and wan, and it was an effort to do anything.

Auntie Ann popped in to hear how the girls had fared. She brought a basket full of goodies for them, plus a whole lot of love and concern which she tried hard not to show.

"Is Suzanna alright, Sally? She doesn't seem herself at all. Why don't you both come out to us for the weekend?"

Sally told her mother the basics of the story, and assured her they would catch up with her once they knew what Pete and Gregg's plans were.

"Neither of us want to be too far from the phone right now, Mum." They shared a hug. Once she had left, Sally tried her 'snap-out-of-it' speech.

"Come on, Suze. You have try and get this into perspective. You'll make yourself ill if you go on like this."

"You're not much better yourself, Sally. How many times have you checked the emails? And picked up the phone to see if there are any messages."

Sally grimaced. "You're right. Let's get out of here and go for a walk or something."

The next evening both girls jumped and looked at the door when the bell trilled. Toby stood outside, holding a very large pizza and two bottles of wine. He sashayed in waving the packages.

"I come bearing sustenance for the body and the spirit," he announced theatrically. "She-Who-Must-Be-Obeyed has decreed you are both too thin and instructed that I remain here until every last drop and mouthful has been consumed." He put the offerings onto the coffee table. "So—let's get started without further delay."

Sally laughed. "You know Mum hates being called that. Where's Amy, Toby? How come you're out on the town on your own?"

"My lady love is performing the vital task of helping her sister run a successful hen's party for an old school friend of theirs. They've been planning a series of dire events for the poor lass for quite a while. I just hope the bride-to-be makes it to the altar in one piece."

He poured wine into three glasses, clinking his against theirs and they settled themselves on the carpet round the low coffee table.

"Don't think you are getting this fabulous feast for nothing, oh sweet Madonnas. I want the whole story, and the grittier the better. Leave nothing out." He opened his eyes wide in mock attention. "Get started, now. I don't have all night."

The girls burst into laughter and poked him in the ribs, spilling his drink on the carpet.

"It must be something in the genes," Suzanna said. "Oh Toby, you would love it at Inkuni. You must take Amy down there—it's a really special place."

It felt good to remember each incident, all the game they'd seen, and recall the people and conversations. Toby was a sympathetic listener and his face either fell or shone as the story unfolded. He clicked his tongue in concern and laughed in the right places.

"How is your arm now, Suzie-wong? I expect you'll have a slight scar?"

Suzanna smiled. "You haven't called me that for years. But I had an excellent doctor and there's hardly any mark now." Suzanna displayed her shoulder. "Pour me some more wine, Toby, I'm sure that's the secret. I have a feeling tomorrow will bring good news."

But another day dragged past and still there was no word from Gregg. Her spirits sank once again. Did it mean that he wasn't going to ring? She was tormented by the thought that perhaps he had succumbed to Rachel's tender touch after all.

'Have a little faith in the man' the voice admonished her. 'Trust the poor guy—he's probably been busy.'

She came to a decision. She decided that if he hadn't rung by that evening she would contact the camp. It shouldn't be too hard to think of some excuse to make a call sound friendly and casual. The day dragged endlessly past. The hours crawled. When she got home from work she checked the phone, checked the computer—nothing.

Right—she would carry out her plan. She sat down in front of the phone, hands shaking in an agony of indecision as she wondered for the millionth time whether to go through with it. Was she being too pushy? What would she say? She hadn't even worked out a script. She studied the black casing of the phone, chewing her nail and changing her mind every second.

Then she took a deep breath. If she could find the number, she would ring.

Sally hadn't got home yet, and it took ages to look through all the papers and mess lying on her desk. Suzanna was on the point of giving up in despair when a small piece of paper dropped out from under a pile of books. The number of the camp was scrawled in Sally's writing across the bottom. With pumping heart and shaking hands, she dialled.

The line was awful, and crackled and popped like something alive and very angry. The ringing tones were distant and faint but she pressed the receiver hard to her ear and hung on, willing someone to answer. Finally the receiver was lifted at the other end, but the voice sounded thousands of miles away and Suzanna couldn't identify who it was, and it was obvious that the person speaking was unable to hear her clearly. Her voice rose in pitch, shouting over the buzzing on the line, desperate to find out if Gregg was there and get a message to him.

"Hello? Hello? Can you hear me? Who is this? Could you speak up please?"

It was no use. After a few loud cracks that made her eardrum ring, the line went dead in her hand. She slumped forward onto the carpet. It just wasn't fair. Despairingly she put her hands over her face and tried not to scream. What could she do? How could she survive this feeling that threatened to choke her to death?

Another day, and then another, slipped past, taking added slices off her confidence like an apple being slowly pared to it's core. She had a big contract to work on at the office, but she was unable to give of her best. Concentration was difficult, and design ideas for artwork just not forthcoming. She doodled on her pad, trying to get something to pull together to present to the client.

"Suzanna, by your standards I have to tell you that this is not your best work." Her boss leaned over her desk, frowning at the layout in his hand.

"I know. I'm sorry. I'll give it another try and re-plan it."

"We're working to a deadline here Suzanna. I don't know what's eating at you, but we can't have our work output decreasing like this. Every single one of our contracts is important, you know that."

With a supreme effort of concentration she started all over again, and this time produced an acceptable layout. She knew she could do better, and so did her client and her boss.

"This will do, I suppose, Suzanna. But I was hoping for a little more depth to it. Still, it is acceptable and we've run out of time on this project." The office manager pursed his lips, flipping over the pages in a manner than thoroughly irritated Suzanna. She thought he was being particularly picky, but she bit her tongue and vowed to try harder with the next assignment. As soon as he'd retreated into his own office, Anthony, her co-worker approached with a sympathetic smile.

"Hey Suze! Don't worry about him too much. He's been a bit stressed out lately."

"Yeah—that makes two of us."

"You do seem to have been a bit quiet since you got back from that trip of yours. What's the problem?"

The unexpected sympathy from someone whom she only knew at work made the tears spring to Suzanna's eyes. Hurriedly she brushed them away, but Anthony leaned forward in concern.

"Come on, it's almost break time. Let's grab a coffee and you can do some off-loading. It sure looks like you could do with an impartial ear."

She allowed him to lead her to the canteen, sit her down and hand her a strong black coffee. Anthony was devastatingly good looking in a fastidious sort of way and was always immaculately dressed. Secretly she had wondered if perhaps he was gay, but nothing had ever been said out loud, and now Suzanna felt she had judged him too harshly. He was just a nice guy.

"OK—spill. If I can help you work things out, that's what I'd like to do."

Suzanna took a deep breath and started at the beginning, telling Anthony about Dave, the trip Sally had won, and meeting Gregg. To her consternation she even found herself talking about Steve, and hastily re-directed herself back to Gregg. She would not go over the ugly scene with Steve even to this sympathetic ear.

"And now I don't know if I'll ever see Gregg again, and if I don't, I think I'll . . . I don't know what I'll do," she finished. She was startled when Anthony burst into laughter.

"Suzie baby. From what you have told me, he'll come. Any red-blooded male would give an arm and a leg to date you, and this guy sounds like he has plenty of red blood. Don't fret. He must just be trying to sort his life out, but, rest assured, you will see him again."

He was saying the words Suzanna wanted to hear, but the note in his voice made her look at him in a different light. It seemed she had completely misjudged Anthony. He was studying her face intensely, and she felt uncomfortable under his clear and direct gaze. He was also a mind-reader it seemed.

"Suze—I'm honoured that you've told me all this. I would like to be your friend, and please don't misread that. I am already in a relationship and have no intention of doing anything to change it. But try to take a step backwards and have faith in Gregg. I'm sure he won't let you down. Now—we'd better get back to work before we both get fired."

Even so, another day dragged past with no word from him.

She found herself writing Gregg's name on each piece of paper—Gregg Mayland, Gregg Mayland and then Suzanna Mayland, Suzanna Mayland. It had a nice round ring to it. Her head dropped down onto her desk. Would she ever see him or hear from him again? The pain in her heart was sharp and intense. It sent shafts down into her belly. She felt so awful that at times she wondered if she was actually ill with something.

To make things worse, Pete had arrived back and phoned Sally regularly, trying to get his plans worked out so that he could get into town to see her. Sally took the calls in her room, talking quietly and for ages, and then emerging with a glow that lit up her pretty features, hugging her arms and doing a surreptitious set of dance steps to the tune in her head.

'At least one of us is happy.' The thought spiralled traitorously into Suzanna's brain. She forced herself to smile and not let Sally see her guilty jealousy.

Sally insisted they both go to their yoga class, and Suzanna did her best to concentrate on the relaxing poses and get her mind to unwind. No sooner had she returned home, though, than all the fears and pressures crashed back in.

Another weekend approached. Pete hadn't arrived as he'd said he would and Sally once again looked as strained and taut as Suzanna did.

"He'll come. Don't worry. He must have been delayed, but he'll come." Suzanna reassured Sally and wished she could be so sure about Gregg.

And then, unannounced, Pete arrived at the door, holding a large bunch of red roses. Sally flew across the floor and straight into his arms, crushing the lovely bouquet. He caught her up to him, laughing with pleasure, and swung her around in a circle, kissing her fervently.

His dark hair had recently been trimmed and his clothes fitted well to his handsome, lanky frame. It was evident that he'd missed Sally as much as she'd missed him, and they couldn't let each other go. Sally hastily changed into a glamorous outfit, while he paced round the lounge, and they set off to paint the town red. Half-heartedly they both asked if Suzanna wanted to join them, but naturally she refused. Three is a crowd, after all.

While Sally was getting ready Suzanna quizzed Pete about Gregg. But he had left the camp a few hours after the girls so he couldn't give her any news.

Sally's radiant face showed concern. "Suze, you'll be alright if we go, won't you? I mean, you won't go and do anything stupid, like... well you know what I mean, don't you?"

Suzanna forced a bright smile. "I promise I will be fine. I'm not the silly girl I used to be, Sally."

They shared a close hug. "You have a wonderful time, dearest Cuz. You deserve to be happy."

Even so, as the two of them bounced out of the door Suzanna sank to the carpet, her arms wrapped round her middle enduring savage pains of longing and loneliness, and fighting tears of self pity.

A little while later, she straightened and headed determinedly for the computer. After the disaster of the phone call she had persuaded herself that if he had wanted to, Gregg would have either phoned or emailed by now. She was definitely not going to email the camp. She would definitely not be the one to make first contact—she wouldn't.

But here she was, resolve vanished like mist in the morning, looking up the address.

She sat staring blankly at the screen, biting at the skin next to the nail on her thumb. What should she say—how would she word it so that it didn't sound as though she was chasing Gregg

'You're not chasing him.' For once the voice was on her side. 'You just want to know if things in the camp are good, and whether he managed to save the kudu or not. Keep it light until you know what the score is.'

'Dearest Gregg' she started to write—stopped and pressed the delete key—too personal.

'Hi Gregg'—deleted—too casual.

'Dear Gregg. Hi there. I wanted to thank you for the great week we spent at your lovely Nkuni Camp. I tried to phone a few days ago, but the lines were really bad and I couldn't speak to anyone properly. Did you manage to save the kudu—we hope so—and also hope you have had no further dramas. When you get time I would love to hear from you. With best regards, Suzanna Scott.'

It wasn't a masterpiece but it was the best she could do. What she really wanted was to pour her heart out to him, plead with him to ring her, come into town and see her, but she realized that anyone in the office could open the email and read it. She went over the message again, not knowing how she could change it without compromising herself and leaving herself wide open to a rebuke of some kind. Or worse—be rejected completely.

She pressed the send button.

She checked the incoming mail at every opportunity, but it was a day later that a reply came through. Suzanna opened it with trembling hands, and then could have cried at the words written on the impersonal white screen.

'Hi Suzanna—thanks for your mail and kind words. We have had a difficult time with our communications from the camp—a vicious and unexpected windstorm blew a huge kigelia tree down and damaged our satellite dish. It has taken well over a week to get everything repaired, and even now we are not back to normal, so I hope this gets through OK. Gregg has taken compassionate leave as his uncle died suddenly. He left camp two days ago and we don't expect to hear from him until he gets things sorted out. He was pretty cut up about it. The camp closes for the rainy season in a few weeks time, so he may not be back till next year. I will certainly tell him you asked after him if he does contact us. Sincerely, Stanley Morgan. PS—Gregg managed to release the kudu, which was great news for us all.'

Suzanna dropped her forehead down onto her arms. Here she was, desperate to hear from him, but she knew so little about him. The doubts flooded her mind. She knew nothing about his family or where they lived. She couldn't be sure of anything about him, apart from the intensity of her feelings towards him. Had she been a one-night-stand? Someone conveniently close for a passionate night of sex? She just didn't know. If he had left the camp two days ago, surely he would have been able to contact her by now. She wondered where his uncle had lived. For all she knew he could have been in another country. Suzanna didn't even know if his parents were alive or not. Poor Gregg, he had obviously had a bad time of it, though.

She almost leapt out of her skin as the phone trilled right next to her ear. She flung out her hand and grabbed it up.

"Hello! Hello? Suzanna here."

Dave's slow voice echoed over the line. "Suzanna? You sound upset, are you alright?"

It took a second to get her blank mind to register and re-focus, but she was completely deflated and had to fight against yelling at him. What the heck was Dave ringing her for? "Oh! Hi Dave. How're you?"

"How was your trip? It seems you survived it then? How long have you been back?"

"We were only away for a week, Dave." She almost added—a week that changed my whole life. "We've been back for ages already." The last thing she wanted was to describe the camp or answer any questions about the incredibly special time down there, so she forced a lighter note into her voice. "What have you been up to?"

His tone lowered, "Suze, would you like to have dinner? I've missed you. You may not realize it but tomorrow is the anniversary of—well, you know, our first time, our first night, together."

Suzanna was stunned. A million retorts flashed into her brain. She was amazed that he had remembered the occasion when she had forgotten it. Well, not forgotten, but certainly she wouldn't have known the actual date. As far as she was concerned their first time had been at her eighteenth birthday, but it could have been a thousand years ago for all she cared—what was he thinking of?

"Suze—are you there?"

She hesitated, wanting to correct him, but not wanting to get into a discussion about it. In comparison to what she had shared with Gregg—well, honestly, there was absolutely no comparison—not even a glimmer. Anger built up in her breast. What had happened to his desire to 'explore other avenues', and what about his casual words that had broken her heart?

"Yes, I'm here."

"I thought perhaps we could go out—have a drink and a meal somewhere. I've missed you and it would be good to catch up . . . . Suze? Are you still there? No strings attached. We could just mull over old times?"

"Look Dave—I don't think it's a good idea. You made your decision and I've accepted it. You told me you wanted to explore—did you call it new horizons? We can't go back—really—it's too late now." She took a deep breath, determined to continue. "And I've, well, I've met someone else." And I may never see him again, she thought silently.

"Oh! That was quick!" Dave sounded peeved.

"Yes, well, it happens. Thanks for the call, Dave. I wish you well. Goodbye."

Suzanna lowered the phone gently, staring at the black case, knowing she had been short off and harsh. But she didn't care. She was past caring.

A few seconds later the phone rang again. She picked it up, sighing with annoyance.

"Dave? I'm not going to change my mind. It's over between us."

"Well, I'm delighted to hear that. What a relief."

She dropped the phone and had to fumble to stop it hitting the floor.

"Gregg? Oh God, I can't believe it. Gregg? How are you? Where are you?"

It sounded as though he was on a long distance line and she pressed the receiver hard to her ear. His voice was distant on the crackly connection.

"I'm fine. I've had a terrible time trying to contact you. All our comms got blown out down at the camp."

"Yes, I tried to phone, but I couldn't get through properly. The line went dead. I also emailed and Stanley told me about your uncle—I'm terribly sorry, Gregg. Where are you now?" Her pulse was beating so rapidly she felt faint.

"Yes, thanks, it's all been a terrible shock. He was so well—it was very sudden and completely unexpected—a heart attack. I'm down at their ranch at the moment and there are heaps of things to sort out and arrange. My aunt has taken it very badly, but Mum is here as well, so we're all doing our bit to help."

Suzanna heard the catch in his voice and her heart went out to him. Memories of her own mother's funeral came back into her mind, and her eyes felt moist. The hole she had left could never be filled.

"Will you be able to get into town—after the funeral, perhaps? I'd—er, I'd love to see you."

The line crackled, faded and came back to life. She'd missed his reply.

"Gregg, are you there? Hello? I didn't hear what you said." Her voice rose. "Gregg?"

There was a continuous buzzing sound as the line died. Suzanna slammed the phone down in frustration, cursing roundly and wailing like a mortally wounded animal. Stupid, darn thing! What lousy technicians would let the lines get into such a bad state of disrepair like this. Didn't they realize that people would have important calls to make? It was too much.

For another half an hour she sat next to the phone, willing it to ring again. Her hand hovered over it, ready to snatch it up. But it sat on the table like a giant black frog—silent.

Overcome with frustration and restless energy, Suzanna leapt to her feet and dug around in the bottom of her wardrobe to pull out an old pair of trainers. She tied her hair back, flung on an old shirt, some stretch pants and headed out of the door for a run.

She hadn't run in ages. In fact she hated running. Ages ago she'd made a pact with herself never to run again. But she was bursting with emotion and had to release it somehow. Running seemed the only way out.

Her feet pounded over the paths and pavements, flew across the green lawns of the park. She barely noticed the people she passed, or the spread of the beautiful purple blossoms clustered on the branches of the jacaranda trees that lined the avenues. Her pony-tail swung from side to side and the perspiration dripped steadily from every pore while her breath steamed in her chest.

She wasn't aware of where she was going. Her feet had a will of their own. Her mind was focused on Gregg and her feelings for him. There was no doubt that she had fallen in love with him and that her life would not be the same ever again. Even if he never arrived at her door, she would not be able to have a relationship with anyone else. No-one else could compare to him—ever.

While her thoughts flew all over the place, her subconscious mind drove her pounding feet to a place she had been before. Suzanna suddenly found herself standing on the pavement outside Dave's house. She stood still, feeling dazed, like waking from a dream, wondering how the heck she had got there, sucking in deep breaths and holding her aching sides. She doubled over to ease the stitch that pierced her stomach, and bring some blood back into her head.

'What did you come here for, Suzanna?' 'I didn't come here—at least not on purpose.' 'So what are you going to do now? Will you knock and go in?' 'No—of course not. It's over between Dave and I, you know that.'

As luck would have it, while she stood confusedly debating, Dave opened his front door and strode out to his car, jingling the keys. He stopped dead when he saw Suzanna on the path, dishevelled and sweaty and panting like a steam train.

"Suze! What are you doing here? You look awful. What's happened?"

She had turned into a pillar of stone. What had brought her here? She stared at Dave's face—once so loved, and the centre of her whole existence. Now she felt as though he was a stranger standing there, staring at her. She searched through her jumbled thoughts but was unable to make sense of anything.

"Suze!" he said again, "you're so pale. Are you alright? Come inside and have a drink of water. I've been hoping that you would change your mind and come to me. Oh, Suzie, come, let me help you."

Fighting off the dizziness, she sank down to her haunches as he strode towards her. She didn't want to go into his house. She'd put everything to do with Dave behind her. Now, just because she hadn't a clue what Gregg's feelings or plans were, she wasn't going to open up any old wounds—for either of them.

"I'm fine," she managed at last. "I went for a run and must have taken the wrong turning without noticing. Are you going out? Truly, I'm fine now. Just a bit out of breath for a moment."

"Please come in, Suze. Just for a moment. I am going out, but I'm early so I've got time to spare. At least let me give you something to drink." He gave her the old familiar look that had once melted her heart, and he took her arm to help her back to her feet. "Come Suzie, lean on me."

His touch seemed to bring her back to life. She flicked the sticky hair out of her face and looked up, squinting against the sun.

"I won't come in Dave. There's no point. You made your decision and now you have to live with it. I know I probably sound hard, but you broke my heart." She held up her hand. "No—don't say anything! It's too late. We had something that I thought was special, but, as I said on the phone, I've met someone else. I don't know if there's any future for us, for him and me, but I'm prepared to wait and see how things turn out."

His face fell, but there was no other way to say it all. He stood back, his hands on his hips. If nothing else Dave was a true sort of bloke and Suzanna knew he wouldn't press himself on her as Steve had done. She sighed deeply, completely drained. She was afraid that if she had to stand here any longer she would sway and fall, and then Dave would have the perfect excuse to carry her inside. Inside the house where they had shared precious moments, and where her resolve to resist him may not hold out.

"If you are driving past our flat I would appreciate a lift home, though. My legs feel like jelly."

She had no idea what an appealing picture she made, with flushed cheeks, her hair in wet ringlets and T-shirt sticking moistly to her breasts and sweaty skin. Dave hesitated, staring at her lovely face, knowing that he had lost more than he'd ever calculated on. Something inside him seemed to suddenly drop. He felt like a candle with all the wax melted and dripping down in lumpy streaks. He wiped his brow with his hand, battling to stay calm.

"Dave? Do you have time to drop me at home please?"

He opened the car door for her in silence, and she climbed gratefully in. She sat right next to the door, on edge in case he tried to change her mind and perhaps put his hand on her knee, or her arm, but he'd got the message, and made no attempt to touch her. They had shared many special moments on the front seat of this car, but the memories attached to her last trip in it were not good. Dave looked across at her as they stopped outside the flat.

"Good luck, Suze. The years we had together were special to me, and I'll never forget you. You were my first love, and that will always stay in my heart."

"Thanks, Dave. Yes, they were special. But we've both moved on. I'm glad I saw you again, and I'm sorry I was short on the phone. Thanks for the lift, and good luck to you as well."

She raised her hand as he drove away, suddenly feeling light and free. As though she had had the closure she had not known she needed.

There was a message on the answer phone from Sally. "Zannie?" The use of her pet nickname said more than the message. "You're obviously not at home, hope you're OK. I just want to tell you I won't be home again tonight. Pete and I—well, you know how it is. I'm still at his place and I have my cell phone if you need me at all." There was a pause. "Grab a take-away and watch a movie. Or go over to Toby and Amy's. Don't mope all by yourself, Suze. See you tomorrow. Bye for now."

She hung up, gulped down a huge glass of water and curled up in the window seat, clutching a fat cushion to her chest. With her chin in her hand, she watched the sun sink and the shadows lengthen across the tiny garden. She closed her eyes and sent a quiet prayer upwards, imploring the Lord above to keep Gregg safe, and help his family through this awful time in their lives.

It was completely dark when she roused herself, turned the sound up high on one of her favourite CD's and headed for a hot soothing shower. She washed her hair and pampered herself with some luxury face cream, stroking it down her neck and massaging it into her skin. Her old robe wrapped tight, comfortable and familiar. She tied it at the waist, and wandered into the kitchen on bare feet, poking through the fridge for something to nibble on. Her hair hung down her back, soaking her gown, but she didn't care.

She poured a glass of wine and sat on the sagging old couch, eating slowly, and flicking through the channels on TV trying to find something of interest, rejecting snippets of programs that were full of killings, explosions and death. And then, suddenly, a documentary that had been filmed in the Zambezi Valley was on the screen. She was stunned. How amazing!

She sat up and watched avidly, wishing she had found the channel earlier to see the whole program—absorbing everything the announcer was saying, and loving the views of the river and the surrounds. She wanted to shout, 'I've been there, it really exists and it's incredible.'

Once it had finished she sat in a trance, going over the week down at the camp. She thought of all the sightings of animals, the roar of the lion in the silence of the night, and the beautiful lioness about to have her cubs. She remembered the wild dog and the close call with the bull elephant. The pool area drenched in moonlight as she and Sally frolicked naked in the silky water. But most of all she ran her mind over Gregg—even the sharp words that had passed between them. She smiled at the episode of her sarong being caught on the splinter and wondered if it had been he who had ringed the spot in red pen.

'Come on Suzanna. This is getting us nowhere. Tomorrow is another day. Let's go to bed.'

The covers were cosy but she couldn't concentrate on her book. So she lay in the darkness listening to the faint sounds of the traffic, and wondering if she should take a sleeping tablet. She grinned wryly to herself. Despite her anxiety and stress at not seeing Gregg she hadn't once thought of resorting to the bottle of pills, and she realized again what a drama queen she had been over her break-up with Dave.

She imagined Sally and Pete hugged up close in each other's arms. The only thing she had to hug was her pillow and she gripped it to her chest and curled up on her side, staving off the ever existent waves of longing and loneliness.

Chapter 20

THE STRANGE HOUSE was masked in a gloomy, ghostly light. Vaporous mists swirled under the eaves and curled like hungry tongues that licked the life and sucked the colour from everything but the glinting windows.

How had she got here? What had drawn her to this frightening place of hidden threats and unseen presences, prying eyes glowing from dark corners and amorphous shapes hovering against the walls and rising soundlessly towards the ceiling?

She strained her eyes, struggling to open them wide but feeling as though they were still closed, the lids glued together. How could she ever make her way through to safety when she couldn't see properly? Something brushed at her legs. With a cry she stepped sharply aside, but it reached out with evil tentacles and wrapped itself round one of her ankles, tripping her, trying to hold her back, growing ever larger, a formless black shape that filled her with terror.

A long trail of wispy spider web swayed from the beam above, clinging and suffocating, descending downwards, floating through the air and settling into her hair and over her arms, sticking to her skin like a poisonous veil. She twisted and writhed, desperate to escape. Fighting against the ties that held her hostage. Terrified mewing sounds, trapped kitten cries, escaped her lips.

A distant and repetitive sound echoed. But from where? There was no door—no way out. No-one to help. She whirled as the sound came again. But the blackness was gripping and absolute—like treacle pulling her down into the sticky depths of a bottomless pit, determined to smother her and stop her breathing once and for all.

The knock came again. Somehow she knew she had to get towards it—that this sound was her salvation. Her only hope. Frantically she tore at the bonds that held her, as soft as silk but as strong as nylon rope. Her mind screamed for the sound to be repeated, to set her free and let her overcome this terrible pressing weight of darkness.

There! And again! At last the knock penetrated her subconscious mind and her eyes flew open.

She lay absolutely still, staring blankly at the dark ceiling, her heart hammering, while the horrible panic of the dream left tendrils of fear across her mind. The bedclothes were tightly wrapped round her and she was soaked with sweat. She waited, listening intently, trying to control the heaving of her chest. Had it really been someone knocking, or had it been part of the awful dream?

No-one knocked on your door after midnight in the city. It was dangerous to answer the door in the middle of the night. Not long ago there had been a savage case of rape when a girl had opened her door to a stranger claiming he needed help in the small hours, and everyone had shaken their heads and agreed she had been a fool to let him in.

She lay rigid, clutching a fistful of sheet, listening for the sound again. Sally would have her key, so it was definitely not her. Perhaps Dave had decided to come round, after all? Maybe he was feeling a little maudlin after a few drinks, and wanted to persuade her to patch things up.

She started violently as it came again. Insistent and urgent. Not going away. Real. Not in her dream. Suzanna's pulse knocked just as hard. Summoning all her will power she slowly crept out of bed, wrapped her gown round herself and tiptoed to the door, then jumped in fright to hear it louder and right next to her ear.

"Suzanna? Suzanna—are you in?"

Oh no! She was hearing things. She fumbled at the door, dropped the key, scrabbled around in the darkness, found the light switch, found the key and wrenched it into the lock.

Oh, sweet Heaven!

He filled the doorway—tall, broad, handsome, and looking exhausted. She gaped at him with her mouth open. Was she still asleep? She rubbed at her eyes and then reached out towards him, checking he wasn't a figment of her imagination. His hand came towards hers, but something in her expression made it hover in the air without touching her.

"Did I frighten you? I'm sorry. I've been driving for hours. I hoped to get here earlier, but I had a puncture . . ."

He was here. He had come. How could she have known that the knocking would save her? Free her from all the misery of the black dream.

"Suzanna? Are you OK? I'm sorry to just arrive like this—and especially at this time of night. Once I'd set off I couldn't go back. And then I had that damned puncture, and it took ages fumbling around in the dark to change the wheel."

Wordlessly, moving like a robot that hadn't been wired correctly, she pushed the door back and the whole room felt small as he stepped through. He stood still, regarding her in silence, trying to read her expression. Her eyes were huge as she stared up at him. She hugged her dressing gown close, shivering and suddenly aware that she had nothing except a clinging nightie underneath it.

"Were you asleep? Perhaps I should have found a phone along the way to ring you. Warn you I was coming. I just didn't think! I was in such an all fired hurry to get here and see you, that I didn't think . . . and then I had that infernal delay." He rubbed his hand over his face. "Suzanna? I'm so sorry if I scared you."

She had been pining for him so badly. Desperate to see him. To feel him and touch him. Aching to hear his voice. And now, here he was, standing right in front of her, and she couldn't move, couldn't speak. What was the matter with her? Her eyes were like huge pools of dark water and her body was quivering with spasms of shock.

Somehow, he seemed to understand.

Ever so slowly, as though gentling a wild fawn, he stretched out his hand, and brushed a strand of hair back from her face. As softly as a whisper his finger traced the line of her cheek, moved gently round the back of her neck to her shoulder and slowly, quietly, he pulled her towards him. He wrapped his arms round her and held her tightly against his chest, willing away the tremors that ran through her, soothing her with the power of his hold.

She snaked out her arms and clung to him, her cheek pressed to his shirt, drawing strength from him, breathing in his smell. A huge sob escaped unbidden from the depths of her soul.

"Oh, Gregg! I've missed you so badly. Why didn't you call me? I didn't know what to think. I wasn't sure if I'd see you again."

He stroked his hand down her back, combed his fingers through her tangled hair.

"Sshh. It's alright. I'm here now."

He lifted her chin and kissed her lips, softly, gently. He smiled into her eyes, kissed her eyelids and her temples. She reached up with her mouth and found his.

The endless days of longing were over. He had missed her as much as she had missed and ached for him. Despite his family crisis their mutual need had taken precedence and he'd decided to come to her. All the frustrations had built up in him, like they had in her, but now he had her firmly and safely in his arms, and it felt as natural as if it had been written into her destiny from the beginning.

Their kisses probed deeper, their tongues entwined, their lips melted and crushed together.

The fire was building in her belly. The urgency mounted between them as they discovered all over again the depth of the bond between them. Suzanna reached up and wound her arms round his neck. Her robe opened slightly and his hands slipped inside to feel her soft skin. He moaned deep in his throat as his touch ran down her back and over the roundness of her buttocks. Slowly he eased the silky material of her clothing backwards, kissing the exposed curve of her shoulder.

The gown fell away from the swell of her breasts and revealed the full length of her body. She clung to him, standing in nothing more than her bare skin. The roughness of his clothing scratched at her, making every pore scream out for more.

Gregg bent and lifted her into his arms. In the bedroom he laid her gently on the bed and leaned over her. For the longest moments he just looked at her. His eyes travelled over her face, all the way down her body and back to her eyes. She lay supine, absorbing his adoring looks. It didn't occur to her to feel awkward or embarrassed under his gaze. It just felt natural and wonderful—as though her whole life had been leading to this point in time.

Now his wide hands stroked downwards from her neck, over her breasts and caressed her stomach. There was a tiny sparkle of a tear in the corner of his eyes and the sight of it moved her more than any words could have done. She put her hand up and ran the back of her fingers gently over his stubble lined cheek, soothing him with her tender touch.

"You look tired," she told him softly.

He took her hand in his and kissed each fingertip, one after the other.

"I've missed you so badly." The words were music to her soul.

His bent his head down, kissing her lips. And then his hands and tongue set about their devilish task of sending her wild, licking, sucking and kissing every soft fold and secret place. He was still fully clothed and somehow that made it more erotic. She cried out, holding on to him but pleading with him to stop. He stood up and in a few swift moves he unbuttoned and unzipped his clothing, leaving it in a pile on the floor. His beautiful body was above her and now it was her turn to look all the way up and down. Then he lowered himself into her outstretched arms and lay beside her. He moved over her and at last his weight pressed her down.

Their love-making was slow, sweet and beautiful, then demanding and urgent, building, almost verging on violent.

Soaring and flying and carrying them both into orbits of ecstasy. At last fulfilling their desperate need.

They clung together, their bodies slick with moisture but both reluctant to release each other from their deep hold. They dropped sweet kisses onto each other's necks, foreheads and shoulders. Gregg found Suzanna's mouth once more, and licked along the line of her top lip.

"You taste all salty," he murmured, "quite delicious actually."

He rolled onto his back, tucked the sheet round their hips and drew her into the curve of his arm, her head on his shoulder.

"Now I'm glad I came." He grinned sideways at her, gripping her raised fist as she playfully made to punch his shoulder.

"When the phone cut out," he went on, "I almost went mad with frustration. I'd had such a bad time getting through to you, it was hard not to smash it when the damn thing died on me."

"I felt the same way," Suzanna replied. "I wanted to rip it out of the wall and crush it to death."

She smoothed her hand over his shoulder, glorying in the feel of him.

"Gregg? I'm so sorry about your uncle. Have you had the funeral? I thought you would stay with your family until it was over. I've been longing for you so badly, but I just never expected to see you so soon." 'If at all!' Her unspoken thought hung in the air.

"It was Mum who told me to come to you. She saw the state I was in when the phone died. She could see my dilemma of wanting to be there to help them, but needing to be with you." His tone became more serious. "The funeral is in a few day's time. In fact, my little one, I wanted to ask if you'd come back with me—come and meet my family. I know it's not under very happy circumstances, and it's a lot to ask," he grinned, "and I should warn you that we are quite an imposing bunch when we're all together."

He smiled sideways at her and kissed her hair. He'd called her 'my little one'—an endearment that spread warmth right through her. She gave him a fierce hug. God, how she had longed to be with him again like this!

"I meant what I said to you at the camp, Suzanna. I haven't been able to think of anything or anyone else but you. I nearly went crazy when the comms went down in the camp and we couldn't contact anyone after that storm. I worked for eighteen hours straight, trying to get it all back into action. But we had to wait for a part to be brought in, which took forever and nearly drove me mad. And then I got news of my uncle via another ranger who drove in, and everything fell apart completely."

Suzanna's heart twisted at the sad note in his voice.

"Mum is pretty upset. He was her only brother and they were very close. She's been a brick, though. Between us we've almost sorted everything out. I would really like you to come and meet her, and Dad, of course, and I know they would love you."

"Love me?" The words were out before she could control them. Her heart beat rapidly against his chest and she could feel the pulse drumming in her throat.

He raised himself up onto one elbow, smoothed his hand over her cheek and looked into her eyes. His expression was very serious.

"I said once before that I am not in the habit of seducing beautiful women, Suzanna, and I meant it. I have never felt like this before, about anyone. The time we were apart was a living agony for me. I thought about you every moment.

I know we haven't known each other for very long, but from the moment I saw you, I've felt an unexplainable pull—almost like an invisible tie." He lifted the side of his mouth, "almost like I've known you in a previous life. It's as though we're meant to be together."

Her fingers fluttered against his mouth and she could hardly breathe. His words dropped like precious jewels deep into her soul. She lay on her back and watched his eyes as he spoke, and knew that he was speaking from his heart.

"I love you, Suzanna. I feel like I've waited my whole life for you, and I want to spend the rest of it with you. I love you. I want to find out all about you, and tell you everything there is to know about me. I want you to have my babies," he chuckled, "a boy and a girl at the very least."

She couldn't help it. The corners of her lips were curved into a smile, but the tears filled her eyes and dripped wetly down into her hair.

Her heart nearly burst when he brushed them away and said, "Don't cry, my darling. It's all very sudden for you, but I've been over and over it in my mind. I love you and want you to be with me forever. I just hope and pray that that's what you want too."

Suzanna needed a little time to absorb all that he'd said. "I know nothing about your family, Gregg. How can you be sure they will even like me? Do you have a brother, sisters?"

"There are three of us. Danny is two years older than me. He runs my dad's farm, in conjunction with the old man. Danny's wife's name is Annabelle and they have two great kids, Sam and Angie. And then there's my sister Janie. She's eighteen months younger than me and is expecting her first child after three years of being married, so it's a huge forthcoming family event. We are all close, and things can get pretty noisy when we're all together, I can tell you."

He leaned down and hugged her.

"I just know that you'll all get on well. Janie can be as fiery as you can. She's had to hold her own against two big brothers, but she's a darling at heart."

Suzanna turned it all over in her mind, trying to picture what his brother and sister, and his parents looked like.

"There's more Suzanna," he went on. "My aunt and uncle, Daphne and Bob by the way, only ever had one child—a daughter—my cousin. Last year she married an Australian and they now live in Perth. He's an IT freak and knows the innards and workings of a computer like I know the bushveld. They will never come home and run Bob's ranch. The will hasn't been read yet, but Daphne told me that she and Bob had discussed things a while ago, and they had already planned to leave their ranch to me—they just hadn't planned for it to be so soon—poor things."

Slightly shocked she asked, "What about the camp? You love it down there, and you're so good at running it. Stanley told me that you've really turned it round, and the occupancy rate has soared under your control. How will you be able to leave it?"

A look of pain spread across his face.

"I know," he replied. "I've worked my guts out at that camp, and I love it. I love the layout, the challenge of the day-to-day problems and everything about it. But it's not mine. I'm about to be given the chance to own my own ranch. That's huge for me. There is already quite a large population of game there, and I would just love to develop it, bring in more animals and turn the whole property into a photographic safari outfit. There's a huge opening in this country for tourists to come in and bag the best photo of wildlife, rather than take the horns or skin home to pin on the wall. So many of our species are on the edge of becoming extinct and we need to protect them and do our best to preserve them—not just for future generations of mankind, but because we owe it to the whole animal kingdom to see that they have a future in this world."

He saw how wide and round Suzanna's eyes were and lifted one side of his mouth again.

"Sorry, it's a pet topic of mine. I didn't mean to go on or to bore you."

"No," she assured him, smiling widely. "It's just that I think that's the longest speech I've ever heard you make."

He threw back his head, a gesture she now knew was characteristic of him, and gave a snort of laughter.

"Oh, I can wax pretty eloquent when I want to." He stroked her cheek. "Do you need time to think things over, Suzanna? I've never been more serious in my life, and I've never been more sure of my feelings, but I don't want to rush you into making a decision too quickly. I love you and I can only hope that you feel the same way about me. But if you need more time, you can have it—as much as you want. If I have to I'll wait for you forever."

A sudden look of concern made him frown.

"I promise to take care of you if you come with me. All that I want is right here in my arms. I need you, Suzanna. I want you by my side. I want to marry you and have you share my life, help me make decisions. With you next to me I know I can make a success of anything."

Then he grinned wickedly. "And from time to time we can enjoy some really great sex."

She struggled up and drew her knees under her, the sheet round her waist. She tugged it up to cover her breasts and knelt on the bed facing him. She had no idea of the effect she made, with the white sheet clutched to her chest, eyes huge and limpid, and hair tousled and free round her shoulders. Gregg admitted later that she looked like a water nymph sitting on a lily pad, and he'd had to physically restrain himself from grabbing her before he heard what she had to say.

"These days of being apart from you have been the longest and hardest I've ever had to endure," Suzanna told him. "I have missed you with a terrible pain that I've never known before. It's as though half of me has been missing. Never in my wildest dreams would I have expected to meet and fall so totally in love with someone in such a short time. I always thought that true love would be something that would flower and develop slowly. But—I love you Gregg. I think I have from the first moment I saw you." She looked at him sideways. "Even though you were so cruel to me when we first met."

Gregg was totally unrepentant. "You sent my emotions and feelings into such a spin, I had no way of knowing how to deal with them—or with you. Every time I saw you I was thrown off balance, at a loss for words. I couldn't concentrate on my work, or sleep properly. You have the power to make things happen to my mind, and to my body I might add, that are beyond my control. I just didn't know what to make of it all. I was afraid that you would be married, or have a steady partner—that you would be beyond my reach."

Suzanna took his wide hand in hers and lovingly stroked the backs of his fingers.

"When you weren't there to say goodbye, after—well, after we'd been together, and it had been so earth-shakingly wonderful, I thought I would curl up and die," she told him. "I hated leaving the camp, but it cut me into tiny pieces to leave without seeing you, or having the chance to speak to you again."

"I hated it too," he said. "I have to admit that I drove my team of men harder than they deserved to find that snared kudu. If we had stumbled across the poachers along the way, they would have been dead meat. And then to loose all means of communication just when I'd sorted out all my jumbled thoughts and feelings . . ." he laughed shortly. "I was like an angry buffalo for days."

He put up his hand and tenderly tucked a lock of hair behind her ear.

"Do you think you could marry me, Suzanna? I would be so honoured to have you as my wife."

She leaned down and kissed his beloved mouth. She let her lips roam over his throat, that special place where his shoulder joined his neck. The sheet fell away and exposed her breasts to his touch. She kissed his chest, flicked her tongue ever downwards, working her fingers in tune with her mouth, loving the taste of his skin, the smell of him, the texture of the thick curly hair low on his belly.

She ignored his groans as she took him into her mouth, sucking and deliberately inflicting sweet agony with her teeth. It was her turn to drive him crazy. He arched against her mouth, clutching at her shoulders. His hands closed on her hair and his chest rose and fell with the intensity of his breathing.

At the last moment, when neither of them could endure it any longer, she enclosed him within her body, triumphantly above him, feeling him press right up into her heart. Her movements were primordial, wildly intense, pleasure seeking and exquisitely giving, as old as mankind itself, but as new as a shimmering ball of fire.

The waves built intolerably until they crashed and exploded on the shore of their emotions, like a million bubbles racing and hissing over the beach to arrive, now spent and quiet and totally beautiful, dissolving into the sands of time.

Slowly their senses returned. Still locked against him Suzanna leaned forwards and kissed his forehead and his lips. Her smile was wide and loving.

"Just in case I forget to tell you? I love you with all my heart and all my being. And the answer to all your questions is an irrevocable—yes, yes, yes."

He threw his arms round her, laughing and hugging her to his chest.

"And just in case I forget . . . ." He leaned over the edge of the bed and reached down with one hand to lift his pants off the floor, digging in the pocket and drawing out something that he held easily in one palm. With a mischievous grin and a deep chuckle he said, "I have a gift for you. But I may have to teach you how to use it—now don't get mad. This, my darling, is just for you."

How could she resist him?

In his hand he held a neat little camera enclosed in a smooth grey case.

On the outside the letters *G* and *S* were written in gold—intertwined forever.

About the Author

JEAN WAS BORN in Rhodesia—later called Zimbabwe—a small and beautiful Country lying in the heart of Africa that was later to be subjected to radical changes no-one could have foreseen in those halcyon early days.

Jean taught at a small country school and subsequently met and married a man of the land—a tobacco farmer, who encouraged and developed her inherent love of the African bushveld. Their most precious times were spent exploring remote areas, and viewing the wonders of the natural bird and wildlife that abounded in the northern regions, specifically in Kariba and the Zambezi Valley.

After losing their beloved home and farm during the infamous Government Land Reform Program Jean and her husband left Zimbabwe to join their family now living in New Zealand. It is hard to completely sever one's roots however, and a large part of her heart will always remain in the wild and beautiful bush she once knew so well.

Jean has longed dreamed of writing a book, and now that she lives in a land where dreams can be made to come true, she won't give up on hers. "Destiny in Wild Africa" is the start.